WHERE FIRES ARE TO BURN

Copyright © Mark L. Watson, 2019

All rights reserved

No part of this book may be reproduced by any means, nor transmitted, nor translated into a machine language, without the written permission of the publisher.

Mark L. Watson has asserted the right to be identified as the author of this work in accordance with Sections 77 and 78 of the Copright, Designs and Patents Act 1988.

Condition of Sale
This book is sold subject to the condition that it shall not, by way of trade or otherwise, be lent, resold, hired out or otherwise circulated in any form of binding or cover other than that in which it is published and without a similar condition including this condition being imposed on the subsequent purchaser.

Mark L. Watson Productions
www.marklwatson.co.uk

Printed and bound by KDP Publishing.

ISBN: 9781081197551

Where Fires Are To Burn

Mark L. Watson

Prologue

The tower was three storeys from bottom to top and the blackened wall was crumbling, as all walls in that place were. He kept close to the brickwork, his back to the wall.

Ryan slowed his breathing and listened.

The voices were there, ahead of him and behind. He was stooped just slightly, his arm bent at the elbow to keep the pistol levelled.

He crouched down behind a rubbish bin, overflowing with rotten waste, and waited.

He could see, further along the alleyway, the three men standing in the doorway, partly silhouetted by the evening glow. They were talking to each other in Spanish though he couldn't understand what they said and it didn't matter regardless. He rounded the bin and approached the fire escape steps on the side of the hospital and watched where he put his feet in fear of betraying his position and alerting the men and others like them. He placed his foot carefully up on to the first step and the metalwork creaked a little and he turned with the pistol but nobody was watching. He bounced up the steps as quietly as he could, trying to step lightly, as a cat might, while moving as fast as was possible. He could hear the metalwork squeaking and rattling but he had no alternative. He had to run one way or another, he couldn't stop or the whole thing would be over. As he rounded the top of the fire escape onto the hospital roof he practically threw himself to the floor.

He lay for some time under the white sky, catching his breath and listening and praying that nobody had heard him or seen him there.

The place was silent but for his breathing and the thumping of his heart as it practically battered its way out of his chest.

After a few minutes, when he was sure he was not followed, he stood and hurried across the grey roof, around the old air conditioning units and vents, and reached the door leading to the stairs down into the hospital building. It was locked with a pushbar from the inside as he knew it would be, but he was prepared. He swung the cloth pack from his shoulder down onto the ground and removed from it two screwdrivers. He set about removing the door from its external hinges so as to quietly enter the building from above. He removed the three screws from the bottom hinge and then from the centre one and the door dropped slightly on its own weight and then disappointment and fear suddenly surged through him as he saw, through the gap, the barricade which had been built on the other side.

He stopped.

There were voices again, calling from somewhere.

He listened. His life depended on it.

They came from beyond the door, down on the top floor of the hospital building beneath him. He knew bandits came and went from that place looking for provisions to use or to sell but he had watched the building for three days and was sure they had gone.

He was obviously wrong.

Perhaps they had set a small camp inside or perhaps there were people injured there who had chosen the building as a safe house. Whoever was using that place as a refuge had secured it well to prevent others from doing exactly as he was intending on doing.

He checked the sky. It was darkening. He knew he wouldn't get through the barricade quietly enough to ensure his safety and the raid would have to be cancelled and reapproached at another time.

More voices. He listened.

They were beneath him, inside the building, but they were also all around him, down in the town beyond, calling loudly across distances to each other in the dusk.

Then he heard it.

A rattling he recognised.

The fire escape.

Footsteps were coming up the metal staircase on the outside of the building. He scurried over towards the edge of the roof and crouched down behind an air conditioning extractor unit. He readied the pistol. He was more than ready to shoot in the head any person who discovered him there but that was the final option he had. A gunshot out there, where gangs moved in packs like dogs and each man was armed, would be like a siren sounding and he was in no position to hold his own in a gunfight with a gang of bandits.

At the very least he could use the pistol on himself he reasoned.

He positioned himself in a manner which allowed him to peer around the straight edge of the metal unit and see across to the top of the steps. After a moment a man walked into view and stood, regarding the rooftop before him.

Ryan pulled his head backwards slightly and watched. He was sure the man couldn't see him from where he stood but whether or not the man had watched Ryan ascend to the roof was yet a mystery to him.

The man walked to the edge of the metal framework of the steps and called down to somebody below.

Ryan couldn't hear what was said, growled in a thick Mexican accent.

A moment later the steps rattled again and Ryan watched as four more men came onto the rooftop, some carrying packs, and the last man carrying on his back a basket of wood scraps and all armed with rifles and pistols.

Ryan's heart raced.

He knew they must have seen him go up those steps to that roof and that he was now indeed cornered. He looked around the metal unit as best he could for an exit strategy and couldn't see another way down and knew he was three storeys up above the broken concrete alleyway. He considered the jump from the edge and weighed in his head the distance and the impact of his fall, and knew that even a twisted ankle would spell the end for him there. He knew also that a twisted ankle was the very best that could be hoped for from that height.

He would wait. He was a good shot and a fast runner.

There was no alternative.

He reasoned in his head that should he succeed in slinking his way silently along the air conditioning units towards the top of the steps that he could make a dash for the steps and could jump from a lower point if required.

He watched the men on the roof.

They didn't appear to be searching for him at all, talking and laughing, their rifles swinging on straps.

The roof was flat across the rear of the building but rose into a tiled peak at the front side and the men moved to that place and took their packs from their backs. They unrolled blankets and produced other items they would need there and the man with the basket of wood set it down and went about making a small fire and another produced an iron kettle.

Ryan caught his breath, his assumption being that should the men be there simply to make camp then there would likely be some safer time to make a silent escape without incident. The assumption was short lived.

One of the men, dressed in a faded black poncho and a small cap and wearing high black leather riding boots and a slight limp, crossed back to the top of the steps and set across the metalwork a tripwire and clipped the end to a bell and sat back on the vent housing with a shotgun pointed directly at the top of the steps, and from that place he did not move.

The men were experienced, as they had to be out there in the nearly lawless lands of the north. They would not build a camp without also ensuring that it was in a place well protected with weaponry and such and the men would rotate their duties as sentry. The location of that watchman at the top of the steps also clarified to Ryan that there was indeed no other way down from the building, other than through the doorway into the staircase that had been barricaded from the inside and of which the men did not seem to be too concerned.

Ryan waited for he had no option.

He was relieved that he had , at the very least, positioned himself at the featureless rear of the building, and he prayed to whoever may listen that the men should not find cause to venture back that far, though he knew he could not bet against it.

He kept a firm grip on the pistol.

The sky darkened slowly and Ryan waited in that place as the men stoked their fire and ate and drank and took it in turns throughout the night to watch the tripwire and guard the top of the metal steps.

The air was not cold, but Ryan shivered through the night, trying to rest his eyes without falling asleep, until eventually the light spread out behind the white clouds at the horizon and another day broke.

He had crawled silently to the edge of the building twice over that night in the hope of seeing in the shadows a way down from there but the drop was severe and unbroken and on to only concrete below. There were no neighbouring buildings anywhere close enough to jump to and he knew his options were to plummet the distance down, clamber somehow, blindly in the dark, down over the edge onto a window frame or gutter and most likely fall doing so, or to wait out the men and hope he was not discovered.

He waited.

As the light came the following morning he was wrapped in his poncho in a small bundle on the cold stone, the muzzle of the pistol protruding from the fabric. He had not slept.

The bandit who was currently charged with guarding the top of the steps was slouched back where he sat with the old shotgun resting in his lap. He looked to be sleeping, or dozing at least, and the group of other men were wrapped in their blankets across the roof, their fire dead and cold and the tequila bottles empty and smashed.

Ryan watched the guard for some time, considering the opportunity to slowly move his way, and either silently pass the man or to garrote him where he sat, though he knew that should he be detected at any stage of that plan, which was likely, he would be dead or worse.

He watched out across the crumbling rooftops and the greying sky beyond. There was barely a sound but from the whistling wind, no bird called or insect chirped. He was worried that Kiara would not know where he was and would think some tragedy had befallen him and he was worried she may come looking for him, though he hoped she knew better. She was aware that these things did not always unfold as planned and she would surely just wait there where she was safe until he returned or until he didn't.

When the sun was up fully, the men awoke and packed away their blankets and began to cook meat on a new fire and they sat and smoked and argued with each other over everything and nothing.

They milled around the rooftop without cause, passing their time there by fighting one another and they began to drink from big glass bottles and they fought more and all the time Ryan sat behind the air conditioning unit and waited like an injured bird. They took their turns to watch the steps and sometimes they all watched from the roof and sometimes there seemed to be nobody guarding it at all but there did not, at any stage, present a reasonable opportunity of escape. It was twenty feet or more between the end unit and the top of the metal steps and all the men carried guns. They came near to the edge of the building where Ryan crouched and he held his breath and pulled his poncho up to cover his face and aimed his gun at them and this happened once and then twice and then again but the men were by then drunk and he was, somehow, not spotted.

He sat all day until the sun went down a second time. He was bubbling with hunger and thirst and had urinated twice were he sat for he had no other option.

When it was dark the rain came.

Slow at first and then heavier and he pulled his poncho up around his head but it was soon dripping and the rain poured from the wide brim of his leather hat. The bandits' fire sputtered and hissed and eventually went out and the men pulled themselves under an awning and the man guarding the steps shouted to them to protest his turn at sitting out in the rain and they laughed and threw bottles at him.

The sky was entirely black and no light shone from anywhere around.

Ryan's mind started to play tricks on itself and his feet and legs were numb. He began to feel very sick and it was, at that time, that he saw the guard rise from where he was sitting and move to the top of the steps with the shotgun raised. There was a sound somewhere below and the guard moved to investigate it further.

He called to the men under their awning but there returned nothing more than a muffled reply and he carefully stepped over the tripwire and descended the steps.

Ryan waited and listened.

He listened as hard as he could against the rain, the metalwork of the fire escape rattled on its old fixings and he heard the man descend all the way to the ground alleyway below and call out again in the night.

He glanced to the rest of the posse who were not moved from where they lay.

He swung the poncho down and rose to his feet, the pistol readied. He leaped through the gathering rainwater to the next metal unit and stooped down and then moved to the last one and stooped again and listened. After the briefest of moments he darted to the top of the steps and hurdled the tripwire and danced down the staircase as lightly as he could.

As he turned at the first platform he could see the man below with the shotgun, walking slowly along the alleyway, calling out at what noise he had heard. Ryan jumped down the second set of steps and threw himself over the railings to the ground below where he crashed onto the old concrete with a loud splash of rainwater.

He didn't look back to see whether his landing had alerted the man though he knew that it must and he heard the man call out.

He ran.

He ran out of the alleyway without looking back once and around the edge of the building and across the cracked old road at the front and threw himself over the metal traffic barrier and across the open scrubland beyond and away into the blackness.

Chapter One

Ryan was concerned that the cartwheel might need replacing entirely. There were only three of the original eight spokes left and they too were rotten. He had been looking for weeks for a wheel which was suitable to hold up the cart, though it would need to be the same diameter as the other one otherwise he would need to find two of them.

He watched as his son pulled the rickety cart, rattling across the stones.

"Careful, take care with that thing"

The other wheel wasn't much better.

His son looked over to him and nodded once and slowed. It was too many miles to Linares for them to walk in what remained of that day and Ryan was sure the cart wheel would not make that distance regardless. The road west to Montemorelos was not a safe road to take and he had been told that no military patrol had stopped there for weeks, and any which passed would simply pass and go. They had been forced to take their cart along the farm tracks through the hills and they were approaching the north shore of the Rio San Fernando at Guadeloupe, yet a day's hike from Linares.

His wife, Kiara, walked at the rear of their group, the sack strapped around her.

She called out.

"The sun dropped behind that hill some time back, we should make camp while there is light"

The son stopped with the cart and looked at his father. He walked a few more paces and stopped too and nodded and surveyed the landscape around him. The hills were low and dusty and hot and the track ran bolt straight through the pinyon and shrub at the valley floor. There were no berries or fruits there to eat and they had not passed a water source for over a day.

"We can make the river" he called back, "but we must try to move quicker"

The son said nothing and slowly began to tow the cart forward.

By the time the track approached the woodland at the edge of the river the sky was completely black and they walked in darkness. The wind had picked up, as it always did, and blew the dust down from the hills and they pulled their ponchos and shawls over themselves and hurried the cart to the shelter of the trees.

"The land is too dry here to risk making a fire" Ryan remarked as his wife took her pack from her back, "we should move a little further to the river"

Kiara watched him and looked at the ground and again at her husband. She could not bear to walk a step further but she knew also that he was right.

"I don't really think making a fire on the side of the river is safe either, somebody might see it" she said.

They thought for a moment and the boy volunteered to go to the riverside and check for a clearing there and to see what cover the trees provided and the viability of camping secretly there. Ryan crouched to their cart and reached under the front beam and unclipped the metal box that was fixed there, hidden from sight. He sat it on the floor and took the key from where it hung around his neck and unlocked the thick padlock. Inside, everything they cared about and everything of value was piled into the tin. There were three photos of their son Dylan and daughter Mia together and a photo of Ryan's parents standing shoulder to shoulder and staring blankly into the camera lens, as was once customary. There were eleven matchboxes set neatly beside each other in two lines, each filled with different seeds. Theirs was a time when the old currency of paper and metal was rapidly becoming valueless, though not entirely yet, and trade was conducted primarily in the commodities of more practical use. There was nothing of more use to the ongoing survival of mankind than the seeds of fruits and plants, as from those any man with access to soil could grow himself a future. One box contained seeds of Magnolia and one of wild Geranium, which whilst of mild medicinal usage, were of low value and easily scavenged. There was a box of Agave seeds from across the border to the north and the Blue Agave seeds of that land, both of which were bound together with a rubber band. Two boxes were full to bursting with corn kernels which they had found and, of significantly more importance to them, the seeds of apple, mango, tomato, chilli and cacao. Each of the boxes was guarded well and Ryan knew exactly the inventory of each for it was those boxes which provided his family with the means to trade and beyond that, should they find a place, the means to grow.

The rains had come for weeks on end and the lands were fertile but they had left their own pastures for the south, and with them all crops. There were other items in the tin also, jewellery, some pesos and dollars and a small case of .357 shells.

Laying atop it all was the Colt Python with an 8-inch Royal Blue barrel and wooden grain grip.

He took the pistol out and swung open the cylinder and looked through the empty chambers and swung it closed. He spun the gun around in his hand to face it the other way and handed it to Dylan and tossed him the box of shells

"Take it with you"

Dylan nodded and took from inside the box the required six shells and loaded them into the chambers of the pistol. He tossed the box back to his father.

"Careful" Kiara shouted and the boy nodded and raised a hand as he set out into the black.

Kiara sat down on the dry ground and Ryan stood and regarded nothing at all for there was nothing to see.

A few moments later they heard the boy returning through the trees.

"And?" Ryan asked.

"There's a farm further upriver, old buildings, probably not used now I guess The river is wide though dad, I don't think we'd get across"

Ryan smiled.

"No son, we won't get across the river"

"Is there a bridge?"

Dylan shook his head.

"And across?"

"Trees. Mostly. It's dark"

"You see any lights or anything?"

The boy shook his head.

"Nu-huh. It's real dark"

Ryan nodded.

"Is there a place to make a fire"

Dylan smiled.

"Yessir, the river bank is open. We might catch fish too, dad, I guess"

Ryan nodded again.

"Maybe. I'll bring the cart down there, help your mother will you. Take her ahead and y'all get both yourselves a drink. Keep the pistol with you. Careful with the damn thing"

"Can we shoot it later?"

"No we can't. Go on"

On the north bank of the Rio San Fernando they left the cart in the trees away from view and Ryan dug a small hole in the sand and put into it some rocks and then some wood and in an instant had a small campfire burning.

He took water from the river into the metal pot and made coffee and they ate rough flour tortillas and beans and shared a single orange between them.

"Should we go and see what's in the farm buildings?" the boy asked.

"In daylight we will. Not now. Eat your food"

"Maybe you can teach me to shoot the gun some more, dad. If we find somewhere safe, you know."

"Maybe"

They ate and talked and the boy fell asleep at the fire and they lifted him into the cover of the trees and wrapped him in a blanket and the three of them lay there under the stars listening to the river.

At daybreak they rose and drank cold coffee and packed the blankets onto the cart and Ryan put the pistol back into the box under the wooden beam and buried the firepit in sand completely until there was no trace of it.

Beyond the trees to the east they could see the top of the metal barn roof and they set out along the shoreline and through the trees and up onto the track.

There were two long barns with corrugated steel roofs and three old wooden stables which were rotting and burned and an old cottage to the north. They stood a hundred yards back in the treeline and watched for any sign of life there. There was largely nothing to fear from the simple folk of that area, who welcomed travellers from the north and the south who provided them with opportunities to trade, and who brought news across the country that may otherwise not reach them since the loss of radio.

The national emergency radio had been transmitted for just over four years after the disaster but then the fuels which powered it since losing electricity began to dwindle in supply and eventually that too went.

Though not everyone there was to be trusted, many had taken to lives of self-serving greed and brutalism. There roamed hordes of bandits and thieves across that land and beyond, comparable in number to small army regiments and armed as such. Some held entire towns under their control, and they occupied without contest the forests of Chiapas and Oaxaca and the borderlands of the south, of which terrible stories were told. They had seen many things and heard many tales in their time there, enough for them to know well what barbaric and terrible people walked those lands.

The nation had been under military law for many years and they enforced their rule with a heavy hand, but their number was not great enough to protect the entire country and all its settlements.

The cities were the safest places to be as they were policed and patrolled but the roads which led to those places through the expanse of hills and forests were practically lawless. Military patrols and convoys would routinely travel the major roads to the north and south but they were infrequent, especially at the extremes of the country at the points furthest in distance from the capital. National Service had become compulsory and the age of enlistment had been brought down year on year and at that time stood at only fourteen. Dylan was into his final two years before he would be drafted. Many people of that place hid their children from conscription, lying about their ages when questioned and living as far into the countryside as they could to avoid detection. In those dark ages there were not the means to be traced that there had once been, and it was easier, if not quite unavoidable, to live off the known grid. The military were thorough in their checks, and on their routine patrols would take any child deemed to be the age of conscription, by force or otherwise. Failure to comply with what was seen as a national security measure would invariably result in the excessive force for which the military had become known, and penance for those seen to be aiding or harbouring a child of conscription age.

Ryan had no intention of still being in that country when that time came.

They would continue to head south and cross the border into Guatemala within the year. He had sworn it to his wife and son.

He had heard of a place by the flooded Amatique Bay, far south at the borderline between Belize and Guatemala where there grew plentiful fruit fertile soil and where the waters were clean. It was a whisper to him, a secret, a dream, a longing from months prior but it was something to aim for and there were times when that was enough. To stay in one place in the country which they walked was to accept the slow grip of hunger and disease, and a future in which his son would soon be taken from him. After losing one child that was something he would die trying to prevent, if that is what should come of it. He knew nothing of what future lay ahead of him or his family, and he could only listen to the teaching of that which had already occurred.

But yet he also had a dream, idealistic he accepted, that there was something more than what they had there. For that, they would walk, step by step, cart in tow, until they reached the southern border of Mexico and they would leave and they would not return.

Step by step.

"There is nobody in there" Dylan called from where he crouched in the treeline.

The farm buildings were silent in the morning light.

Ryan nodded.

"Go on then"

He rose and nodded Dylan forward and the boy walked away into the open farmyard and Ryan followed behind him, the pistol levelled, vigilant as always. Complacency was fatal. His wife waited at the treeline with the cart, watching. For the first few months of their journey the three of them had always stayed close to one another and to the cart, moving as one and not leaving another behind in any situation so as to maximise the protection they could offer one another. They only ever had the single pistol, and thus the problem had arisen as to whether it should be left with the cart to protect their belongings, which could be raided and stolen at any time, or whether Ryan should carry it into the many buildings which they scavenged.

Ryan had taught her how to shoot, though they could not practise for there was not the ammunition to spare. To that end, she had also become particularly adept at swinging a staff, which hung in two iron hooks along the side of the cart, and at wielding and throwing a blade. Whilst ammunition for their Colt was difficult to come by, they found old knives and an axe along their route, and they had sharpened each of them as much as could be done.

Kiara sat on the back of the cart, sewing at the edge of her boot with a leather needle, a wooden-handled field knife sticking point-first into the wood beside her right arm for protection.

Some time later, Ryan and Dylan came back to her across the dusty yard carrying what few items of vague worth they had found. Ryan walked ahead with two lengths of cut wood under his arm and a metal bucket, Dylan behind him swinging a length of cable.

Kiara watched.

"For the wheel?" she called to them.

"Hopefully, let's see" replied Ryan, setting the wood down beside the cart and holding it up to see if he could replace or refurbish the broken spokes.

"What do you want with that?" she asked her son.

"Dad said he'd teach me to fish in that river" he said excitedly.

"With electrical cable?"

The boy shrugged.

"I didn't say I'd teach you to fish in *that* river, I said I'd teach you to fish in *a* river. We don't have time to do it today, we need to try and get over to Linares by sundown"

"Isn't it just over that hill?"

Ryan nodded.

"Yes, but it's going to take most of the day to get across there and we're the wrong side of the river to start with. The river must run straight through the town or close to it, I would guess, perhaps we can fish tomorrow. Put that cable onto the cart for now"

The boy did as he was told.

"Hold this" he said, motioning Dylan to him. He held the wood against the wooden wheel rim and Ryan knocked some old nails through it to brace the wheel slightly, though the spokes didn't pass through the axle.

"It'll do for now" he said, sitting back and looking at the wheel, "you ready?"

Kiara nodded and Dylan took hold of the front of the cart and the three of them set back out along the riverside to find a place to cross.

By mid-afternoon they crossed the water at La Escondida and traded some items from their cart for tortillas and coffee and they all sat in the shade and ate in silence and then they were on their way again. They stayed away from the main road, as they always did, and followed the track through the low farmland until it reached the outskirts of Linares.

It was always a relief to reach civilisation, if that was what it was to be called. There were many dangers in passing through those places, especially after sunset, and it was no place to relax or let one's guard down. There were no full-time active law enforcement forces present in those smaller towns, though they did pass through on occasion, and some still garrisoned patrols of soldiers. It was deterrent enough to prevent obvious crime and provide some protection to those who lived there or who passed through, though on the open roads, none of that existed and a group of roamers could easily take their belongings or their lives with neither struggle nor repercussion.

They found a busy street where a line of metal crates had been lit with fire to provide crude flickering street lighting and people sat and talked and traded and gambled for commodities. Gambling, especially in the cities, was one of the most effective ways to amass wealth. There were small games of chance, most often rigged, on every street corner where people wagered coffee beans or screws and nails or cigarettes. Though if a man truly wanted to take risks, there were places set in old bars where everything could be gambled on the roll of the dice or the turn of a card. Men wagered ammunition, weapons, food, especially fruits, and even livestock. It was high stakes and much could be won, but Ryan had known men personally who had not paid off gambling debts and who had lost their lives for it. The bars that offered these wagers of real value were often military-owned or run by cartels, and whilst they remained friendly when winning, they were far from it when they lost. An example was nearly always made of somebody and often in the most public manner. Blood stained their hands and their walls and it took a certain man, either brave or desperate or foolish or all three, to walk through their door. The absence of law enforcement and the increase of cartel-rule brought about the regression in morality and castigation, and those who were so inclined took a resort to medieval-era punishments. Fingers were taken, men were shackled and flogged in the street and though Ryan had not seen it himself, he was told of men dragged through towns by horses until they were torn and broken. The military would punish by death such behaviour, but they not present to do so. Their priorities always lay elsewhere.

They headed south along the roadside, past the stone-walled houses. The iron gates were chained and windows shuttered with panels of wood and metal as though a storm were expected, though it was not. Dogs roamed the yards and barked at everyone who passed. Cars and trucks were still parked in many of the driveways and along the roadsides though they were rusted and smashed and wheels and seats and wires had been taken and none driven in many years.

Once the fuel ceased to be imported, the population relied on what gasoline and diesel was already in their possession or what crude alternative could be fashioned. Those who stockpiled managed to keep it for almost two years before it degraded but most of the country and any other country like it stopped fuelling road vehicles within a couple of months of the disaster. Fuels became the source of widespread civilian warfare, protected fiercely and fought over daily. At the first evacuation, the roads south were blocked by mobsters and gasoline syphoned at gunpoint from those who travelled the country without a convoy. Within a year, travel methods jumped back some hundred years of progress and the people relied on horse or mule or ox and goods had to be shipped by cart or boat. Goods increased tenfold in value. Factories and farms ceased production for they had no method of powering their machines and crops were farmed by hand where possible and guarded ferociously.

Half a mile or more along the road they again reached the river and took a place under the raised railway line which crossed the river by bridge. There were camps along the water's edge where others rested and a man played a guitar with only two strings and he played well given its state. They sang old Mexican folk songs and two children danced and laughed at each other and the smell of cooking fish and tobacco floated through the calm evening breeze. The railway above them was held over the river with giant red iron struts and they were rusted almost entirely through and flags hung from the bridge and the whole structure was overcome with huge purple rhodochiton flowers as though it were a twisted vision of Babylon itself.

They swung the cart up against one of the old supports and set to making a fire.

Ryan took the old kettle from where it hung and opened the sacking and took some of the coffee grounds in his hand and tossed them inside.

Kiara went to the water's edge with the pan and took up some of the cool water and carried it back and filled the kettle and set it down on a stone in the centre of the growing fire.

"Can we fish?" asked **Dylan**, watching the water.

Ryan thought and nodded.

"Sure. We can try. Get the cable"

Chapter Two

They camped at Linares for three nights whilst they waited for the next convoy of travellers to leave to the south. A group of twenty-six walked together, smaller parties joined as one unit to pass more safely through the troubled countryside, south down highway 85. It would be a two day walk to Villagrán and they would take rest at an outpost in El Guajolote, just before crossing the state border. Travellers from the south passed word of safe refuge there, a place with good visibility of the highway and the surrounding country and the group were confident of their safety, given their significant number.

The group gathered at dawn at the southern end of Linares.

A man in a long black coat and a headband had assumed the position of captain. He stepped to the front and spoke.

"Están todos aqui?"

The group nodded and mumbled though none knew how many were due to walk so to confirm that everyone was present was an untruth.

There were men and women and children with them. One man held two mules laden with packs and baskets, another held a pony which pulled a steel trailer behind it. A young boy held two dogs on chains which pulled forward on their chains for no reason.

"Hay alguien armado?" the man called out.

Once more the group nodded and mumbled the affirmative.

Some of the men held rifles openly and another held two pistols in chest holsters like a bandit and the boy with the dogs said that his weapons were in his pack.

The man nodded and turned and waved the group forwards and they set out to the long road south, a clattering of hooves and boots and creaking wheels and jangling pots and chains.

There was not one thing to see on the road and it was bolt-straight through the open flatland. Either side there lay beyond them mile upon mile of absolute nothingness where farms had once stood and which had been stripped of their crops and barns and fences, and even the old telegraph posts that lined the highway were without wires.

In the distance to the west the dusky purple mountains owned the horizon entirely.

The group walked at the pace of their slowest which was not fast at all. The man with the two mules allowed them to be harnessed to one of the carts to aid with the progress though there was much to tow and the day was hot. The men pulled the heavier of the carts and the women walked with the rifles and the children. The boy let the two dogs from their chains and they trotted along some hundred yards ahead of the group, sniffing and pawing at the ground as they went, searching for food that wasn't there.

The man with the long coat and headband walked at the front and, though he was keen and alert and stern-faced, he was quick to halt their progress when needed and he pointed out plots of trees and bushes where berries or fruit could be taken and he knew where a tiny stream tracked through a field margin where the water canteens could be filled. He had a small leather knapsack strapped across his back which was dusty and beaten and could not have held much at all, and from which the muzzle of a revolver protruded throughout the day.

They reached El Guajolote long before sundown but they stopped their progress regardless and made camp inside a line of abandoned homes there a short distance from the edge of the highway. There was nothing of any remark about the place and no building left to scavenge and no plot of earth growing anything worth foraging. The old stone well was as dry as it could be and many of them gathered again in the small roadway outside the homes to trade goods and stories.

The settlement there had been a transient stop-over on that highway for many years, and though the walls were intact, window frames and roof tiles and wiring and piping had long since been removed to various ends. Fires had been made time and again in the yards and in the homes themselves and some appeared burned out entirely, whether accidentally or otherwise. El Guajolote was the dry, dusty skeleton of a place but it served as somewhere to rest nonetheless and was better indeed than the open country.

There were others in that place with them, travelling south to north, people of their kind who were honest and god-fearing and looking to trade goods or seeds or foodstuffs or simply advice of what lay ahead of them on their passage. Three toothless roamers circled the peripheral of their group and, though the party was wary of them at first, it became apparent that they were of little threat and not armed and barely dressed. They were the battered and forgotten who had no means to survive and no skills with which to flourish, who simply existed in vast numbers to go one day to the next on the leanest of existences until their day came to die.

As the sky at the horizon grew pink, coyotes could be heard on the flatlands. The man with the long coat sat in the dusty open, smoking and talking to other travellers. Another, a squat man with his hair tied back messily, held to them an open case of rifle shells and the men examined them and traded some for various items.

Dylan sat on the back of the cart and watched them, the Colt Python turning over and over in his hands.

One of the travellers saw him and called to him.

"Hey Bandido, es eso tuyo?"

He stopped swinging the gun and nodded.

"Yeah it's mine" he replied in English.

The man nodded his approval.

"I like this gun" he said, pointing with a cigarette between his fingers, "are you a good shot?"

Dylan shrugged.

"I never really have enough shells to practise"

The man nodded.

"You can practise with mine"

Dylan looked over to his father who was sitting some distance back on the step of the home and who had been listening to the interchange. He rose and nodded his son onwards to the man. He would allow it for it was a good opportunity for the boy to learn but he would also insist that nothing happen without his oversight.

The man held the old M1 carbine to the boy.

The boy shook his head.

"I want to practise with the pistol"

The man in the long coat spoke.

"The rifle will shoot twice the distance of the pistol, and is much higher calibre"

He held out a .30 shell in the palm of his hand.

"I don't have a rifle", Dylan replied, "I have a pistol, and that is what I should learn to shoot"

The men nodded and agreed.

"Use this" said the man in the coat, swinging an old revolver from his belt and handing it to the boy, "you can practise shooting the sign across there, if you shoot it with your American pistol you'll take it out of the ground"

The boy weighed it in his hand and levelled it and the men stepped back.

Ryan moved in behind him.

"Steady your breath" he said softly, "be calm when you shoot"

He squeezed the pistol and fired a shot into the twilight and it rang out across the quiet country.

He levelled it again and took another shot and missed a second time.

The man in the coat leaned in and held the boy by the shoulders and turned him slightly to adjust his stance and he fired a third shot into the dark.

Ryan watched.

"This time", he said, "take the breath in before you squeeze the trigger. Don't hold it in, but use the stillness"

The boy nodded.

He took a breath and waited just a moment and squeezed the trigger and cracked the shell into the metal roadsign and it clanged loudly and the men cheered.

Ryan applauded softly behind.

"Again bandido" the man called.

The boy took another breath and fired a second shot into the sign.

He looked to his father and the cheering men and turned and fired another shot wildly into the evening.

"Ah" called Ryan "you stopped concentrating didn't you? Always focus when you fire a weapon"

The boy fired a few more shells into the roadsign and a few more into the dark and then he took some shots with the rifle until his mother approached.

"Come on you boys, come to eat please"

"Ahh let the little bandido have his fun" called one of the men.

"My boys have many hours of the day to have what fun they need, but they must eat now" she smiled.

"The boy should know how to protect himself" called the man in the coat.

She nodded.

"He should. But he also has a mother who can protect him too"

She smiled slightly to them and shepherded the boy away towards their cart and the small fire where the pan hung.

"You can't offer the protection a gun can offer though, surely lady?" called the squat man, playfully.

She turned and approached him and gently took the handgun from him and looked down its length and spun the cylinder with her finger.

She levelled it at the roadsign with a single hand and launched three shots straight through the centre of it, one after the other and then pivoted her body a few degrees and put the remaining three shells through another metal sign thirty feet further back. She swung the pistol in her hand and offered it back to the silent man. The other men all laughed as she pushed Ryan and the boy back towards their dinner without another word.

They ate together in the shelter of the old building whilst watching the cart and their belongings. Ryan had acquired some .357 shells for the Colt and he positioned them into the ammunition box as they ate. He was still smiling at his wife's actions earlier with the man's old pistol, feeling at once proud and undeniably impressed. Neither of them had ever picked up a firearm until a few years prior, when his father-in-law had taught him to shoot from scratch, picking off glass bottles from increasing distances in the barn and the yard. He had passed those teachings on to Kiara in time, and she had taken to it well, as she had just proved.

That was all back when they had more ammunition and less concern.

They were both American by birth, having been born and raised north of Santa Fe, though Kiara's parents were of Mexican heritage. They met each other whilst they were both in their early twenties and soon bought a small apartment together on the north side of Albuquerque. A few years later their first child, a son, was born. Within the first two years of his life, Kiara's uncle died and her parents retired back to the family farm south of Monterrey in the north of Mexico to continue the uncle's work, and at the first opportunity Ryan and Kiara followed them south of border and took jobs and a small flat in the city. That was where they remained through the birth of their daughter, until they were forced to leave there that fateful day.

The news broke across national media outlets in the March, a predicted impact date of late May. More than one hundred million US citizens crossed the southern border and flooded into the Mexican deserts with what they could carry and tow. Those in Monterrey were told they would be outside the blast radius, but that there may be dust storms brought down from the north and to expect rough weather for some time.

It was fatally miscalculated.

Two days before the impact, they boarded their windows and doors and stockpiled what food they could. No emergency services would be on call until after the damage could be assessed and they were instructed to turn off all electrics to prevent fires which would not be fought. The looting had been and gone and men ran the streets proclaiming the second coming of the lord and the end of humanity itself.

When morning came, they had been sitting awake all night. They were not able to watch televised broadcasts as their building manager had turned off the power and they had no idea what to expect or when, if anything at all. Just before eight that morning, the building shook lightly and the crockery rattled and then it shook more and the pictures fell from the walls and then the very ground beneath them shuddered and the widows cracked and the plaster crumbled at the corners where the building began to change shape.

"Out" Ryan shouted.

His wide-eyed family stared at him.

"Out" he shouted again and grabbed the five-year-old Mia around the waist and scrambled to the door.

Kiara and Dylan jumped too and the boy, still only seven, began to cry and Kiara pushed him to the door of their apartment and out onto the stairwell and down the stairs. The steps shook and the building shook around them and other tenants ran and fell as they tried to carry gathered belongings and items of worth and they screamed at each other over the shaking and the children all cried.

In the street they were sure it was an earthquake.

Whilst the roadways remained thus far intact, the world around them shuddered and alarms rang from all around and people ran in every direction for nobody had anywhere to go.

They clicked open their little car and threw the children inside and started the engine and spun off along the road, swerving between other cars and people darting left to right and back again.

They crossed Highway 30 south onto Calle Aramberri and as they passed the cemetery they slowed slightly and took breath.

"Where are you driving us?" called Kiara, raw desperation in her voice.

Ryan didn't reply, he was tapping the steering wheel with his palm as he frantically considered his options. His only thought was to flee the city, but they were yet in the very heart of the place and it was not a quick drive at any time of day.

At the end of the road Ryan threw the car south towards the river and the bottom edge of the city.

"We need to get away from these buildings. And all these people"

"Is it an earthquake?" Mia called from the back seat, fear shaking her tiny voice.

"It's ok" replied Kiara, turning in her seat to calm the children, "it's just a little earthquake, but it's nothing to worry about. Remember how we talked about going on holiday when everything was over?"

The children nodded.

Mia clutched her stuffed panda to her chest with both hands.

"Well we're going now. We're going to go to the country for a little while and we're going to have lots of fun. You hear me?"

"Are we going to bela's?" asked the boy.

Her eyes widened and she looked at Ryan behind the wheel.

He nodded.
Her parents were only an hour or so south of the city.
"Yes, that's it, that's exactly where we're going, honey"
Ryan nodded.
"So just sit quietly and everything will be fine, ok?"
Neither child spoke.
"OK?" she asked again.
Mia nodded, unsure.
"OK Dyl?"
Dylan looked out of the window as the world fell apart.
He nodded.
"OK"

They crossed the highway and passed over the winding brown river and the traffic slowed as they entered the slipway into the Loma Larga tunnel.

"Is a tunnel the best idea?" Kiara asked.

Ryan didn't reply.

He agreed that it almost certainly was not, but it was the way out of the city to the south and that was all there was to it.

The traffic on the road crawled into the tunnel and the rumbling of the ground echoed around them and the place glowed red from taillights and smelled of petrol fumes and within a few hundred feet they stopped entirely. They sat for nearly an hour without moving until people began to leave their vehicles.

Their engine was off and Kiara was playing word games with the children to keep their minds calm.

Ryan kicked the door open.

"Wait here, I'll be back soon"

He handed the keys to Kiara and stepped out from the car and walked up between the parked vehicles through the tunnel. The Loma Larga was nearly two kilometres long and it took some time for Ryan to reach the front of the traffic, where a fuel tanker lay jack-knifed across the lanes with four cars smashed into the side of it, blocking further progress to the south. The traffic behind them to the north had queued back out of the tunnel and up to the highway and many had abandoned their vehicles altogether and continued on foot, rendering all vehicles inside the tunnel trapped completely.

As the people in the tunnel grew angry, they tried to turn their cars around in spaces that wouldn't allow it, creating a mess of vehicles that could not be moved.

Around the place there grew a blackening of the sky. The tunnel would ordinarily have been lit with electric lighting, and fans mounted in the concrete ceiling kept the airflow moving to stop polluted air from building up inside the structure, but neither was functional and the place became heavy and dark and still.

Though those in the tunnel could not witness it, a storm cloud one thousand miles wide pulsed southwards across the land, turning the sky black and yellow and raining down on the place everything which the wind could carry. Sand and earth from the deserts of the north and the borderlands, tiny particles of glass and metal and splintered wood from the city, tumbling in the air and tearing through everything it encountered. Wind whistled and screamed through the Loma Larga, though the debris in the air didn't carry far into the underground structure and the people remained as protected there as anywhere.

They hid in their cars and their trucks for nearly three hours until the darkness lifted and light could be seen at the ends of the tunnel again.

The people gathered by the jack-knifed tanker to determine what, if anything at all, could be done to move the thing enough to get their vehicles out, or if attempts should indeed be made to move the many vehicles which spread out behind them, though they numbered in the hundreds and many were without drivers.

They spent that afternoon there, growing hungry and thirsty and, though the kind and charitable amongst them shared what provisions they had, there was not enough to go around the group once and would most certainly not last the night.

Eventually Ryan determined that there was indeed no decision to be made, and he gathered his family from the car where Mia was sleeping and took them onto the pedestrian carriageway in the centre of the tunnel to leave on foot.

"When will we be at bela's?" the girl asked, rubbing at her eyes as she was lifted from the car.

Kiara lifted her up and held her in one arm and took Dylan by the hand.
"We'll be at abuela's soon, we have to walk for a bit"
"I'm hungry, mommy"
"I know"
"When can I have something?"
"Soon"
"But I'm hungry now"
Kiara nodded.
"I know"

Chapter Three

It took them nearly four days to make the journey to her parents' farmland near Palmitos. They were forced to spend the first night sheltered in a fuel station with others where they took food from the shelves without paying and, though they knew it was a matter of survival, they were yet plagued with guilt for it. On the second morning, they woke to ash and dust which blanketed everything there was to see like a heavy snowfall. They began to walk south to the city limits, past smashed buildings and abandoned cars and fires in the street. Occasional helicopters would pass but they saw no emergency response of any kind, neither law enforcement nor medical nor military and the city had deteriorated to a level of civil unrest and been left to fend for itself.

They kicked through the detritus and huddled together and moved swiftly, and by the evening they reached highway 85. They headed south and walked along the inside of the carriageway with hordes of others and spent that night at the roadside sheltering with only the warmth of each other as vehicles of all description sped by them.

Before dawn on the third day they made headway along the road, turning their ordeal into a game for the children and challenging them to spot things of interest and collect what they found and to look out for busses or trucks which may be able to take them further. It was the boy, sometime in that afternoon, who managed to flag down a passing tractor pulling behind it a steel trailer once used for moving livestock and the old man in the cab allowed them to climb into the back and took them slowly southwards. They drove as far as Huajuquito, the place at which they should begin to cross the Cerro de la Silla hills to the farmland on the eastern side.

They thanked the man with as much gratitude as they could find in themselves and the girl hugged him tightly and called him her superhero and told him that she would pray that night for him and for his sheep, which she insisted he had lost from the trailer, and he smiled and wished them well.

The third night was spent in that town where they took shelter in a shopping centre which had been opened to accept refugees and those without homes or those fleeing from the city. The shops had been ransacked and looted long before, and a restaurant there prepared coffee and rice and distributed it to the hungry who were scattered across the country, trying to find places to go or places which they had lost or those with simply no place at all. They took a large blanket from the store and slept together on the ground and Ryan sat awake all night and watched them.

Such duty was laden on any father, and the weight of responsibility was something that a parent carried regardless, though with that changed time Ryan felt the weight greater than ever. He watched his children wrapped around each other in his wife's arms.

Simple and innocent and utterly helpless.

They were not tainted by the wrongs of that world but they were thrust into the very fires of it nonetheless, and Ryan vowed to his own heart that he would shield them with safety and love in a place where they could not be reached by darkness, until the time came where they could fight for themselves. He vowed to have them well-prepared for when that day came, for he knew it would. He wondered what their future held for them, what may become of the dreams they had and the dream which he had for them. Every step along a given route changes the scenery which lay before it, and that which lay behind, but some steps take one to a place from which they cannot go back, and Ryan feared that these few days had taken them to a place from which they would not be returning. Whether that city, and other cities like it would recover and repair themselves was inconsequential, their lives would go on as they must, but he knew that there was no way of turning around to the life which was, regardless of what happened from that day onward.

They woke on the fourth morning and Ryan walked them to the edge of the road and stood the children next to each other.

"Take this water, and only drink it when you must. We have to do one more walk, but we will be there today, ok?"

They nodded.

"No quiero caminar, daddy" said Mia.

She alternated comfortably between languages, often in the same sentence. The children spoke only Spanish at their schools and with their friends, but Ryan encouraged them to speak only English in their home so they would not ever forget it.

"I know you don't want to walk, none of us do sweetheart, but you want to get to bela y belo's don't you?"

She nodded sheepishly.

The boy said nothing.

"We have to cross the hills, and much of the walk will be uphill. But what do you get after an uphill?"

"Downhill" the boy responded.

"Exactly. And downhills are easy, aren't they? Remember that. Every uphill has a downhill"

"We need one more big effort and then tonight you can play on the big swing and eat ice cream and we can play any game you want" Kiara spoke.

Both children smiled.

"Can we play with Belo's tractor?" Dylan smiled.

She laughed.

"Maybe not the tractor. We'll see. Come on"

She nodded them forward and they set out along the edge of the Presa Rodrigo Gomez which glistened blue and calm under the rising sun. The dust had settled but even out there in the countryside they could smell the fires and the cloud of dust and smoke still blackened the horizon to the north where Monterrey lay in ruins.

They crossed the dusty hills slowly, following the old road as it wound through the terrain. The sun was hot and they drank most of the water and rested where they could in the shade of big trees, and again they tried to make games to keep the children's minds busy and their energy levels from faltering. At some point in the mid-afternoon, they came down from the pass and saw before them the small town of La Boca.

They rested and ate fruits from a tree and tried to wash themselves in a small winding stream but the water carried dust and dirt, and when Kiara tried to wash Mia's face it left her with little spots of dirt and Ryan told the children not to drink it at all.

From the centre of La Boca, they knew it was only a short walk through the fields to reach her parent's farmland.

They took the road south through the open pastures and within the hour they reached the familiar old tree at the foot of the driveway, as dead and twisted as it ever was and yet refusing to fall. Kiara's grandmother had lived on the farm since she herself was a little girl and she tended the land and the animals with her own hands since her husband did not return from war. She kept the farm running well until she was far too old and her children deemed her a danger to herself, her stubbornness to give up and her undying insistence on operating machinery with impaired vision and failing dexterity.

Her two sons took control of the farm for the last years of her life and managed to gently ease her into what retirement they could, though she would regularly follow them about their business with a critical eye, reprimanding when tasks were not conducted in the traditional manner. Years after her death, the two sons split the equity in half and the eldest brother continued on with the land whilst the younger brother left to seek his fortunes north across the border. He married and had a single child, Kiara. It was the death of the eldest brother five years prior that had taken her parents back to that land, and they maintained both land and business well, despite their increasing age.

When the children saw the old tree they began to skip and there was relief in both their hearts and voices as they shouted and sang down the long driveway.

Their grandmother heard them coming and, as the track straightened out, they saw her standing beside the house with a broad smile across her weathered face. They ran to her and she bundled them both up and squeezed them in to her with her eyes closed and held them both as tightly as she could until their grandfather rounded the corner and they transferred their embrace to him.

Their rooms were always ready there, with small toys which they had left and there were clothes and the cupboards were always full of food.

They prepared a great meal and discussed the events of the past days and they each fell asleep early in their warm beds.

Three years went by.

The cities became wrecks. They were barely policed, and gangs flourished and roamers and thieves walked without reproach.

The storms came and went.

There were times when it rained for weeks without stopping and the cities ran with black water and the lands flooded and the trees came down and the animals drowned. Then would follow weeks of drought. The flooded cities dried and then burned and the sands of the northern deserts blew across the country and battered through old buildings and killed what crops remained.

The Federal government issued nationwide curfews that could not be enforced and eventually martial law. They supervised the organised demolition of huge swathes of the cities in places where structures were deemed dangerous, and left in their wake mountains of wrecked stonework.

Shockwaves from the initial impact triggered tsunamis to pulse out across the world's oceans from both coastlines and caused extensive flooding at practically any place on a waterway. International import and export ceased completely, with the small exception of manual trade across certain relaxed borders. Thus ceased the import of the fuels needed to power transport and machinery and manufacture, and within the first year there had occurred the almost complete cessation of all trade in new goods.

People hoarded what they must, stockpiled fuels where possible and began to live off what the land beneath their feet offered. Crops were stolen openly and it was not long before farmland was heavily guarded. Farms that neighboured each other would combine forces in joint security arrangements to better protect what food and livestock they still held, and it was common to see sentries in trees with rifles in even the most desolate of places. Disease spread and sickness prevailed, overrunning the nation's hospitals, which in turn could not get access to medications that would otherwise have been flown in by air.

Even those with money began to lose the power to travel. In the first year, their money got them access to whatever they desired, but the time slowly arrived where liquid gasoline began to deteriorate and no money could change that.

Drug cartels that had once run vast areas of that great nation began to lose the ability to make their money and to export their produce, and they turned their attentions to any sort of organised crime that they could.

The roads became a danger to travel. Gangs would stake out the main interchanges and tunnels and bridges and stage roadblocks and raid whatever transport passed that way until no transport passed at all. The stock in horses and mules rose so high that to own a beast capable of travel or pulling a cart was deemed something worth killing for. The people of the land bunkered themselves into their homes and armed themselves, and those who could not shoot soon learned and they stockpiled ammunition and there rose a great market in the manufacture of shells and bullets.

Though the towns would run dry, the water often became diseased and undrinkable and the people were forced to move on or die there. Eventually the peso lost value altogether and the value was transferred to goods of true worth such as tools, weaponry, seeds which could be cultivated and items from the past life that had been preserved, such as cleaning supplies and tinned food and fossil fuels for burning.

Ryan and his father-in-law made the journey back to Monterrey two weeks after their arrival at the farm, though the road into the city was completely impassable, and indeed they reached nowhere at all near their apartment.

They had intended to salvage what they could and to bring their belongings back to the farm but they were forced to abandon their quest for it would have involved walking much of the burning city by foot.

The heavy and difficult decision was made then to leave all of their old life and their belongings there, and to start again in the country refuge. The memories alone would suffice, the rest of it was material, and could be replaced.

They had no way of knowing that day, how far from the truth that was, though regardless, they were all safe and they knew that that was all that truly mattered.

Their land had once been vast, a number of acres of open pasture that grazed criollo cattle and rambouillet sheep and grew wheat and beans. An orchard next to the house had been filled with blossoming lemon and guava and guanabana. As time went by and the storms and droughts and thefts ravaged the land, they pulled their perimeter in to a smaller area which could be guarded more practically and fenced around it.

They pushed the cattle to plough the closest fields to the house, though they were not ploughing beasts, and reseeded the land there. Their yield was smaller than it had been in any of the years that their family had held that land, though it was sufficient to feed them and to provide a means of petty trade for other goods that they did not grow, coffee and corn and rice. The seeds from every fruit they ate and every plant they harvested were carefully extracted and stored in jars and boxes in the cool basement and the door which led down there was reinforced and locked with numerous locks at all times.

It was to them a vault for the most prized and protected of their possessions and the key to which remained around the grandfather's neck at all times, with a spare one buried out in a jar beside the stone well.

The children were taught the ways of the land, and the great-grandmother would have been proud to see them adopt the traditional practices of farming. The boy was taught how to lead and muster the cattle and how to shear the rambouillets. The milk and the wool was used and stored and what wasn't needed was traded in the town. Mia was too young for the manual work, though her grandmother taught her how to prepare food and darn clothes and to gather the fruits, though she resorted almost entirely to shaking the trees, laughing and screaming as the fruit fell.

Half a mile to the north was the neighbouring farmstead.

The landowner who farmed there was a long-time friend of that family and had watched them all grow. He too had brought the perimeter of his farm in to a more manageable and protectable size, and so for the first time in memory, the boundaries of their lands did not meet. He grew coffee in vast amounts and employed a small number of workers to harvest and prepare the berries. His land was fenced at the perimeter and he sat a number of riflemen at places along the boundary to watch for raiders and thieves and they signalled to each other with whistles. His friendship to the family was such that he acted, as much as could be achieved, as the sentry for their land too. There had been, over those past few years, numerous travelling parties who had crossed the land, scavenging and looting. Many were chancers, people of desperation who had no place to call their own and so simply wandered. They went from place to place, sometimes alone or in pairs and sometimes in small groups, taking what they could and offering little threat. The simple sound of the warning whistles piping through the air or a couple of warning shots from a rifle was usually adequate deterrent to move them along. Many weren't looking for trouble, simply a way to survive.

Though others existed there too.

There were, with increasing regularity, bands of dedicated raiders, their sole purpose to ransack and take every thing that they could. They came with horses and carts laden with wares, and with rifles and pistols and knives. They were the ghosts of the night hills, riding in darkness and swallowing what they encountered. Combat did not fear them nor were they afraid to take the life of any person who stood in their way. Though these raiders of the land, the displaced gangs and cartels and criminals were preceded by reputations of brutality and ruthlessness, they were yet simple men. They were not educated and readily out-smarted or out-gunned.

The neighbouring farmer's sentries sat through the night in shifts and listened for the hooves of horses or the rattle of carts. The town there, as with towns everywhere, offered effective community protection between those who lived and operated there and each house watched out for the next, prepared to aid their neighbour should the situation call for it.

But Kiara's parents' farm was a mile or more from the town and the whistles of the sentries could not be heard by the townsfolk unless the land was quiet and the wind blew right. Thus they recognised what importance there needed to be in being able to protect themselves there.

When the chores of the day were done, Kiara and Ryan and her father would often walk out on to the land where they would erect targets of old artefacts and they would practise firing the grandfather's old hunting rifle.

Despite the sun setting over the hills to the west and casting a low and blinding light across the yard, he would insist they faced into the sun to shoot. To the east of the yard the colossal ceiba tree grew higher than all else and was the grandfather's complete pride and utter joy and he would not allow a rifle so much as pointed in its direction, should it discharge accidentally.

It had been that way since Kiara was little.

The tree was sacred he would say, full of the spirits of the land and the tree itself could see. Kiara would laugh as a girl and call her father crazy but he would just look at her and nod.

Its huge star-like green leaves spread over their land as though the tree protected all below it, and its rough hard thorns climbed its own trunk and protected the thing itself. She had been told since young not to touch the great old tree, for not only would the thorns hurt her hands, the tree was not hers to touch. When the seeds fell, each wrapped in cotton, they would cover the yard and the lawns as though it had snowed and the place would turn completely white.

Her father had three rifles in total, though they each took different shells and some were easier to source than others. They would practise with the air-rifle, which took simple pellets that were in abundance, and then occasionally move on to the long rifles to familiarise themselves with the recoil and the kickback that more powerful weapons had when fired.

The old man was a sure shot, picking bottles from the old wall without trying, and he and Ryan held competitions between themselves to hit the smallest or most distant targets, and the grandfather nearly always won. In time, Kiara learned to shoot. She favoured the smaller rifle for its weight and agility, and favoured even more so her father's revolver, a Model 64, though it was kept indoors as the .38 Special cartridges it housed were rare and the gun held great value itself. On occasion the boy was allowed to join them there, though his mother was not ever pleased at it.

"One day he'll need it", the grandfather would say and his mother would pretend she hadn't heard. The grandfather taught him the stance and how to line the weapon with his shoulders and steady himself and where to place his weight, as he fired and the boy took to it as any 11 year old would do, with great enthusiasm if not any talent.

In the late summer of that year, Ryan returned from the town one warm afternoon, where he had been trading woollen blankets and hats which his daughter and her grandmother had made. He brought back a stack of pesos which were of ever-decreasing value, and a bag of goods for the family.

Kiara was trimming the fruit trees, which were by that time harvested, so as to encourage their growth the following spring.

"I have something for you" he called as he neared the orchard.

She stepped down from the wooden stool and walked to him.

He reached into his overcoat and swung out the shiny blue Colt Python. He presented it to her on his palm.

"What is that?" she asked without taking it.

"It's yours"

She narrowed her eyes.

"You bought me a gun?"

He smiled.

"Now you have your own. I bought a big box of shells too, though we don't waste them. The guy who sold it to me said that he doesn't even know a place to buy more"

She took it and turned it in her hand and studied it.

She had not at any stage of her life until those last few years been, inclined to buy or fire or even hold a weapon, and though their situation dictated that she must, she was still a little uneasy and uncomfortable with it.

"Practise with it" Ryan said, "and keep it on you if you're out in the fields or the town. Yeah?"

She nodded and thanked him and held the gun out slightly, as though unsure what to do with it.

He took it from her hand and swung it around his finger and turner by the hips slightly so as to push the muzzle down the back of her belted jeans.

She smiled.

"There you go Annie Oakley, now you can get back to your trees"

Chapter Four

Four summers came and brought drought and four winters passed in famine.

The grandfather grew older, his fingers losing their abilities with the tools required to farm and the family took on his workload alongside their own. The grandmother educated the children on every topic she was knowledgeable on and she bought books in the town with which to show and tell them about the things of the world that they would likely never see. Gradually, the memories of their past crumbled away and the children barely remembered what had been before. The country fell into decline, as countries across the planet did. The towns and cities there became pockets of trade and commune and offered reasonable safety under the blanket of lawlessness that lay across the land. There still remained in Mexico City a sitting government, though they governed without election and corruption poured through its heart. Regardless, its powers were relatively restricted and it held no command over divisions of healthcare or infrastructure or transport or sanitation as those services no longer existed, and any effort to maintain them stood with the people themselves.

The Secretary of National Defence held most of the political sway as he commanded the vast armies. Whilst he and the Director of the Navy were answerable to the President, they operated autonomously and were not governed or questioned on their decisions in any manner.

It was late one June afternoon and the sky was pink.

There had been no rains and the stream trickling down from the hills had become a trace-line of grey pebble and dust. Dylan and his mother had been walking for most of the afternoon, trying to locate the four remaining cattle which had escaped their enclosure before dawn. They rounded two of them and led them slowly along the worn track, back towards the farm. The other two cows had bolted, split from the little herd of escapees and Kiara and the boy were forced to choose only one of the two groups to chase and had to watch the others scarper away down the hillside.

They were standing at the crest of the hill looking for their trail when they heard the whistles.

Long and shrill and cutting through the birdsong and the breeze. Unmistakable in that place, the most unnatural sound.

They looked at each other, their eyes wide.

Kiara pulled the pistol from her belt and the two ran back along the track towards their land, leaving the two rounded cows where they stood and the other two to their fate.

In the valley, the men had surrounded the farmhouse.

Six men were positioned along the driveway, two more sat stooped on the gentle hill that led away to the north where the beans grew, their rifles on the farmhouse. Two men were walking the fenceline between their land and the neighbouring farm and it was they who had triggered the alarm whistles.

The neighbour's three sentries left their posts, rifles and pistols in hand and fired shots into the air at the approaching men.

"Larguesen!" they shouted, running at the men. They blew their tin whistles as they went, notifying men in the surrounding land of their situation, or indeed hoping to do so.

As they neared the fenceline the two raiders levelled their weapons and fired at the sentries and one fell and tumbled and bounced in the dust. Another sentry fired back and hit one of the raiders in the neck. He fell to his knees and clutched at himself as the blood pulsed through his fingers, pouring down his shirt to the ground and he coughed and fell.

The second raider ducked in behind the wooden fence and more shots rang out across the dusky hills. Three more of his comrades joined him there and eventually all of the sentries lay dead in the dirt and the echoing of the shots calmed.

Inside the farmhouse, the grandmother had taken Mia down into the basement and the grandfather locked the door behind them.

He took two of the rifles to the top bedroom and positioned himself at the window and loaded the rifle with shells and took a knee.

Ryan took the remaining rifle and the Model 64 and walked into the front room.

Five men approached the front of the house and stopped short of their porch.

The grandfather aimed his rifle straight at them but did not fire.

"What do you want?" he shouted, hiding down behind the rifle.

The men looked up to the window.

"What have you got?" the man asked.

"We have nothing for you, we are just a simple farm" Ryan shouted from behind the front door.

"Ahhhh" the man called, smiling, "you have something for us. Don't be difficult with me my friend"

Ryan moved to the front window with the rifle.

He watched the five men standing in the yard, and though he knew there were likely others, he had no idea how many.

"Go" Ryan called, "all of you. Go now and you won't get killed. Men will be coming from all around us, you'll see. We're not alone here"

The five men laughed.

The man at the front who had been speaking raised his old rifle at the front door and fired a round straight into the woodwork.

"We're not scared of you" Ryan called, "now go"

The man bolted the rifle and fired again and then a second time and then a third.

He shouted, far more aggressively.

"You are lucky we are giving you this warning, amigo. Bring the old man outside, this is your one chance"

"You have no chance" shouted the grandfather from the bedroom window, volleying a stream of rifle shots straight into the men, grounding three of them who lay in the dust screaming and holding their wounds as they spat blood.

The other two men leaped away and began to fire on the house.

Their accomplices came in from the surrounding land and added firepower to the barrage being levelled at the old farmhouse.

In the shaking and ringing of the shots, Ryan heard the grandfather cry out from upstairs.

He ducked away from the window and took a breath.

"Papa" he screamed up the stairs, "are you ok?"

The few moments seemed eternal before his father-in-law's voice was heard from the bedroom.

"Yes. I was shot. I'm ok"

"Shit", Ryan said to himself.

He knew he would have to get the old man somewhere safe to be treated.

He scrambled up the stairs on his knees as rifle shots thumped into the front wall and smashed the windows and he found the old man sitting back against the bed, dripping thick blood through his clothes onto the wooden floor. The blood followed the grooves in the timber and stretched out across the floor like the branches of a dead tree.

The rifle-fire ceased.

Ryan put his finger to his lips for the grandfather to be quiet.

"Let's get you downstairs quickly" he said, stopping down next to him, "hold on to me"

He lifted the man by the shoulders and they staggered together towards the door.

As Ryan took the first step down the wooden staircase, holding the grandfather against him, his arm tucked underneath his own, he heard the front door smash open and the men enter the house.

He let the old man drop to the floor and pointed the pistol down the stairs into the hallway below.

A man in an old dusty coat and hat rounded the bottom of the steps with a rifle and Ryan put a single shot through his hat into the top of his head and his eyes stopped and he staggered two steps forward into the wall and dropped slowly to the floor.

He looked down at the pistol and the empty cylinder.

He threw it onto the bed and scrambled to the window for the old man's rifle, and as he grabbed it and turned back to the steps, two men appeared in front of him, weapons levelled.

"Drop it" one said sharply.

Ryan lowered it slightly.

"Drop it" the man repeated louder and Ryan slowly stooped to put the rifle on the floor.

"Take whatever you want" he said slowly.

The men smiled and one moved into the room to start looking through the drawers and cupboards for items of value.

Ryan stood in the centre of the room, his father-in-law sat outside the door at the top of the stairs, pooling blood across the floor and not speaking.

"Let the old man go, he needs help" Ryan said.

He knew if he could get the grandfather help with the wound that he stood a fair chance of survival but time was critical.

The man in the doorway looked round at the grandfather on the floor. He turned to look at Ryan.

"This old man?" he asked, turning his arm and firing a single shot into the side of his father-in-law's head.

He had been motionless before the shot and the bullet toppled him slowly into the wall in a spray of red.

Ryan's world went silent and everything spun.

For the briefest of moments he stood and stared, dazed and lost and numb, before running at the man in the doorway and throwing himself through the air at him, the two of them crashing to the floor in the hallway.

He grabbed the man's face in his palm and in a blurred fury of impulse and rage of which he had no control, he smashed the man's head backwards into the floor and then again and again and again until the back of his skull split and blood spat out across the wood and dripped from the man's eyes, and though he kicked and struggled beneath him, Ryan continued the crash the man's head to the floor until a shot rang out and Ryan felt the intense burning.

The power in his arms, a few seconds prior so strong that he could not temper it, drained completely and he went numb and could not hold himself up on his knees and he rolled slowly off the dead raider beneath him to the floor.

As he rolled onto his back, he saw the second man standing above him with his pistol still aimed.

Ryan watched him, wide-eyed, and tried to speak but could not and he croaked and spat blood and thought then that he was at the doorway of death, though he could still feel the burning in his shoulder where the bullet had seared through his flesh and it encouraged him.

As his world clouded, he attempted to push himself up but could not control his arms and he lay there as the man stepped over him and headed back down the steps.

The others in the building ransacked the place and laughed at him on the floor as they turned the rooms upside-down and they took items of worth and items of interest and items that seemed of no value at all, and within a few minutes they had what they had come for and moved again to the front yard.

Ryan called on all the power and determination within himself to push himself to his elbows.

There was blood everywhere, across the bed and the walls and the doors and dripping down the stairs, and the place was wet with water that had been spilled from something the men carried and it flowed the blood quicker.

He rolled and pushed himself to the top of the steps and allowed himself to tumble from the top to the very bottom of the wooden staircase and he crashed to the floor and the pain inside him roared like nothing else.

The stairs were dripping wet too and the blood trickled through the water in strange patterns and swirled and clouded like cream in hot coffee.

He forced himself upright and watched the men carrying what they had taken out through the front door of the farmhouse.

The man who had spoken from the yard came into the house and walked to him and stopped.

"You were warned" he said, and threw his cigarillo to the ground beneath him.

It sat for a moment, its tip glowing, before the floor turned blue.

It billowed outwards from the man's feet to the walls and up the back of the sofa and the kitchen door and orange flames took hold of everything.

Ryan realised then that it was not water which was dripping through the house and the smell of the kerosene flooded his lungs.

In an instant the place was ablaze and the man smiled and left through the front door.

Ryan tried to stand and couldn't and his mind raced as he tried to figure out what to do. For a moment he considered the best way to extinguish the fire, and as he rolled himself to the kitchen to find water he began to realise the scale of the fire was beyond him and the kitchen itself was in flames itself.

His mind turned to survival and he knew that he had to get his daughter and his mother-in-law out of the basement immediately and out of the house to safety and he summoned every strength that he could from within the deepest parts of his soul and with a scream he pulled himself to his feet and staggered through the smoke-filled hallway to the basement door.

He tried to shout to them but his voice was hoarse, and the sound of cracking timber and exploding glass began to fill the house behind him as the blaze took hold of the building.

He could hear them shouting from within and he pushed his weight against the door and turned the burning handle and couldn't turn it enough to open it.

Then he heard Mia's voice, cutting through all cacophony as though it was not there.

The only sound in his ears at that moment.

"Daddy, belo has the key around his neck"

His heart disappeared from his chest.

He looked back along the hallway to the stairs and they were no longer there.

Black smoke swirled along the ceiling and up into the hole that once led to the upper floor of the house.

It began to fill his lungs.

He pushed and pushed at the door and threw his body into it until the blood poured from him and he stood back and lifted his leg and kicked at the wood, and as he lifted it a second time he lost his balance and fell backwards into the wall and his vision flashed white and then slowly everything faded to orange and then to black.

At the far end of the plantation, Kiara and Dylan were running at full speed towards the blaze, crashing through crops with no regard. As they flew into the dusty yard the men were walking away from them towards the track and they spun and fumbled for their weapons and tried to aim them.

Kiara squeezed the trigger again and again and put two shots straight into the first man and one into the next, and another man tried to get in front of her and she put the next round straight through his eye.

She pulled her shawl over her mouth as she ran and without hesitating she thundered through the flames and into the burning house, and her hair singed and her breathing nearly stopped as she choked on the smoke.

She tried to scream for her family though there was no sound.

Dylan staggered in beside her and she grabbed him by the neck of his clothes and threw him back towards the front door.

"Get out" she screamed, coughing.

Ryan lay on the floor beneath the black smoke, motionless.

She flung herself to the ground on top of him and held his face and looked at him and saw no life, though she felt his hand try to reach for her and she grabbed him by the shoulders and pulled him backwards through the room, through the spitting timber and flame and into the yard beyond.

The boy was crying.

Behind her, the roof of the building collapsed inwards in an explosion of flame and sparks and smoke and debris.

As she turned to look at it, the side wall fell too and the flames blew outwards and she pulled the boy to the floor, on top of his father as the sky around them went black.

The raiders watched silently from the driveway.

They said nothing nor looked back again as they silently left the land and moved off down the old driveway to the track beyond.

Kiara and her son lay out in the dirt on top of Ryan's blood-covered body, as the house fell apart, grandfather's body with it, grandmother and granddaughter silently asleep beneath it.

Chapter Five

At the foot of the white stone steps the two old men played their instruments to nobody. The smaller man sat on the bottom step with the marimbol between his knees, plucking at the sticks without rhythm, his long poncho wrapped around himself and his instrument so that only his hat and the toes of his old boots showed.

The rain continued to fall though had subsided overnight and people began to emerge from their shelters again. A brown stream rolled along the edge of the roadway, carrying what filth it collected. The taller man, wet through to his skin, danced in front of the other, his hair matted to his face as he jigged clumsily, shaking and rattling the old jawbone of a donkey in his hands. His boots were torn although he either did not notice or did not care.

Ryan, Kiara and Dylan steadily pulled their cart past the men and Dylan stood for a moment to watch the musicians, and the dancing man smiled at him and accentuated his dancing further to entertain the boy and Dylan smiled.

Ryan smiled but did not stop, the cart still pulling behind him.

They reached the old square in Huajutla de Reyes where the festival had been some days prior. The buildings there, once prettily ornate and delicate were crumbling and forgotten and neglected, tied in strips of coloured fabric which dripped with rainwater.

They stopped under the stone archway and Ryan split the buñuelos between them and they wrung the water from their hair and Kiara took the cover from the cart and shook the water from it and reattached it with the hooks.

"Dad" said the boy as he ate.

Ryan looked at him.

"Did you know, in Mexico City there are lions and bears that walk around the streets?"

Ryan smiled.

"Where have you got that from?" his mother asked.

"From that boy I was talking to at the festival"
"Which boy?" his mother asked.
"The boy" he said, finishing the bunuelo, "the boy I was talking to, with the red hat"
His mother looked at him and then at Ryan.
Ryan shrugged and gently shook his head.
"There are no lions walking the streets" he said.
The boy thought.
He dusted the crumbs and the sugar from his fingers on his trousers.
"There are" he said, "and bears"
"I'm sure the boy in the red hat, whoever he was, was mistaken. We don't have lions in Mexico, Dylan. I guess there may be mountain lions possibly, way up north, but not in the city"
"And bears"
"The bears are in the hills too, not in the city. Don't worry about them"
The boy thought.
"Dad?"
"Yes"
"I think they escaped from a zoo and they don't know where to go"
Ryan nodded.
"Ok, well when we get there, maybe you'll see one"
They began to walk.
"I hope not", the boy said, walking behind.
They walked away from the town square towards the southern edge of the town.
"I do hope I see a killer whale, that would be awesome"
"That is one thing you are definitely not going to see in Mexico City" Ryan said without looking back, "come on, keep up"
They reached the edge of the town before midday and took the cart onto the raised highway 105 where it followed the river at Tecorral.
"Are we walking alone?" the boy asked.
Ryan shrugged.
"We'll look out for others, you see if you can see anyone as we go, ok?
The boy nodded.
There was always risk to walking open country alone, but the walk south west to Tehuetlán could be done in an afternoon if they didn't stop.

The festival which was held there a few days prior had drawn in people from the surrounding hills and towns and caused those passing to stay longer, but it had also attracted opportunistic criminals and petty thieves who had used the cover of the rain storms to ransack carts and steal horses. Fights and violence had broken out in pockets of the town and many of those who had come to enjoy the revelry had quickly moved on.

The road where they stood was empty but Ryan was confident that if they moved swiftly, which they always did, they would spot another caravan or convoy which they could join to reach Tehuetlán, or indeed further.

The road cut through the valley floor, shouldered high on either side with the green hills of Hidalgo, full of sweetgum and sacred fir where birds could be heard.

"Do you think we can get more buneulos when we get there?" the boy asked as they walked.

"I don't know" his mother replied, "they were made for the festival"

"They were really good"

"We'll see if we can find somewhere that might make them for you"

"I'm really bored of tortillas now" he said.

"We all are" Kiara nodded, "we'll find something better soon"

"When will we reach Mexico City?"

"Mexico City? Not for a while. We are nowhere near it yet"

The boy didn't reply.

They walked as they always walked.

"How long do you think?" he asked eventually.

Kiara shrugged.

"Ryan" she called.

Ryan walked at the front with the cart, his head down as he pushed forward like an ox with a plough. His poncho was wet through but he had no option but to wear it regardless.

He didn't look around to her though she knew he had heard her call.

"How long to Mexico City do you think?"

He walked for a moment, thinking of the answer for them.

He had no map, no physical plot to follow and no way of discerning distance nor time. Routes were discussed with other travellers on the roads, of which there were many, tens of thousands moving in each direction along the highways and tracks, as vehicles once did. They made roadside camps and makeshift trading posts at riversides where fires were stoked and information was shared. The people told each other what dangers lurked along certain roads, where to go and where not to go and places where places one should never go. It was there that a traveller could learn the walking distance to the next town, or the next place to trade or to find shelter.

"A week's walk" he called, "if we don't stop. Which we will"

The answer made the boy think more and they walked on in silence as his head turned.

"Will we be there by Christmas?" he asked.

"Christmas?" his mum asked, "Dyl it's the middle of November, when do you think Christmas is?"

She smiled and the boy nodded and smiled too.

Halfway along their journey, the road turned south in a sweeping curve and a track led from it into the hills to the north.

The sign read *Tetzacual.*

At the edge of the roadside, a gathering of travellers had amassed by a cluster of old white stone buildings, and they watched as Ryan and his family approached slowly from the east.

"Hola viajeros" called a man in a blue overcoat, standing at the edge of the party with his dog.

Ryan nodded.

"Hola señor"

The travellers nodded and greeted the family.

"A donde van?" one of the men asked.

"Tehuetlán. Today Tehuetlán, but we walk to México City eventually. And then the south"

The group nodded and smiled.

"Do you have anything to trade?" one of the women called to them.

She stood over her young girl. They were wet and dirty and without belongings.

"We need dry clothes, or blankets" said another.

"We all need dry clothes" Ryan replied, trying not to sound blunt, though his statement was an obvious one, "you should make a fire while the rains have slowed and dry what you can now".

He looked across to the old buildings.

"What's inside?" he asked.

The people shook their heads and mumbled that they had looked already and that there was nothing of worth.

The man spoke.

"There has been, er" he thought of the word and clicked his fingers as he did so, "fuego, er, fire"

Ryan nodded.

"Is not safe for sleeping here, is black" the man concluded.

Dylan pulled fruit from a tree at the roadside and inspected it and took a bite and his face screwed at it. His mother watched.

"Have you come from the south?" Ryan asked.

"Si" nodded another of the men, older and with a wide straw hat that frayed around the brim.

"Is the passage safe?

The man shrugged slightly and thought and nodded.

"Si"

"No bandidos?"

The man shook his head.

"Militar" he said.

Ryan nodded.

The military could not hide their presence, even in small numbers. As convoys moved around the country from city to city, conducting their general peacekeeping and recruitment, word of their location moved a few days ahead of them, allowing the gangs and criminals and raiders to remain a step ahead. Despite the lack of telephony or other digital communication, word travelled fast along the roads from town to town. Every highway in the land had become a direct method of transferring information and as so many people travelled, information about a place was shared freely.

The presence of the military was always a reassuring thing.

They were heavy-handed, corrupt and badly governed but they provided an order and a safety where they travelled, and it was known that groups would follow behind their convoy to guarantee safe passage.

They thanked the group and wished them well and moved out along the road, the hills to the south of the road cascading away into mist at the horizon. Kiara took an old blanket from under the sheeting of their cart and wrapped it around the wet little girl and pulled it around her shoulders and the mother thanked her and drew the crucifix across her chest and Kiara smiled and waved away her gratitude.

The air was warm and humid and the rain had stopped.

A sign at the roadside told them the Parque Ecologico was one and half kilometres further along the road, an area that had once been preserved from development. Its preservation was no longer required. Development of highways and towns ceased almost immediately after the disaster and nature had long overrun huge swathes of the country, climbed its way up buildings and bridges and pulled stonework apart where it could. Land that was not farmed had overgrown and encompassed anything that stood before it, and the trees and bushes that once grew at the roadside snaked and bloomed out over the tarmac, unrestricted and not tamed by the hand of man.

A few miles further, old cars, rusted and smashed and torched, began to litter the roadside.

Behind the low metal fence, buildings spread out to the south.

"What is it?" called Ryan.

Kiara paused and peered through the trees.

"A school"

Ryan stopped.

"Should we look?"

"For what?" she asked.

"For anything. Screws and nails maybe, I need something to fix the back plate on the cart. Or books"

She shrugged and nodded.

They took the cart from the road and walked it along the cracked driveway and stopped it outside the first building, wrapped in creeping vines and dark inside despite the daylight.

"You want to stay here with the cart?" Ryan asked.

She thought.

"No, I'll go, you watch the stuff", she nodded to Dylan, "come on, you're with me".

She took the Colt from the box and tucked it into the back of her trousers and pushed the broken door open and it creaked and clicked where the hinge was broken. They walked inside the dank hallway, stinking of rot and damp, the plaster on the wall blackened and crumbling. In places the walls were still coloured blue and yellow where they had once been painted brightly, but the paint had faded and the colours now seemed haunting in their innocence.

The place was silent. They passed along the hallway and peered inside the first classroom. The chalkboard still hung on the wall at the front and the whole room had been spray-painted many times over so that even the graffiti was faded. There were old wooden chairs, mostly broken, and the metal legs had been removed from all of the tables. The light fixtures were gone and the foam square ceiling panels hung from their fittings.

In the second room, a great black hole had been burned into the floor where a fire had been made and then most likely abandoned whilst still alight.

In the third room the bookcase was turned over and the ground was littered with old textbooks.

"Here" Kiara called.

The boy caught up with her and they entered the room.

"Look through these. Put over here the ones that are still usable, not the wet ones or the torn ones, the good books that people will want to read"

"What are they?" he asked.

"I don't know, they're just books. Go on"

She ushered him into the room.

"I'm going to look in the other rooms ok? Shout if you see or hear anything"

He nodded. He knew the protocol.

The boy crouched to the ground and began looking through the books for anything worth keeping and his mother left the room and moved further down the hallway.

A painting hung along the corridor wall of horses running through water and she stopped and smiled at it and lost herself for the briefest of moments. She took hold of the frame and lifted it down from the wall and set it carefully on the ground and took the hooks and screws from the back of it and then the hooks from the wall and dropped them into her pocket.

In the next room the smell got worse. She pushed open the door, scraping backwards the chairs which had been piled up behind it. They clattered to the floor and the noise seemed deafening in the silence.

The boy called out to her.

"It's ok, it's me" she called back.

The room had been the school dining hall. Chairs and tables were strewn across the floor, and the back wall opened into a serving hatch and small kitchen beyond. She rounded the counter and pushed open the swing door into the kitchen. The room was windowless and the metal wall cupboards danced with what little flickering sunlight crept through the open doorway. The smell was overpowering. At her feet, four bodies were piled before her, bloated and rotten and crawling with things that she could not see. She jumped backwards and fell out of the door and instinctively pulled the pistol from her belt and aimed it at the kitchen.

She caught her breath and listened.

There was only silence.

The dead had been in there some time, though she could not be sure that the hand at which they had fallen had moved on. She darted back out the dining room, kicking through the old chairs and out into the hallway.

"Let's go" she shouted as she neared the room with books.

The boy was sorting through them and had made a small pile to his side.

"Come on" she called from the doorway, urgency in her voice.

He looked around from where he sat.

"Now" she barked.

He stood.

"I put some books there which we can take"

"Leave them, it doesn't matter. Come on. Right now"

He hesitated.

"I'm not telling you again", walking away along the corridor to the door.

The boy quickly grabbed the top book from the pile and ran to catch her and they both burst out of the doorway into the sunlight beyond and along the driveway without stopping.

Ryan was sitting on the cart by the side of the building and began to ask what had happened to instigate such urgency, though instead simply picked the front of the cart from the ground and pulled it after them to the road.

By late afternoon they reached the boundary of Tehuetlán.

Low adobe buildings spotted the roadside, white and brown or painted red with stone overhangs at the front.

A sign read *El Toritos Tacos* and a cartoon bull held the snack with a toothy smile.

The door was boarded with heavy wooden struts and on the roof an old man sat in a metal chair with a hunting rifle and watched them as they walked. Ryan tipped the brim of his hat to the man as they passed and the man nodded very slightly. The place had not sold tacos for some time.

A long articulated truck was jack-knifed in the road and its tyres had been taken and children ran along the open back where the goods had once been strapped. Two women sat high up on old stone steps between two buildings and called to them to be careful and the children ignored them as children do.

They found the centre of the town where stalls sold beans and rice and pastries and coffee and Ryan bought each of them a tortilla wrap filled with beans and corn and loroco.

"Quieres pesos?" he asked, holding out the paper notes to her.

The elderly lady shook her head. Pesos were of little value to her, and whilst they were still active currency, there were no banks to honour them and the true value to her was in reusable commodities.

"No" she said, "what do you have?"

Ryan shrugged.

"I have lots of things. What do you want for the food?"

She pointed at the cart, its luggage covered with the sheet.

"I'm not taking the cover off it all for you to see, what is it that you want? We have seeds?"

She looked at him.

"Semillas" he repeated.

She cocked her head.

"Books, tools, some old clothes?" he continued.

"Books" she said.

Ryan nodded.

He reached under the sheeting and pulled out a stack of old books, some fiction, others textbooks on all manner of subjects.

He put the stack down on the wooden countertop and the woman looked at them for a moment and took one and turned it in her hand and nodded to Ryan.

"Gracias" he said and the woman nodded again.

They ate together at the roadside, sitting on the high stone kerb and watching an old man trying in vain to swat two dogs away from his rubbish bins. He would chase one with his straw broom and as it ran the other would pull the bins and he would turn and chase that dog away and the first would return again. They smiled as they ate and the man swore and shouted and swung his broom around and the dogs continued relentlessly. Neither man nor dog had anything better to do and, at the very least, it provided a cruel entertainment for them whilst they ate.

"We'll camp here tonight" Kiara said and Ryan nodded.

As the sun went down, they found a place where other camps were made and positioned their cart against the front wall of an old building and pulled the biggest of the blankets from it. Ryan had fastened metal hooks into the fabric and he hooked one side of the blanket onto the side of the cart and pulled it outwards so that it was taught and took two thick nails from the box. He pushed them through the blanket and hammered them into the old wall until they held the blanket up a few feet from the floor as a makeshift tent roof, protection should it start to rain again overnight. There was no place to make a fire but the night was warm and they had already found food so there would be no need to cook. They had coffee in the flask and they were happy with it cold.

They sat. The sky grew dark and the town grew quiet, but for the low chattering of the travellers who slept in the open there, a scattering of homeless roamers with blankets and carts or trolleys and with dogs and ponies and donkeys or oxen.

"I have a book, dad" Dylan said, pulling it from the side of the cart.

"Great. What is it?"

The boy didn't know.

He read the cover aloud.

"Baja nuestros mares: Estudianos los océanos", he thought of the translation, "Under our seas"

Ryan nodded.

"Learning the oceans" Dylan said.

"Studying" Ryan corrected.

"Studying the oceans"

Ryan nodded.

"Exactly"

Dylan looked at the book.

"Para niños. For children"

"Good. Perfect Dyl"

"Can we read it?"

"It's pretty dark. We can try"

The boy sat next to his father and opened the book. He held it closer to his face in the darkness and tried to read it.

"It's too dark to read this now son" he said, and saw the boy's disappointment, "we can look at the pictures though, yeah?"

Dylan smiled.

"Do you know what that is?" he asked pointing into the book.

"A squid"

"And that one"

"Er, a fish"

"What fish?"

"A swordfish"

"Close Dyl, it's a marlin. It's like a swordfish though"

They turned through the book.

"What's that one?"

"A spider"

"A spider?" Ryan laughed, "that's not a spider, it's a book about the sea"

"You can get spiders in the sea"

"I don't know if you can"

"You can dad. They're called sea spiders and they swim underwater and they eat dead sharks when they fall to the bottom"

Ryan smiled.

"Ok. So what is that?"

Dylan shook his head.

"I don't know, what is it?"

Ryan shrugged.

"I have no idea, a crab or something. It says underneath the picture what it is"

Dylan held the book close to his eyes.

"I can't read it"

"OK, well we can find out in the morning"

Dylan nodded and kept trying to read it regardless.

Ryan smiled. Across from him, Kiara smiled too.

"Dad"

"Yes?"

"Do you know what my all-time favourite fish in the world is?"

"What?"

"A killer whale. They live right out at sea and they can eat anything they want"

Ryan nodded.

"They can. Do you want to know something, though?"

The boy looked up from the book.

"They're not fish, Dylan"

The boy looked puzzled.

"Of course they are"

"Well, they look a lot like fish, like really big fish. But they're whales, and whales aren't fish. They're mammals"

"What's a mammal?"

"It's lots of things. You're a mammal"

The boy thought.

"I'm nothing like a killer whale"

"I know"

"They're called Orcas actually dad"

Ryan nodded.

"Indeed they are"

The boy thought more, sitting in the dark.

"Dad"

"Yes?"

"If I'm a mammal, then a killer whale must be a fish"

Ryan nodded.

"OK sure, that's fine"

Chapter Six

At dawn the camp began to awake and the tents and coverings and blankets were put away and the carts packed and the animals gathered.

The rain had held off through the night and the morning sky was pink at the horizon and silhouetted birds flew low and jumped between trees and flowering plants. It was still early, but those who travelled onwards gathered together to do so as a group.

"Van al sur?" a man called over to them as they packed the blankets onto the cart.

Kiara nodded to him.

"Si, al sur. Y usted?"

The man nodded and said that he was also heading south.

He asked if he could travel with them as he otherwise walked alone. They agreed and told him they were heading back up onto highway 105 to make the journey to Acatipa.

The man asked where they were heading beyond there, beyond only Acatipa.

"Cuidad de México", Ryan answered, "finalmente"

The man thought.

He pushed his fingers through his long greying beard and straightened it downward. He shook his head. He told them that Acatipa was almost due west, and that much of highway 105 wove north and south as it snaked through the woodlands. He told them they would likely walk all day on that road, and though they may reach Sor Juana by sundown, they would have walked no more than ten miles as the crow flies.

He asked them what map they were following.

"We have no map" Ryan admitted.

The man nodded.

He said that without a map it was foolish to try to travel.

Ryan told him that they knew exactly where they were going and the man agreed that, in principle, that was indeed true. He said, however, that the knowledge of people travelling those roads was temporary and what they did not know was the tracks and trails that intersected the hills and countryside around them.

He pulled a stack of old yellowing papers from his pack and called Ryan over to him.

"Look" he said, holding the top sheet of paper out to him, "here".

He pointed on the map to the town in which they stood and showed them the highway 105 as it worked from town to town in an easterly direction.

"Not south" he said.

He showed Ryan the track south of the town, through the hills.

"Tochintlán" he said, tapping the map, "by tonight"

Ryan nodded.

He walked back to his wife and son.

"This guy has a map, there's a track through the hills to the south. What do you think?"

She thought.

"Do you trust him?"

Ryan shrugged.

"I don't trust anyone. But he has a map"

"Where is this place?"

"What place?"

"The place he says we'll reach?"

"A day. The road goes due south. The highway doesn't"

She shrugged.

"We camp there tonight and tomorrow we can make Lolotla in a day"

"Sure", she pulled her shawl over her shoulders, "but you watch this guy"

A group of others, two men and a woman and her young daughter, joined them at the edge of the town and were convinced also to take the track south into the hills. The two men travelled with packs and the woman carried a sack bound up with twine. The young girl pulled behind her a small travel suitcase on casters with a handle though it was torn and the wheels squeaked where they bobbled over the earth. They greeted each other warmly and Dylan smiled to the little girl though she was too shy to return the gesture and kept close to her mother's legs.

The end of the street opened into a wide gravel-covered car park where the chassis of cars still sat and the shell of a rusted bus was without its bonnet or engine.

In front of them, the bridge spanned the river to the endless countryside at the far side, the brown water beneath it running in channels through the silt and stone, a white truck upended in the middle.

As they crossed the road bridge they saw the military camped at the opposite side.

A group of sixty or more soldiers gathered in the morning light, breaking down their camp. They were dressed uniformly in standard-issue green combat trousers and black boots, with shirts and t-shirts of all shades of green that the spectrum could create. Some wore berets, others didn't, and some carried their rifles strung across their backs even whilst they worked.

Black and brown horses were lined at the riverbank, each harnessed to a wooden cart. The carts were of varying description, some with four wheels and some with two, painted and branded in all colours, and all carrying boxes and crates and some covered in tarpaulin or sheets. The men bridled the horses and prepared them to move.

The group crossed the bridge towards them and some of the soldiers' attention was drawn.

As they left the bridge on the other side of the river, three officers stepped in front of them, carbines in hand, though one held an HM-3 submachine gun by his side.

"Buenos dias senores" said the man with the grey beard who led their party.

"Buenos dias" replied the lead soldier, a young man with a thin moustache and sunglasses, "a donde van?"

The man replied that they were heading through the hills to the road at the south, and he went on to explain where that route would take him though the soldiers did not care.

The young girl held tight to her mother although her mother was not threatened at all by the military presence there, indeed the contrary.

"Es suyo el muchacho?" the soldier asked the man with the beard.

He shook his head and pointed to Ryan.

"It's his" he said.

"The boy is mine" Ryan called, pointing to his own chest, "mío"

The soldiers looked at Dylan and the lead soldier stepped forward to him. Dylan stood where he stood and met the soldier's stare at eye level. He was still young but he knew enough of that world to know not to show weakness.

"Cuántos años tienes?" the soldier asked.

His mother stepped quickly forward to them.

"He's twelve", she said, putting her hand across onto her son's chest and gently pushing him backwards, "twelve".

The soldier nodded.

He looked at Kiara.

"Here" she said, reaching into the wooden box on the front of the cart, "look".

She pulled out the boy's papers, the birth certificate and identity card which were government issued and proved the boy was who they claimed him to be and his age correct.

"He's twelve. Doce" she repeated, pushing the papers to the soldier's hand.

"El debe venir con nosotros" the soldier said, handing the papers to the soldier behind him.

His father jumped forward and grabbed the boy.

"No way is he going with you, he's twelve years old, dammit. The age of conscription is fourteen, we all know that. Back off"

He pulled the boy backwards and stood between his son and the soldiers.

"No, es a partir de los doce años de edad" the soldier said, flatly.

"It's not twelve, it's fourteen" Ryan cried, his voice growing with anger and his face reddening, "the boy is staying with me, now get out of our way"

He pushed the soldier slightly to one side with his arm.

The soldier jerked himself back into place and snapped the sunglasses from his face.

"The age is twelve" he barked in English, "the age is what age I tell you it is"

The boy was nearly in tears, his mother wrapped around him and pulling him in to her.

The man with the beard and the others in their group had drifted slowly across the road and stood awkwardly at the far side, offering no protection or otherwise from the situation in which they found themselves.

Ryan looked desperately to them but their faces were blank.

Other soldiers from the camp walked across to where Ryan and his family stood.

"And you touch me again and you will be going nowhere" said the soldier.

Ryan took hold of the cart and began to turn it and walk it back the way they had come.

"Go, now" he yelled at Kiara and Dylan.

The soldiers began to shout, and two of them grabbed Ryan by the shoulders and pulled him backwards and held him as he struggled. He kicked and pulled and managed to throw a headbutt backwards into one of the soldiers who cried out and loosened his grip enough for Ryan to pull himself free.

He turned to run to Kiara and Dylan, back across the bridge, but as his front foot hit the ground the long muzzle of a rifle appeared at the side of his face and he instantly stopped.

Four more soldiers stepped past him and grabbed hold of Kiara and the boy and pulled them apart from each other. The boy screamed and his mother screamed too. She kicked at the soldiers and put her boot into the groin of one and floored him and pulled hair from another's head but more came and they eventually restrained her, and soon she too was held on the ground at rifle point.

The lead soldier stepped to Ryan.

"The age is twelve. The boy has national service. Defying national duty is an offence of the state. He comes with us"

From that moment their world blurred.

Ryan could feel himself shouting and thrashing though it seemed in slow motion as though he moved through thick air and, without knowing it, he fell to the ground as his crying son was pulled away into the military camp. He disappeared backwards into the blanket of green uniforms as though falling slowly through a swamp.

The soldiers stood and stared, expressionless. They had seen it before. They had all held screaming parents back. They had all carried sons away as they cried. Most had been that son themselves. But the country came first. That was the way.

In a blur, silent and spinning, Ryan jumped to his feet and threw himself through the soldiers after Dylan. One grabbed him by the chest, big hands clinging to his shirt. The soldier's mouth moved but the words weren't heard, and Ryan swung a full-arm punch at him and the soldier went backwards to the ground and Ryan ran further, and without knowing where it had come from, a rifle butt swung into the side of his head and he blacked out before he hit the ground.

When he woke it was silent.

He could feel the sun on one cheek and the dusty ground on the other and a throbbing pain in his head.

He rolled onto his back and opened his eyes slowly. For a second he had forgotten everything. For only a second.

He spun to his knees.

He was alone, kneeling on the grass. A blanket had been laid over him and there was blood on its fringe.

He knelt for a moment and looked around the place and waited. Kiara came up from the river slowly and saw him and walked to him.

"Are you ok?" she asked.

He said nothing.

A bird soared silently to the water and stood and did nothing.

"Where are they?" he asked, croaking.

Kiara looked at him.

"Are they gone?" he asked.

She shrugged.

"Are they gone, Kiara?" he cried.

"Of course they're gone" she said angrily.

He rose to his feet and his head burned. He touched the side of it and it was sticky with blood.

"Hey, hey" Kiara said, "stay there, I've got some water here to clean that"

"We have to go after them"

He got up and staggered.

She shook her head.

"Let me clean your head. Be careful, it's quite a bad gash"

"I don't care" he snapped, "which way did they go, into the town?"

She poured some of the water onto a cloth and reached it to his head. He batted her hand away.

"I don't care about my head, I care about my damn son" he cried.

She looked him sternly in the eyes.

"They'll kill you where you stand Ryan" she yelled at him, snapping his attention to her, "they took him for service, what can we do? What the hell can we do?"

"We can go after them"

"And what, Ryan?", she started to cry, "look at you, you're covered in blood as it is. What are you going to do, fight the whole damned army?"

He dropped back to his knees.

Kiara stepped forward and held him and began to gently wipe the blood from the side of his head and the red water dripped down his side to the ground.

He looked up at her.

"I'm going to find him, Kiara"

She said nothing.

"Which way did they go?"

She shook her head.

"Tell me"

"Through the town, Ryan, ok?"

She shook her head and spoke softly.

"If you go after them you can go alone"

He pursed his lips.

"So be it"

She stopped cleaning him and walked back to the cart and threw the bloodied cloth to the ground angrily. She picked the front of the cart from the ground and began to walk it along the road, south into the hills without looking back.

"You're ridiculous" she said without turning, "you'll be dead the moment they see you. You're coming with me. We'll find him again in the city, this country isn't big enough to stop us"

She walked away along the track as Ryan knelt in the dirt.

He called for her and she ignored him. He wiped the dripping water from his face and spat red into the dust.

He stood and watched her disappear around the bend in the road into the shady hillside and he stood for a while longer, staring into the filthy river, before eventually following.

It was three weeks before they made it to Texcoco.

The first days after the army had taken Dylan were a blur for both of them. They walked in silence, snapping and sniping at one another for the slightest of things. Tears were shed until their eyes were red and swollen and Ryan had drunk every drop of wine and tequila and mescal they happened upon.

He vowed to find Dylan again and to exact some revenge on the men who took him and left him bleeding in the dirt. No amount of logical reasoning or justification of the legality of what had occurred could convince him otherwise and Kiara had given up trying. She reasoned that, regardless, she would be there to prevent him from doing anything exceptionally foolish should it come to that.

On the windy road south of the small town of Malila, the rain began once more, thundering and relentless. The roadway became a river, torrents of filthy water poured from the hills and gathered in the valleys and they were forced to take shelter in an abandoned cotton factory for nearly three days.

There, they met others from the road, roamers and ramblers and in that old dusty concrete shell a camp was formed until, on the third night of their stay there, a group of bandits ransacked the place and three men were shot and belongings taken. After half a bottle of mescal Ryan's lingering bitterness and anger surfaced and he shot one of the men in the knee with the Colt and his accomplices had to drag him from the place screaming.

Kiara took the gun from him and told him that he was a danger to himself with the thing whilst in that mental state and that she would not permit him to carry it again and reminded him that the pistol was indeed hers after all.

They left in the early hours of that morning and walked through the rain until the wetness of their clothes became inconsequential. They made small fires in the shells of buildings and cooked rice and corn and drank mouldy cold coffee and talked very little, although their allegiance to one another was unbreakable for it was all they had.

They suffered silently, speaking little of their losses but for their determination to find their son again.

Ryan blamed himself entirely, as he did for the loss of Mia. He said that if they had not approached the soldiers there or listened to the old man tell him about the pass through the hills, then they would have evaded questioning and ultimately still have their son. He said that if he had not insisted on his daughter and mother-in-law bunkering themselves in the basement of the farmhouse, and not keeping a key himself, or indeed remembering where the existing key was kept, that they too would still be with him. He knew that if he had done as the bandits asked that day, stepped outside and allowed the family to be robbed, then his father-in-law would be with them also and that they would have the farmhouse and thus no need to wander endlessly across the country like desperate nomads.

He was burdened greatly with the weight of such regret, and he found every day he carried them with him a greater struggle than the last. The fury and pain burned him until he physically hurt and the thought that he could not hunt those men down one by one and avenge his family was often too much to bear. The one thing that carried him through those darkest of days was an unbending and unwavering dedication to getting Dylan back to safety, wherever that was.

He knew also that should they find Dylan again, serving in the military forces in the city or elsewhere, that he was bound by law to national service and that to break this was a capital offence. There would be no trial or investigation or negotiation of the matter. The capital punishment would be implemented immediately and could not be argued.

He didn't care.

He would find a way, and his son would comply and Kiara would have no choice when the day came. Or they would all die trying. What he would not accept is that a boy of twelve could be conscripted into a corrupt government force and would be worked to the ground and put in the path of endless harm.

As the roads converged on Mexico City, the environment of that country changed to one which they had not experienced since the fateful day that they were forced from Monterrey. There were stores still trading and bars selling beers and wines and tequilas and there were people everywhere. They passed mile after mile of old homes, mostly still inhabited, though nearly all decrepit and boarded and fenced for protection. The roads were lined with parked vehicles of all types, yet missing wheels and tyres and windows and most missing their interiors. As much as could be expected, the place operated as a normal city.

But beneath the veneer there was far more to it.

Men with rifles and pistols sat on rooftops and in shaded alleyways and behind the counters in the stores. Where once there had been a peripheral drone of traffic in the midday sun, there existed there a ghostly silence where the only thing to be heard was a quiet and suspicious chatter and the distant dogs and birds and occasional gunshot.

They walked that place with care.

Kiara had the muzzle of the Colt Python tucked in the front of her jeans and all the chambers securely loaded.

They decided between them that their aim in that city was to trade in as much of their cart-load as they could so that they could travel lighter and to gather simple provisions and ammunition and seek information on where the military strongholds were. They walked the streets toward the centre of the city until the sun went down on them and they took refuge in an abandoned construction site at the boundary of Avenue Palmas. They pulled the blankets over the cart to shield the dust and made no fire for fear of attracting unwanted attention and slept for only three hours each.

When Kiara woke, just as the very faintest glow of dawn rise up from the horizon, Ryan was sitting out on the stone foundations turning a photograph in his hands. It had been taken years prior, Ryan holding his son under his arm in a plastic firefighter's hat and Kiara holding their infant daughter, only a few months after she was born. The photo was faded and the corners were turned and fraying but it was everything to him. The memory was of unbridled joy but the sight of the image brought tears of pain and loss.

The guilt which Ryan carried for the loss of both of his children consumed him. He had flashbacks to pulling himself through the smoking wreckage of the old farmhouse before the flames were out, his own blood hissing in the heat as it dropped from him, screaming and crying as his fingers burned on everything he touched. It had been too hot for him to reach the stairway into the basement, though the basement itself was undamaged by the fire. When Mia and her grandmother were found, they were cuddled together in the chair, also untouched by flame. The smoke had overcome them. Such mercy was the slightest consolation to him, to know they hadn't burned and suffered, and it had given them the opportunity for a proper burial.

Such was not the case for his father-in-law.

Kiara pulled the blanket away from the cart. She crossed the dusty ground to him and held him from behind. He took a deep breath in and settled himself.

"We'll find him" she said, softly.

He nodded.

"He's not gone forever, Ryan. He has a job to do for this country"

"He won't know where to find us though Kiara. What if he gets away from them, he won't know where to go to find us"

"We've been through this", she said, tucking the blankets back onto the cart, "he knows where we're heading. We will find military somewhere and get word to him. Let's write a letter"

He stood and nodded slowly.

"Yes. OK"

They hugged and Ryan put the photograph carefully back into the box and fastened it back under the cart. The sky was a dusky grey though the world was yet silent and the air was cool and calm.

She poured him cold coffee from the flask and they drank together and moved on.

Chapter Seven

It was Christmas day.

They followed the canal south out of Mexico City and headed west along highway 10. The south of the city was quiet compared to the ceaseless noise of the centre, where a man had no time to think and must have his wits about him even when he slept. There were men and women there, city folk whose entire existence had been in the close confines of a bustling metropolis, who lived that way without undue concern, knowing each street and each back alley and where to find what was needed. They were the people, in the tens of thousands, who moved around the city like mice at work, sleeping with their eyes partly open and with one finger hovering over a trigger at all times.

Ryan and Kiara could not bear to be there. They were both more accustomed to the countryside, having space to breathe and to move freely without watching over their shoulders wherever they went. Though they had spent many years living in Monterrey, they had spent many years since that living alone with the land. They were used to the silence that the countryside offered, and that was indeed not what was found in central Mexico City.

They arrived into the city in late November, tired from walking that country without rest. Their boots were worn and their clothes were torn and stained and their provisions had dwindled almost entirely. They traded away most of their belongings, the items which had been salvaged or scavenged along their journey, items of little value in the previous world which had taken more value in that new one, as all items had. There was not a thing in that country or any country that had not assumed a new value. No new goods were being created, and nothing could be imported from elsewhere, so every item was sacred.

They still pulled the cart behind them, cracking and bent, though it was not laden as it had once been. They carried with them two iron pans and a kettle, an old barrel of water from the river, a stack of blankets and old clothes, each as damp and rotten as the next, some split timber that they used as fire kindling and a box of tools. They had three small sacks of coffee beans, a bag of mixed rice grains and some dried beans. Ryan had also bought a single smoked rabbit in the city for them to eat for Christmas dinner that evening, and two bottles of old red wine from California which had cost him more than he was comfortable with.

The first place they headed on their arrival in the city was the military headquarters at the old international airport. The airport itself, being the largest and most expansive complex in the city, and indeed the country itself, had been commandeered many years prior to act as a centre for operations for all branches of state military. In the first couple of years after the disaster, the place and the surrounding roads buzzed with army trucks and military cars and the thundering drone of helicopters and jets as they were despatched across the nation. But that was long ago, in their place were hordes of black and white and brown horses, led by men in green. They carried goods in packs strapped to their backs, and pulled carts and trucks of all description. As they neared the airport they saw the old trailer from a goods lorry, stacked up with boxes and crates and harnessed with chains to nearly thirty horses, ploughing along the roadway as men cracked whips and led them with ropes, a commander standing atop it all shouting orders as though king of the twisted parade.

The white wall was crumbling and the twisted barbed wire that spiralled along its perimeter was rusty and lethal. At the old gates, painted still in flaking mint green, four guards stood with rifles.

Ryan approached.

"Be careful" Kiara instructed from behind him.

The guards faced him as he neared.

"Hola" he nodded.

They nodded back.

He spared the details. He knew they wouldn't care.

He told them that his son was in the military though he did not know where, and needed to get word to him. He asked how best this could be achieved.

The soldiers shrugged.

They asked which division he was stationed with, and Ryan replied that he did not know.

One of the men, the only one seemingly interested in helping him at all, told him that the country was split into forty-four divisions, each operating in its own territory, with a little overlap in places.

Ryan again bent the truth. He told the man that the last they had heard of him he was with a division in Hidalgo, somewhere in the hills away from anything of note.

The man shrugged.

"Where is that division stationed?" Ryan asked.

The man pointed to the ground.

"Aqui"

Ryan's eyes widened.

"Here?"

The sign next to the gate read *Campo Militar No. 1-L*.

The man shook his head.

"Not *here*" he said, pointing to the sign, "but in Cuidad de Mexico. Somewhere in this city"

The soldier told Ryan that, even though that may be the case, soldiers were not formally listed by name in any centralised way, and that only the commanders of each division truly knew who was in their group. He said that the groups left their command bases for weeks at a time, circuiting the countryside in patterns, recruiting and gathering supplies and fixing infrastructure, and that men were gathered and men were lost along the way without anybody knowing they were there.

He shrugged and stepped back to his post.

"Sorry"

Ryan stood there for a moment longer. Kiara watched from the road, leaning backwards against the old cart with the Colt swinging around her finger.

He turned once more to the soldiers and asked them if they knew the location of any other camps that he could try and they nodded and said there were many, spread across the city in every direction.

The soldier briefly described where the bases where, and though the names of roads and suburbs were of no meaning to him, he remembered each of them. That afternoon he sat with a blade and carved the names and locations, as best as he could remember, into the wooden cart so that he should not forget, and for the month of December they walked the city relentlessly until they had visited eleven of them.

They were shrugged away from most by soldiers and airmen and cadets, unwilling or unable to help. As the first soldier had told him, nobody would even know his son's name but for those who he travelled with.

Such information would not deter them from the hunt.

No parent could give it up, walk away, move on. They would search until the end of everything if that was what it would take.

They knew that, even if they were to find him in person, they would not be able to simply take him from his duties, at least not without a fight that they would be unable to win, but if they could reach him then they would be able to arrange a place and a time where they could meet again once the opportunity arose, however long that may be.

At one base, Ryan was given a short piece of notepaper and an envelope and he wrote for Dylan an instruction.

He told his son to meet them in Villahermosa and the instructions for where to go, and that they would go to that place and they would wait forever for him and that they would not ever give up on him, however many years may pass.

Nuggets of information came to them here and there, soldiers who thought that they perhaps knew the location of the battalion with which he travelled, or thought they knew where he may be stationed, but each lead came to nothing at all and they walked until they were sore and tired and weak.

The roadway west to the suburb of Avante climbed up onto the concrete overpass, lined with the short white metal fencing, twisted and wrapped in vines. They crossed underneath where camps had been made and fires burned and music played and men and women watched them from beneath their blankets. The business of the city had been overbearing at times but there was safety there for the numbers of people present, and in those quiet suburbs they felt vulnerable.

They had been given information that the base in the south of the city, once home to the command of paratroopers and fusiliers and of naval cadets, would be a good place for them to search, as that place kept records of military goods shipments and would have some idea of when last a group came in from Hidalgo.

The sun had dropped and the air was cooling.

Despite the temperatures during the day still maintaining their warmth, the winter nights were cool and they would struggle through the nights without fire.

Kiara pushed open a tall iron gate to a yard beyond, spraypainted and derelict, an old basketball hoop still screwed high into the concrete wall. They pulled the cart inside and closed the gate and tucked themselves around the corner where they could not be seen from the road and made a small fire. Ryan pulled the blankets from the cart and laid them out and hung the largest over the top as he always did. He took a pot from the cart and poured water inside and added herbs which they had picked and put the rabbit inside. It was smoked already so they had no need to cook it but they would warm it and flavour it more than had been done, and prepare some rice and grains in the pot along with it.

As it cooked, Kiara sat on the ground with some of the wine in a tin mug and held Dylan's book on the oceans in her hand.

"Happy Christmas Dyl" she said, mostly to herself, and held the book to her chest and then kissed it and put it carefully on the ground as though the paper somehow embodied her son and all that he was worth to her. She crossed her heart and looked to the skies and said in her head a prayer for her son and for her lost daughter and told them both that they were the dearest things to her and that she would not forget either of them. She flicked a tear from the corner of her eye with her thumbnail and took a big sip of the wine.

Ryan was stirring the pot at the fire. He looked over to her and raised his cup.

"Feliz Navidad" he said to her softly.

She smiled.

"Feliz Navidad"

They both drank.

She wished her children were there with her and she remembered back to Christmases of the past. She remembered spending Christmas as a young girl in the United States, the music playing and eating too many sugarcookies and snowball fights in Cathedral Plaza with her father. She pushed the thoughts of her father from her mind, unable to completely block the flashing image of his burned body when it was pulled from the farmhouse. She remembered clearly the first Christmas with Dylan, him rolling around in the wrapping paper whilst their old dog barked and jumped in the commotion, and the first Christmas with Mia when it snowed so heavily that they were stuck indoors without power and how they lit every candle they owned to light and warm the place and played every game they could remember to entertain their son. She remembered the first Christmas they had spent in Mexico once moving south, how everything was different and how they missed the traditions to which they were accustomed, and had their old friends send them goods across the border to ease their transition.

Then the first Christmas in the old farmhouse after leaving Monterrey. They had no belongings there, no toys for the children and no stores to buy more. Ryan had walked for more than a week to Reynosa at the border to find gifts and American produce from McAllen and came with cured ham and tins of peaches and dried fruits and small toys for the children and returned to the farmhouse wearing a red Santa hat. The children had shouted in joy when he returned. There was no effort at all to force the joy of Christmas together because they did not need to and on that day they realised the true value of their family, and Kiara knew that things from that point would work out for them.

Everything changes and nothing can be foreseen.

Once the weather had taken the crops and the nation felt the weight of dwindling resources, everyone had changed.

She sat there in that dirty concrete yard under an old ripped blanket which smelled of damp and firesmoke, her boots worn and her nails long like a gypsy woman, drinking Californian pinot noir from a bent tin mug and eating a wild rabbit.

No children in sight.

Everything changes and nothing can be foreseen.

She knew inside her heart that she would see Dylan again, it was her intuition as a mother and for this she was not worried, but the memories of Mia were only that, memories which in time would bend and fade and though she wished she could avenge her daughter and her parents and take closure for the loss, she knew there was nothing that could be done and the burden would be carried forever. There was no sympathy for her grief, no salvation to be offered and she knew her world would be darkened slightly for the rest of her days.

But she would not stop. She would not let the loss of Mia, the loss of her mother, the loss of her father or their home, rule her into despair. She would walk on. She would get word to her son that their quest would continue to the southern border and they would leave that country and find a place where food was bountiful and crops would grow and the water was clean and they would start a life there. They would start a life in a new world as they had done before, time and again since she was a little girl. She was adaptable and resolute. She was the mother of two children and that would always be the case to her, and she was strong enough to face anything that faced her, and she knew that even though she cried for what had been, that life was long and she had much left inside her yet.

She finished the wine in her mug and poured more.

It was cold there and she shuffled closer to the fire and brought the blanket up around her shoulders and leaned in to her husband. He wrapped his arm around her and held her there, as they stared into the dancing flames and gave thanks for each other, for there was nothing else.

The following morning she woke to a steel-grey sky. Her head was heavy from the wine. She was not used to drinking as she had done, even though it was only a bottle to herself. She could hear people passing beyond the gate and she knew the day had begun. She did not like to camp where others could see her, unless they were in a place where others camped. She felt that laying there on the street under old blankets made her look homeless, though she indeed was homeless in every sense. She knew that there was not a person on those streets or otherwise that would pass judgement on her for her situation but she hated it nonetheless. She knew she looked unkempt, and though she washed and brushed her hair daily and cleaned her teeth and tried where possible to find clean clothes, which was all more than could be said for much of the population, she knew also that she was not the presentable and pretty woman she had once taken pride in being. She had not found make-up of any kind for so long that she had stopped looking, and though there was not a person who cared, not least her husband, she cared for it herself and took care in her appearance. She pulled the old blankets together in a bundle and threw them onto the cart.

"I want to find some new clothes, these are horrible" she said to her husband.

He nodded.

"Sure"

They used some of the water from the container to clean the pot and the mugs and hung them onto the cart.

"We can look today, yeah?"

She nodded to him.

"Yes, once we've been to the military camp. There are houses everywhere here. We can look through some of the ones that have been abandoned"

Ryan tied up the last of the things.

"Of course. Feliz Navidad"

She smiled.

It was a short walk to the camp by the old zoo. The glass enclosures were long abandoned and the place was overgrown and the trees hung out across the road and grass grew from between the cracks in the concrete and dogs sat amongst the shrubs and watched as they neared.

The long black metal fencing at the perimeter of the camp was guarded by men with automatic rifles. They left the cart in the road and approached the gate.

A tall guard with a long beard stepped forward, his rifle at his side.

"Hola" Ryan called.

The man nodded, his black sunglasses hanging onto his nose.

"Inglés?" Ryan asked.

The man shrugged and nodded, pursing his lips.

"We're looking for somebody"

The man said nothing.

"Mi hijo, my son. He joined the military in Hidalgo some weeks ago. Do you know where we might go to find him, or to get a message to him?"

He reached into his pocket and pulled out the note they had written to their son, wrapped in a plastic bag to protect it from water damage and with his name written on the front. The note gave the simple outline of the plan though did not mention any plan to cross the border should the letter be intercepted or found in Dylan's possession. Such intentions may lead to worse outcomes for him on grounds of desertion. Dylan was young but he was tough, as had been proven to them, and they knew that if their message reached him, that he would in time find a way to get to them.

Ryan lifted the letter from his pocket and the guard looked at it and read the name and shook his head and handed it back.

"I have a message to get to him. Is there anybody here?" he motioned beyond the guard, through the gates to the bustling military yard beyond, "anybody who can help us?"

The guard thought.

"Hidalgo?"

Ryan nodded.

"Sí"

"Cuando? This month?"

Ryan shook his head.

"Last month. November"

The guard turned and called to his colleagues who were standing back from him and they talked quickly in Spanish and then the guard nodded and turned back to Ryan and Kiara.

"Have you been to treinta y siete?"

Ryan shook his head. He looked to Kiara and she frowned and shook her head too. They had obsessed their time in that month on walking the city from camp to camp and had visited each military establishment in turn, each with its own name and designation and camp number and they did not recollect visiting camp thirtyseven"

"Treinta y siete B" the guard repeated.

"No. Where is it?" Ryan asked.

"South of Chalco" he pointed, "you can walk in one day, maybe two"

"Do troops from Hidalgo base there?" Kiara asked from the road.

The man shook his head.

"No, but many military from here are moving south because of the fires"

"The fires?" she asked.

The guard nodded.

"Fires burn in the south"

They shrugged.

"We don't know of the fires"

"The south of Mexico burns. Military from every state is being directed there. Hidalgo, Veracruz, Oaxaca. You will find your son in the south I am sure"

Ryan and Kiara thanked the man and Ryan shook his hand and the man nodded.

"I had a boy" he said, "Good luck"

They thanked the man again and he stepped back to his post and they turned and left.

Ryan took the knife from the metal box and rounded the cart and with the tip of the blade scratched *Chalco – 37B* into the wood.

The guard called across the road to them.

"South to the Teuhtli volcano and then the ciento seis to the east"

They thanked him again and he smiled.

The roads through the south of the city were wide and sparse and the commercial buildings that lined their way were hulking shells of what booming industry had once inhabited them. The roads themselves were endless snakes of abandoned cars and trucks, many parked neatly at the roadside though many left where they had stopped, fuel tanks empty as the people had tried to flee the city or to indeed reach the city. They had been mostly stripped, tyres had been used as fuel to keep fires alight in the coldest and wettest of times, fabric taken for shelter and small items of interior used for all manner of survivalist techniques.

No longer did the people create waste. Finally, at the end of it all, when it was too late to make any difference, their need for recycling became paramount. Nothing was discarded. Even the smallest piece of fabric or plastic, the screws from an old contraption, the clothes on a child's doll, an old tin that once stored food. Each thing became something more than it once was, time and time again.

There was no alternative.

They followed the main roadway south from the military camp, the giant palms than lined its centre bent and stripped of their leaves, past old car garages and superstores, until they took their route a few blocks east to find a residential area.

The roads there were quiet.

They walked for a some time, scoping out each property they passed for what valuables it may hold.

Tall gates were chained and locked and some held dogs and men and boys with rifles who watched them carefully as they passed, walls painted yellow and blue and spraypainted and bulletholed and the streets smelled of sewage.

They found a sideroad between two tall houses where the sun itself couldn't reach, the walls covered in dead vines from top to bottom as though they were being engulfed by the web of some great spider.

The Colt was already in Kiara's hand.

They tucked the cart into the side behind the burned-out shell of a red Honda.

"Are you waiting here?" Kiara asked.

Ryan shrugged.

"I can come if you want"

"No. I'm ok. Watch the things"

He nodded and watched as she walked into the darkness of the sideroad and approached an old screen door. She pushed it and it was locked.

"There's one more further back" Ryan called.

The next door was locked too but they were sure the building was long abandoned.

She put her boot against the door and pushed again, and then kicked it.

"You want me to come and see if I can help?" Ryan called again, turning back to the street to check that nobody had heard him shout. There was nobody to be seen.

"No" she shouted back out of the shadows.

She crashed her boot against it again and the door flung backwards on its hinges and rattled on something inside and bounced back until it nearly closed again.

Ryan saw her wave to him from the darkness and he waved back and watched the road.

She disappeared inside.

The house was dusty and smelled of rot. The door opened into the kitchen, the cupboard and shelves practically empty. The place had been turned over and very faint footprints led through the dust, covered themselves with yet more dust. Kiara opened each cupboard door and looked inside and there was little trace of anything edible. There were tins of beans and fruit but they were years out of date, even though they were deemed long-life products. Whilst food was scarce, and many of the items that were once commonplace were now luxuries, they were not starving and they had plenty of dried rice and beans on the cart. There were places to buy flour and spices and some fruits and other items from the forests of the south and, very rarely, fish from the flooded coastlines.

In the back of the house sat an old sofa and a smashed television on an old wooden stand, a broken cabinet against the end wall with trinkets and photo frames all blurred under an inch of dust and a dead palm in a ceramic pot in the corner. The wooden crucifix still hung above the doorway, ornate and painted in red and yellow and gold.

The wooden stairs to the upper floor creaked and the wood crackled under her feet and the air upstairs was heavy and hot and she struggled to breathe in the circling dust. In the main bedroom the bed itself was neatly made and there were personal items on the dressing table and a pair of eyeglasses on the bedside table.

The clothes still hung in the carved wooden wardrobe.

They smelled stale and needed washing and airing but they were clean and decent. She peered out of the upstairs window to where Ryan was standing and he noticed her and gave a nod. She took an armful of the clothes from the wardrobe and tossed them down onto the bed in a cloud of dust. There were both men's and women's clothing and she rifled through them quickly to find anything of interest and took from the pile a short black shirt with red detailing and a black pair of jeans and held them against herself in front of the dusty mirror and nodded. She quickly swapped the clothes for her own and left them on the floor where they fell and took to the drawers in the dressing table to find anything else of worth.

She found some old jewellery which she put up on top of the wood and some make-up items which had mostly dried out and were of little use. She found a lipstick and twisted it open and though it was well-used, some still remained and she put some on to her dried lips and puckered and put the stick into her pocket.

Ryan whistled from below to hurry her and she took the items and headed for the stairs. She paused in the doorway and took a few steps backwards into the room.

Hanging on the back of the door was a beautiful long dark red coat, thick and somewhat worn and she unhooked it from where it hung. She stood looking at it for some time, feeling it in her hands as though she were deciding whether to buy it from a store or not. She swung her poncho off and dropped it to the floor and threw the coat around her shoulders. She was amazed at how well it fit.

"This girl had taste" she muttered to herself, smiling.

She dropped the items from the dresser into the deep pockets of the coat and tucked the Colt back in her waistband and headed back outside.

In the afternoon sun Ryan stood staring.

"Wow" he managed, smiling at her in a way that made her feel ten years younger, "you look like a badass"

"That place is a treasure trove, there's tonnes of stuff in there"

"Really? You want to bring some of it out? We could sell it on?"

Kiara shook her head.

"No way. I don't even care. Let's go"

They picked up the cart and moved out to the south through the old neighbourhood where the dogs barked and the men lingered in shadow, with all their eyes now firmly on Kiara as she passed.

Chapter Eight

By the time they had picked their way through the sidestreets of Cuemanco and Coapa they had lost much of the day and emerged onto the dusty shoulder of the Anillo Perficio, the outer ringroad around Mexico City. The road was expansive and empty and seemingly the biggest construction they had encountered which had not broken apart or burned or been swallowed by the encroaching arms of nature, though the trees and bushes that dotted its way were mostly twisted and dead.

They crossed the open highway to the south side and stood regarding the grid of tiny sideroads in the barrio beyond. Gunshots rang out somewhere in the distance.

"Around the volcano?" Ryan asked.

Kiara shrugged.

"To highway one hundred six", she looked at the towering mountain, "though there doesn't seem to be any volcano around here, we just walk south 'til we see it I guess."

They crossed the shrubby bank to where the roads began.

"We're certainly not doing that by sundown" Ryan shrugged.

It was yet mid-afternoon but they both knew that he was right and there was no chance of completing their journey that day, whether their route took them around the ancient volcano or otherwise.

They decided to walk as far as they could by sundown and find somewhere safe to make camp for the night. The barrio they were about to cross through was already in shadow and they were not armed or equipped or practised enough to negotiate their way through places like that after dark.

They took one of the bigger roads into the network of buildings, spaced every few buildings by rat-runs and alleyways through the old yellow and white and rifleshot homes. Many roads were intentionally blocked by old cars, smashed and burned out, wedged across the roads in barricades to keep the people in or to keep them out. There were people in the streets there, sitting around outside their homes, smoking and talking and an old mariachi played his music softly from a street-corner.

The roads were laid into a grid system and they weaved left and right as they followed their course to the south until they reached water and the design of the road layout changed.

They stopped on the corner.

Four men sat around a small fire drinking spirit from a clear bottle and arguing loudly with one another as friends do.

Ryan crossed to them and they did not look up to him with anything more than a glance and continued their loud gesticulating.

"Señores" he said, firmly.

One man looked at him while the others still talked. A man with wild grey hair and a long moustache stood and threw his hands up at the other man who laughed and the man with the wild grey hair turned to storm away but thought of something more to say and spun around dramatically and returned to the group. The man closest to Ryan nodded to him but said nothing.

"Señores" Ryan said again, "hola?"

The men stopped shouting, though the man with the wild grey hair had been offended and he ripped the old boot from his foot and threw it at the man across from him and the others all roared with laughter again and the man who had been hit by the boot threw it yet further across the road and they laughed again.

"Quién es usted?" one man asked, looking at Ryan with a puzzled expression.

"I need your help" Ryan said.

"Why are you just standing there?" the man with one shoe asked.

"Highway one hundred and six"

The men shrugged.

The one-shoed man hobbled into the street and picked up his boot and dusted it down though it was filthy regardless and pulled it back onto his foot.

"Ciento seis" Ryan offered again, though the translation did not improve their comprehension of his request.

"Do you know where it is?" he asked, growing a little impatient.

The men shrugged again.

"How far to the volcano?"

"It's there" pointed one of the men.

"What is the fastest way to get there?

For the first time the men all responded and pointed along the road.

"The road goes south?" Ryan asked.

The man sitting closest to him shook his head.

"There is no road that way. The road is the other way. You want to go to el volcan quickly, you must go through Xochimilco"

Ryan nodded. It meant nothing to him.

"This way?"

He pointed the way the men had pointed, just to clarify their information.

"Sí"

"And this leads to Xochimilco?"

The man took the cigar end from his mouth and tossed it into the fire.

"Barrio dieciocho, then there is water, then you enter the canals"

"So there is no road?" Ryan asked.

"No roads through Xochimilco" one of the men replied.

He was unsure whether the men were relaying the truth to him or whether they were jokers or fools or merely drunk, and he figured they were most likely all three.

He thanked them and nodded his wife onwards into the lowering afternoon sun and the stretching shadows of the barrio.

They walked onwards through Barrio dieciocho until they found the canal and crossed on the footbridge at Tlacoapa.

For the first time in many weeks, the swirling dust and smell of the city subsided entirely and the roads grew quiet and trees and bushes and grasses snaked out from where they grew, enveloping the concrete and stone and they were reminded again of life outside of the metropolis.

The smells of flowers floated through the evening air and birdsong could be heard, and though they were walking through a place with little security, they felt a peace.

The little neighbourhoods of La Asuncion and San Lorenzo were filled with low houses and quiet streets where small cooking fires had been made, and though they were mostly inhabited, the windows were boarded and barred. The noise that swept through the city was replaced by the evening chirping of insects and women calling children in from the streets and dogs barking at everything and nothing.

They pulled the cart through the streets across the network of tiny canals that lay over the place like a web, a distant remnant of the vast lake and the transportation which the place once relied on.

They walked until it was dark.

They made their camp in the north of Caltongo on the water's edge, the neighbourhood growing quiet to the south and the vast expanse of the Xochimilco waterworld to the north and east, cloaked in complete blackness and mystery.

The temperature had dropped considerably Kiara pulled the thick red coat around herself and covered her shoulders in a blanket and Ryan made a fire using wood stripped from the trees there and he struggled to get it to burn for some time and it crackled as it did. They made no effort to heat a pot and ate the beans and rice which they carried in a covered tin which had been cooked some days before and drank the water cold from the jug. They pulled the blanket over themselves and hooked it between the cart and a tree, as was their custom, and huddled together in the darkness, their dancing orange flame the only thing they could see.

As they drifted to sleep beside each other, they heard a voice from the dark and Ryan opened his eyes again and listened.

For a moment he thought he had woken from a deep sleep but their fire still burned and he was still partly seated and he knew he could only have had his eyes closed for a few moments.

Kiara was slumped against him and he jostled her and she sat upright and they listened in silence.

It was a woman's voice.

They heard it again, somewhere outside their makeshift tent.

Ryan took the Colt from where it lay.

"Puede ayudar los desamparados?" the voice called again, frail and old and creaking in the darkness.

Ryan pulled the blanket to one side and looked into the dark. He saw nothing but the fading firelight.

"Come where I can see you" he called into the night.

"Cómo?" the voice called back.

"Come here. Venga donde pueda verle"

There was a pause and the sound of shuffling through the grasses and then from the blackness emerged an elderly woman in a long black embroidered dress that flickered gold in the firelight. She wore a long shawl that was wrapped up around her head and wore hanging jewellery that sparkled and swung as she walked.

"Puede usted ayudar?" she asked.

"Help with what?" Ryan asked.

"Do you have food to spare?" she asked, helplessly.

Ryan looked at Kiara. She looked back at him and said nothing. They did not have food to spare, by any stretch, though they had been desperate themselves and had relied on charity where it was offered and they could not turn the old lady away in the middle of the night.

"Rice" Ryan said.

She nodded.

"Por favor"

He rose from their camp and rounded the fire to the cart and opened the bag of dried rice and scooped two handfuls into the tin mug and held it out to her.

She looked into the cup.

"I can not eat dried rice" she said, dismissively.

"And I can't cook it for you" Ryan replied quickly.

He held the cup out to her still and she just looked at it and made no effort to take it. He tipped it back into the bag and tossed the cup onto the cart.

"Good night then, señora"

She stood longer in the darkness, watching them both.

"What are you doing out here in the night?" Kiara asked and the old woman said nothing, "it's cold, you should find somewhere to shelter"

The woman laughed a croaky laugh.

"I am not cold"

"Take the rice" she said, "find somewhere to rest before it gets colder than this and eat"

The woman watched her intently.

Nobody spoke for a moment as the woman's eyes watched her, dancing gold with the glow of the fire.

She spoke.

"Niña"

Kiara said nothing.

"What is it you are looking for?" the woman asked.

Kiara looked at Ryan, confused and a little perturbed.

"Nothing" she said, "we are just camping here. Take the rice?"

The woman ignored her.

"You are looking for something which you have lost"

Kiara looked again at Ryan, who raised his brow though did not speak.

"You seek something" the woman repeated.

"I'm looking for my son" Kiara said firmly.

The woman watched her.

"You lost another child too" the woman said flatly.

Kiara was stunned.

"How do you know that?" she managed.

The woman smiled.

"I know only what I am told. Cook the rice and I will tell you what you wish to know, though maybe not what you wish to hear"

Ryan was becoming agitated.

"No. We offered you help and you refused it, now go, away with you woman"

He stood in front of the woman.

Kiara reached across and took hold of his leg, pulling him gently backwards.

"Wait" she said to him, turning to the woman, "what more can you tell me?"

The woman smiled.

"Cook the rice"

"We'll cook you the rice when you tell me what more you know" Kiara said.

The woman smiled at her and began to sit.

"I know only what I am told"

She sat down awkwardly in the dark with her legs tucked under her, revealing her thin, bony knees in black tights, ripped and laddered, her black shawl still wrapped around the rest of her body. She swung a small satchel from her back that they had not seen prior. She opened it up and took from the bag a small wrap of red cloth, embroidered in fine silver detailing and set it down in front of her.

She said no more and looked up to Kiara where she was sitting, watching her from their shelter.

A moment passed and she spoke again.

"The rice?"

Ryan frowned and looked at Kiara and she spoke to him with her eyes alone that he should cook the rice for the woman. He shook his head softly in disbelief and crossed to the cart to fetch a pan and water.

The woman unfolded the red cloth and revealed from inside a deck of cards, soft and turned at the corners. She carefully took each corner of the cloth in her fingers, one at a time, and spread it out on the ground between them, and then manoeuvred the deck of cards so that it sat perfectly in the centre.

"What do you want from me?" she asked.

"What do I want from you?", Kiara shrugged, "I don't know, what can you tell me?"

"What do you seek?"

"My son"

The woman nodded and watched her intently and Kiara felt the piercing of her eyes.

"What do you seek? Inside?"

Kiara shrugged.

"Only my son"

"You are looking for peace. You are looking for a place to be, I see it in you. A place to belong"

Kiara said nothing.

The woman was correct though Kiara had not realised that was so. She had not taken the time to think about what she longed for, deep inside herself. She, like everyone in that place, longed to turn back the time and return to what once was. She longed for her daughter again, one more day. She longed for her parents and she longed to find a place, wherever that was, which could return to the time that she once loved.

"You will not find it where you seek it" the women spoke.

"My son?"

She didn't reply. She lifted the pack of cards from the floor and handed them across to Kiara.

"Baraja" she said, and Kiara gently shuffled the pack.

The woman pointed to the ground in front of where Kiara sat.

"Now, make three piles. Here"

Kiara held the pack out and dropped the cards into three individual stacks on the red cloth.

The woman nodded.

"Recogerlas".

She made a circling motion with her finger and Kiara picked the three stacks from the floor and put them back together into one deck of cards, though in a different order to that in which they had begun.

The woman held out her bony palm and Kiara handed her the cards.

Ryan was hanging the pan across the fire and pouring in a cup of rice.

She set the deck on the cloth and closed her eyes for some time and muttered something low in Spanish that neither of them could hear over the cracking of the fire and then, once she was ready, she opened her eyes and quickly turned the first card.

"Your past" she said, and looked at the card.

The card showed a group of people holding burning sticks, though the image was facing away from Kiara.

The woman nodded and held her fingers on the card.

"What is it?"

"Siete de bastos"

"Seven of wands?"

The woman nodded.

"You are tired, yes?"

Kiara nodded.

"Very"

"You are unsure of your quest, you doubt yourself. The man doubts you"

Ryan was stirring the rice.

"I don't doubt her on a damn thing"

She ignored him.

"You are giving yourself to your search but you are ready to stop, to sleep, to end this all for once"

Kiara shrugged.

"I'll never quit my search for my son"

"It is not only your son that you seek. You know that the other things your heart cries for in the night will not come to you. You want to stop tormenting your heart with memories of what once was and longings of what will never be"

Kiara was silent. She did not know what to say to the woman. She knew that her heart was tormented by memories and that she was indeed concerned that their end goal of finding salvation would not be fruitful.

She could not think of the words.

"That could apply to any of us" Ryan called from the fire, dismissive of everything the old woman had to say.

The woman turned to Kiara and smiled.

"He doubts you. You will fight on without him"

Ryan tutted loudly and shook his head.

"If you want your damn dinner leave me out of it, nobody loves and trusts that woman more than I do"

He went back to watching the rice.

"Who did you lose, a child, yes?"

Kiara nodded.

"I lost everyone"

"Turn one" the woman said to Kiara, pointing to the deck.

Kiara leaned forward and slowly turned another card out onto the cloth.

The image showed a stag under a tree hanging with stars.

"Ah" the woman said, smiling broadly, "I understand"

"What?" asked Kiara.

"Pentaculos. Your work will indeed reward you. Do not doubt"

Kiara smiled softly and nodded.

"Find the best route. Find the best way to channel your energy and do not lose hope. Be patient and be reasonable. Do not be frustrated that your goal does not come to you quickly. We fight for what we hold, it is not ours without struggle. If you want it then you will go to it"

The response was cryptic though the messages behind it resonated with Kiara and she took them onboard.

The old woman put her hand on the deck and looked at Kiara.

"Your present" she said and turned a card over.

The image showed a man, possibly an old knight, laying in bed with a sword at his side, three more hanging on the wall by him.

The image caused the old woman to sit back slightly.

"Interesting" she said.

"Why?"

"Four of swords. Las espadas"

"What does it mean?"

The woman thought.

"Where are you walking to?" she asked.

"South" Kiara replied.

The woman nodded.

"You have walked far?"

Kiara lowered her brow.

"You mean today?"

"From the beginning of your quest"

Kiara nodded.

"From Monterrey"

"De Monterrey? It is time for you to think again about what you seek. Remember who you are and what you have been, and remember what brought you here. The road is long, and if you reach what it is that you are looking for then you must be strong and you must be rested. Take time alone, retreat from your pains, banish your stress and find yourself"

Ryan appeared beside the woman, the tin mug hanging from his hand full of steaming rice.

She nodded and thanked him and took it, placing it on the ground next to her.

"Turn one"

Kiara turned another card.

"La reina de bastos. The queen of the wands, you have fire"

She laughed loudly.

Ryan sat down next to them on the ground.

"You have the power" the old woman said, "nobody will silence you when you speak"

Kiara smiled and looked at Ryan, shrugging.

"Your energy is strong, your vision is clear, I am sure now that you are what I thought you were"

"What did you think I was?"

"I knew when I saw you here you were the queen of cats. Maybe it is this coat you wear. You harbour shadow though, don't you?"

"I don't know" Kiara managed, a little confused, "don't we all?"

"Yes. You have the fire in you which burns red and it burns black. You hold darker energies inside you, and they will come out. You are the queen of all cats"

Kiara said nothing.

She did not agree, nor indeed disagree. She knew that every person held something darker inside themselves, especially in those awful times where loss was abundant. She would interpret the cards in time, but at that moment she had nothing to say.

The woman ate some of the rice with her fingers and turned her nose slightly at it.

"You don't like it?" Ryan asked, confused and slightly offended at the actions of a homeless woman on a cold December night.

She didn't reply.

"Your future" she said, holding her hand over the deck again, "you are ready?"

Kiara nodded and the woman turned a card.

The card showed a woman with her arms wrapped around the mane of a lion.

The old woman smiled.

"You have strength, queen of cats. Others can not see your invisible power, but they will know it when it comes. You have stamina for the fight, and you have the composure to win it when it comes. You have lost, and you will lose again, but the battle is yours"

She looked into Kiara's eyes

"Do you feel fear?"

Kiara nodded.

"Yes"

"Good. Feel it. Know it and then go into it regardless. Feel the guilt and the shame and the sadness and grieve what you will, but these things do not make you. Fight, queen of cats"

"I will. I always will"

The old woman smiled.

"Oh I am sure. Turn one"

Kiara turned the card onto the red cloth. An old castle in flames, facing away from her so that the old woman could see it clearly.

The woman nodded and watched the card for a moment.

"Our worlds are fickle places. We build from the ground and then the ground takes it away. We build for the world, the world takes it away. Build, fall, build, fall. Chaos is around us, and you must not fear that things are what they are destined to be. Sometimes the ground on which we build our castles was unstable from the beginning, and when the ground takes it from us we know that the castle was not meant to last. Only once we have lost everything can we build again. From the destruction a new soul will grow. You will lose again, but you will be stronger for it"

"What will I lose? I have lost everything I have already"

The woman looked up to her and her eyes sparkled.

"There is always more to lose, queen of cats, but you will rise from the destruction"

The woman ate the end of the rice quickly and cleaned out the cup with her finger and put the tin mug down into the grass.

She carefully lifted each of the cards and placed them back into a stack and folder the corners of the cloth back over the top of the deck as though it were a ceremony, which indeed to her it was, and put the deck back into her satchel.

"Thank you" Kiara said and the women nodded and waved it away with her hand. When she stood her shawl dropped back around her body and she almost disappeared into the black night of Xochimilco behind her.

"Where will you go now?" Ryan asked.

The old woman cocked her head to the side and looked in to the distance.

"I will go where I am welcome"

"If you need to sleep here, we have a blanket for you"

The woman laughed.

"I will go where I am welcome"

"You're welcome here, we don't own this land"

"Gracias. But no. The night is mine"

Kiara nodded.

She was bemused as to where an elderly lady would possibly go, even in daylight, on the boundaries of the canal system, quite some walk from any shelter or warmth. The night was cold, the sky was black and the woman carried no belongings but what could fit in her tiny satchel. Though she seemed not to care, about that or anything else, and they had at the very least given her food to eat, which despite her resilience was still vital to every man and woman.

"Thank you" Kiara said again, "you seem to know more about me than I know of myself"

The woman shook her head.

"I know only what I am told. Do not be afraid of the power you hold, queen of cats"

Before Kiara could respond, the old woman had gone into the darkness and was lost to the night which she had claimed as her own.

All that was left was the sound of the wind blowing through the eucalyptus trees and the crackling of the fire and the blackness of Xochimilco.

Chapter Nine

The morning was grey and the wind tore in from the hills of the south and they rose early from their camp and pushed onwards. They found the highway again at San Gregorio where market stalls and vendors lined the roadside and the street was a cacophony of noise and commotion and colour and they struggled at times to get the cart through the crowds.

The folk there sold scavenged tools and household items and old toys and books and clothing and a man stood on a building top auctioning off vegetables and throwing them down to the bidders below. A mariachi band loudly played their instruments and a crowd gathered there and women danced together in the street, laughing and swinging each other by the arms and the children ran in circles as the dogs barked at it all. The people there had hung fabrics and flags from the defunct electricity cables that straddled the roads and somebody had painted the road itself in bright paints, though they were fading.

They bought hot tea from a street vendor in their own tin mugs and walked south through Los Reyes and Tepeyeca until the city was behind them and the road snaked through the dusty hills to the south. There was no volcano visible to them and they asked directions again from a man leading mules, and he told them they would not find the volcano on that road but should they continue their route to the south then they could ask again some miles further.

"We will most likely see the volcano from the road though, won't we?" Ryan asked.

The man took the straw hat from his head and scratched his thin hair and put the hat back.

"No"

Ryan nodded.

"It's a big volcano?"

The man shook his head.

"No"

"Right. OK. Thank you"

The man tipped his hat to them both with a nod and took up the ropes tied to the mules and set off again, slowly along the road.

"We'll ask again. Let's just go south"

The road seemed endless.

A thin tarmacked strip of roadway that carved through the lowlands and hung to the side of the hills, overgrown by tall brown grasses and greasewood and thorns that reached across the road. One moment there were tall pine and beech trees spread across the hills around them and the next the landscape was barren and brown and dusty.

At one place some miles along the road they were walking in silence together, Ryan pulling the cart along thirty yards or so behind his wife when she stopped in the road and watched. The place where they stood was raised from the fields to the west and Kiara stood at the edge of the cracked bitumen, watching the landscape.

Ryan slowly caught up to where she stood.

"What is it?"

She didn't reply, though she did not show concern.

Ryan stood and watched too, though he didn't know what he was watching.

A moment passed and he spoke again.

"What?" he asked.

She silently raised a finger to him to wait.

He waited.

"What are you looking at?" he asked again, smiling in confusion at her.

"Look" she said, squinting and pointing to the horizon, "up at the treeline"

A few hundred yards away across the shallow valley of thorn bushes where the hill rose in the west, the oak and beech climbed into a woodland, shrouded in darkness.

Ryan squinted. There was nothing to be heard but the wind.

"People?" he asked.

Kiara shook her head.

"Wait"

He began to lose patience.

"Wait for what, what on earth are you looking at over there?" he snapped.

"Dylan was right all along. Look"

On the far hill, three thin African lionesses emerged from the treeline. They stared silently from the road.

The lionesses walked slowly along the side of the hill, sniffing the air and the ground as they went. They were all equal in size, elegant and slow and powerful, their steady steps silently padding the ground. They looked about them, though if they indeed had spotted Ryan and Kiara on the road then they paid them no notice. They were slim, hungry, their fur dirty, though they were yet alive, all three of them, and that said something to their ability to adapt to those surroundings.

"What do you think they've been eating this whole time?" Ryan asked.

Kiara shrugged.

"Anything. I guess they can catch pretty much whatever they want. Deer, pigs, cattle. Monkeys, maybe", she looked at Ryan from the corner of her eyes and smiled slightly, "People"

Ryan smiled and nodded and he knew she could well be right.

"As if it wasn't dangerous enough out here already" Ryan smiled.

"Dylan was right this whole time. He told you there were wild lions down here"

Ryan nodded.

"He did"

They watched as the three lionesses moved again into the dark trees and disappeared from sight.

"You can tell him when you see him" Kiara said, smiling and starting to walk again.

Ryan smiled and stood for a moment watching where the lionesses had been.

How he hoped.

Some miles further at an indistinct place where the wind blew and the creosote and pinyon twisted around the roadsigns and where they had not seen another soul for some time, they stopped the cart again.

To the west of the highway there lay an ocean of old vehicles, scrapped and twisted and brown, stripped of their parts and their paint. There were at three hundred or more cars and trucks, piled high in towers of twos and threes and fours, burned out to black and some sprayed again with coloured paints in messages and emblems. It was not possible to discern the original nature of the site, whether a scrapyard or an event site, or whether the vehicles had been gathered together more recently to whatever ends.

The place was silent.

At the back side of the open sprawl of twisted metal, there was a small stone building, low and painted white, a single metal door at the corner.

They pulled the cart down from the raised highway onto the gravel of the scrapyard and pulled it through the stones towards the building. The place was situated on one of the bigger routes in or out of the city, and had been passed thousands of times and ransacked until there was little if anything left there. Though there was always reason to check, as one man may see value in wiring that another deems useless, one man may be looking for an item to fix a cart or a home and may need something specific that another would pass on, and they had on many occasions before, searched places that they were sure were bare yet found something worth taking.

The old cars and piles of rubbish and masonry and rusted metal stretched out before them. There was no way they would be able to check each vehicle there, and they deemed it sensible that if they were going to look through the wreckage then they should at least choose some that was less accessible to anyone passing, those therefore more likely to hold something yet unfound.

Ryan pulled the cart under the back of a rusted schoolbus which was set off the ground slightly on top of some boulder-like pieces of smashed concrete and set about walking through the scrapyard. There were cars of every origin, newer and some very old indeed with plates from all over the Americas. They opened doors and leaned in through smashed windows and pried open the trunks and bonnets where they could. The place was dusty and the wind ripped in from the hills and whistled through the metalwork and the hinges creaked and cracked and they stopped to listen for fear of others being there with them.

In an old Buick Skyhawk, Kiara found a nesting boa coiled around itself in the footwell and it flicked its tongue at her and she quickly retreated.

As they searched the wreckage, Kiara heard Ryan call from across the yard.

"Yeah?"

"Come over"

"Where are you?"

"Here, behind the tyres. I need you"

She walked to him.

"What's up?"

"I need your help lifting this"

He was trying to pull a metal barrel from where it was trapped under the rusted shell of a car. His hands were orange with rust and the metal was bending as he pulled it.

"What do you want that for?" she said, confused.

He stood back from it.

"Look under it"

She stepped to the pile of rubble and peered in between the barrel and the car.

"What is it?" she asked.

"I don't know, but check it out" he said pointing.

On top of the rusted shell was a circle spraypainted in white. Inside the circle was the letter Z and three dots in a triangle formation.

"What does that mean?" she asked.

Ryan shook his head.

"Absolutely no idea. But the paint is new and this barrel was put in there intentionally, look, you can see the scrapes through the paintwork of the car where it's been pushed in"

She nodded.

"What's in that bag under there?"

Ryan shrugged.

"Who knows. I say something that's been deliberately left there"

Kiara looked about the place.

The wind whistled but they were otherwise alone.

"Well someone's going to come back for it then. Leave it where it is"

Ryan ignored her and began pulling at the rusted barrel again and he kicked some of the rubble away and pushed it with his foot until, with a creak, it dislodged and bounced across the dirt. Underneath was a black holdall, zipped closed with a thick black handle. Ryan reached into the gap and pulled the bag out and set it down on the bonnet of the car, brushing the dust from it.

He opened the zip.

Inside there were medicines in pharmaceutical bottles with paper labels and blister packs of pills of all colours and bandages and syringes still sealed in foil. There were a stack of plastic water testers with small digital displays and reference cards, all new and in their original branded packaging and a white cardboard box full of foil wrappers.

Kiara read the box.

"Tableta de purificacion"

Ryan smiled.

"I think you should put it back where you found it" Kiara said.

Ryan piled the items back into the holdall.

"Let's take it. This is a goldmine"

Kiara stood and watched him.

"It probably belongs to a cartel or something. I haven't seen this sort of stuff for years. You can't even get this from the state anymore. Water purification tablets? Who the hell do you know who can get their hands on that sort of thing?"

Ryan shrugged.

"Think what it's worth though"

She nodded. Its value was indisputable.

"That bag is probably worth somebody's life" Kiara said, turning to walk away.

Ryan took the handles of the black holdall and followed behind her.

"Let's check out the building and get the hell out of here"

The metal door to the stone building was latched but unlocked and when they looked closer they saw that the lock had been bent away from the doorframe entirely so that the door couldn't lock if it was tried.

Inside was an office that had most likely once operated the scrapyard outside, if it had indeed been a scrapyard.

In the centre of the room, a metal trashcan was blackened by fire, and around it were cast old sheets of plastic and plywood and empty tins where travellers had made camp on many occasions. There remained a metal writing desk in the corner, though it was upturned and had been licked by flames and its drawers were removed.

At the back of the room a single doorway led into a smaller office beyond where the ceiling had been removed and the plaster on the walls had been chipped away and parts of the piping taken. The place was graffitied on all walls in paint and pen, faded over the years. There were bookshelves against the wall and an office desk covered in all sorts of abandoned items and they quickly rifled through the detritus though there was nothing there but litter.

They heard voices somewhere outside and stopped where they stood.

They listened and Kiara pulled the Colt Python from her waistband.

Muffled voices called in Spanish at some indeterminable distance. They knew that the road that passed that place was some two hundred feet or more from the building they stood in as they had crossed the sprawling sea of rusted vehicles before reaching its door.

The voices were certainly closer than the road.

They moved slowly to the door and listened.

The voices moved no closer, men calling and laughing from amidst the wreckage, and they could hear at least three of them.

Ryan and Kiara looked at each other in silence, communicating to each other what they could with their eyes only. Their communication was to stay where they were crouched, and to wait.

They crouched and waited.

The voices passed away from the building and they heard the clanging of metal on stone and the scraping of the wreckage being dragged across the ground as the men searched the place, and after what seemed an eternity, the voices faded away to the north and they breathed again.

Ryan nodded Kiara forward to the door and she stepped slowly through the litter on the floor, the pistol readied in front of her. She stood against the metal door and listened though there was nothing to be heard but the wind and the creaking and cracking and rattling of it passing through the wastes.

She carefully pushed the door open and stood.

There was nothing to be seen that had not been there before. She looked up to the road for the men though she couldn't see well enough over the rusted vehicles and she listened more before stepping outside. Ryan followed closely behind her.

"I hope they didn't find the cart"

Kiara didn't reply.

She thought that the men had not stayed long enough there to have found it where it was hidden, and she assumed that there would have been more noise as they either emptied it of its contents or indeed pulled the thing away entirely, and she had heard neither.

They walked together to where the cart had been and were relieved to see it, still pulled under the schoolbus, the tarpaulin still pulled across it as it been when they left it.

As Ryan crouched to reach for the pulling shaft to turn the cart back around to face the road they heard the man call from behind them.

Their hearts both skipped a beat and they spun to face him.

The tall man, dressed in a blue checked shirt and ripped trousers stepped out from behind the old office building, a dusty black hat low on his head.

Kiara held the pistol steady and they said nothing as the man slowly walked towards them. He had two pistols in a chest holster like a gunslinger though they both remained where they were and he made no effort to pull either.

He walked steadily to them.

He was dirty with a long twisted moustache and high brown boots.

"You can stay right there" Ryan called to him and the man stopped.

He called out across the scrapyard in Spanish and then stood watching the pair, chewing something around in the corner of his mouth.

From beyond the wrecks to the north of the yard three more men emerged in response to the first man's call.

They were raggedy and dishevelled. The front man wore a long poncho that was frayed and torn around the bottom and long hair past his shoulders, the men behind him both in leather jackets and all three with beards.

They walked slowly towards where Ryan and Kiara stood.

They didn't know what to do.

The men were clearly keen on approaching and investigating them further, though Ryan knew they were outnumbered and outgunned.

The men stopped twenty feet back and watched.

"No further" Ryan called.

The men watched.

For a few moments nobody moved but the three men who had approached from the north talked quietly to themselves, the distance between them and Ryan and Kiara still too far for them to be heard.

"What's in the bag?" one called.

Ryan still held the bag by his side and he glanced down at it. They had assumed the men were indeed there for the bag, the intended recipients of a dead-drop, gang members receiving shipments of high-value goods in transit. Ryan had been willing to immediately hand the bag to the men the moment they claimed it as their own, no life should be lost for its claim. But these men had not come to that place to find the bag, they were scavengers, raiders, nowhere-men, walkers of the road and chancers. They had no more claim to the black holdall than he did. He would not risk his life for it but he would also not hand it over to anybody who cared to enquire about its contents.

"Nothing of interest" he replied.

He was aware that it sounded somewhat suspicious and immediately tried to cover his tracks, "our belongings, some old clothes. Nothing of worth"

The man nodded.

Whether he believed Ryan or not was not clear.

"The cart?" the man behind him in the black leather jacket called.

"There is nothing in the cart. Pans, firewood"

Kiara stood firm with the Colt raised at her hip.

The three men mumbled to each other and the front man nodded and they began forward, all three of them.

Kiara raised the pistol at arm's length.

"I suggest you don't come any closer" she snapped loudly.

It caused the front man in the long poncho to draw his old revolver too and they advanced regardless. As they neared they saw the whites of the man's eyes and his nostrils flared. He pulled the revolver from his belt and it swung by his side as he walked.

Kiara's pistol was levelled at his head.

"Another step and I'll shoot you between the eyes" she yelled.

The two men in the leather jackets both stopped advancing, though the man in the poncho continued until he was in front of where Ryan stood and Ryan raised his arms to him to stop him from reaching Kiara and the cart, and as the two men came together the man in the poncho squeezed the trigger of the revolver and two shots rang out in the wind, and the man and Ryan both stopped in time in an embrace and clung to each other and then Ryan's knees faltered and he fell into the man's arms.

The man slowly stepped sideways and Ryan dropped to the floor, crashing face down into the rubble without making a sound.

Kiara's world stopped.

The air swirled and she felt herself silently scream and she broke into an intense heat and dizziness as she saw the wisp of smoke from the man's revolver. He watched Ryan on the ground for a moment and as he turned to her, a slight grin on his dark face and his eyes narrowed and wrinkled and blood splattered across his chest, Kiara, almost involuntarily, launched two of the .357 shells into the side of the man's head.

As his head jerked backwards his hat spun into the wind and his eyes froze and he tried very briefly to turn to look at her but took a step backwards on the uneven ground and fell. The dark red blood poured from his head onto the stone and he lay unmoving on the ground next to Ryan.

She watched the men for a second, though the time was slowed completely and she moved as though underwater, and as she fought for breath, she glanced upwards to see the two men in the leather jackets reaching for their weapons.

That was the very instant that she regained herself and felt at once a rush of cold from the wind and she screamed an ungodly sound and in a single moment discharged the remainder of the Colt's cylinder into the two men.

The first two rounds thudded silently into one man's chest and before he fell the third round glanced through the other's neck, and whilst the fourth round missed entirely, the men fell together to the ground screaming and holding themselves.

She clicked the empty trigger over and over and over until another shot rang out in the silent country and she felt the searing heat in her side. Her fingers seized and she dropped the weapon and clutched her torso, the blood seeping through her hands, warm and thick. There was a dull pain, though it was heady and not intense, and she blurred again and the world greyed and she staggered sideways onto the schoolbus. As she fell against the rusted metalwork, she turned to see the man with the blue checked shirt standing at a distance with one pistol raised and the other at his side, motionless and watching.

Kiara felt her breathing shallow and she tried to call out but there were no words and she didn't know that she had fallen to the ground. She felt her head thud sideways onto the rock, and in an instant, her head filled with so much that she couldn't grasp any of it and then a moment afterwards it filled with nothing at all and all she could hear was the wind and everything went black.

Chapter Ten

There were no thoughts.

A man in shadow, black and misty, floating across the ground away from her into grey. He returned, ghosting over her, shrouded and dark and blocked the light entirely.

There was a sound, a voice.

The cold hand pressed her face and the electricity of it startled her eyes open for just an instant before they dropped again to black.

Another voice. Different.

Her head fell sideways onto stone.

There was no feeling. No pain and no joy, no grasp of understanding of that world or any other. No memory of anything that had been, no longing of anything that may come.

Only an extemporary and ethereal state of nothingness.

There was no feeling above or below, though as her body rose from the cold ground she felt the weightlessness of it ascend to the sky, and the darkness passed away and she saw again the light, shimmering and white and orange through closed eyelids.

For a moment there was wind, a cold on her face, though a numbness throughout which dulled the senses.

In the light the voices continued, speaking without words, speaking without her understanding, words spoken as though the voices were not speaking to her at all.

As she rose to the light, she stopped and again the cold hands on her swung her where she lay, suspended from the ground in shadowy arms.

The shadowman was again over her and the voice was loud, louder than all else and it shook around her head as though that sound was all that existed, and when she heard it she took a moment to comprehend that they were indeed words and that she could indeed understand them.

As she grasped what was said, she was overcome by warmth again and dropped slowly back into darkness.

"Lay still, we've got you now, you're going to be alright"

When again the light returned it did so slowly. The gradual filtering of the orange glow dripped into her consciousness and eased her slowly back to reality.

She could feel herself awake though her eyes were closed and she could feel the softness under her cheek. As she lay there, slowly regaining the understanding of herself, she began to move her body. Her eyelids were heavy and it took great demand to rip them apart and her fingers shook and lifted and she pulled her hand to the deep pain at her side.

The pain roared over her like a wave engulfing something insignificant in an open ocean, and in that moment, the shock of it seared through her until she was awake entirely and she screamed.

She rolled onto her back and watched the ceiling.

The room was dark, a woven blanket hung roughly across the only window, keeping out the grey light, tiny shafts of it dancing through the holes in the fabric onto the opposite wall. The walls were wooden, a cabin or shack where holes of rot had formed and were plastered with clay and an old painting in a frame hung on the wall with tools of blackened metal and mahogany and ironwood. On a table at the foot of the single steel bed, a candlewick burned in a round jar of oil, the glass browned by the flame.

She pulled the blanket aside.

Her torso was wrapped in thick bandage and at her left side it held dressings and gauze against her flank, browned with old blood.

In that moment her memory returned to her and a single image filled her head, the sideways view from her falling place in the dirt, of her husband, motionless on the ground and the man in the poncho laying next to him with his eyes backwards in his head..

The breath left her again and she was filled with an overbearing compulsion to return there and help him. She pulled her elbows underneath her and tried to heave herself up to a sitting position and the pain in her side shot sparks through her entire body and she screamed as loud as she had ever screamed and collapsed back to the bed.

She began to cry.

A moment later, the wooden door of the room was pushed open and a tall man in a brown shirt stood in the door to the dark hallway beyond.

He walked slowly into the room and to her bedside.

Her eyes were wide like a snared animal. She was unable to move and she felt herself shrink from him.

"It's ok lady, you don't got no reason to be afraid"

His voice was warm, familiar, something she felt she knew and it took her a moment to realise he was indeed American and such familiarity relaxed her.

She tried to speak but only croaked.

"It's ok, just relax" the man said.

She tried to raise herself from the bed and he put his hand gently on her chest to stop her.

"You won't be able to get up just yet"

She croaked again and cleared her throat and coughed and tasted blood and tried once more.

"My husband" she managed.

The man watched her.

"Don't worry, just lay down. Do you want some water?"

"My husband" she croaked again, tears in her eyes.

The man called out of the room and a few seconds later another man appeared in the door in a black t-shirt and the first man asked him to fetch the woman some water and he nodded and went again.

Kiara felt the frustration build and she held her breath and pushed herself backwards in the bed so that she was more upright against the wall behind her.

"Where is my husband?"

The man shook his head.

"I don't know darling"

The tears dropped to the pillow.

"He was there" she said, her voice breaking in the emotion and pain and causing her to cough again.

The man took some time to think of his response and thought of the words before he spoke them.

"When we found you, you was the only one there", he looked into her desperate eyes, "the only one... alive, you know? Sorry"

She cried out again and tried to get up and the man held her and she swung her arms at him and the pain in her side flared like fire.

"Where are you going?" the man asked, sternly.

"I have to get to him"

The man shook his head.

She was not his to restrain, and though he knew it best to comfort the poor woman, he knew nothing about her and he allowed her to pull herself to her feet, crying out in anguished pain.

She held herself against the bed and he stood watching her. The other man reappeared in the doorway with a mug of water.

"Have a drink. We'll go back there with you when you're well. You was shot up, lady, you're lucky anyways. We'll help you, but you gotta rest"

The second man tried to hand the water to her, though she batted him away and sent the mug tumbling across the floor. The two men stood there, unsure how to proceed.

"I've got to see if he's ok" she cried.

The man shook his head,

"I'm sorry" he said.

"Where the hell am I?" she cried, tears dripping down her cheeks from her red eyes.

"North of Nushtla. Not really anywhere"

"How do I get back there?"

"Where?"

"Where I was?" To my husband"

"To the scrapyard?"

"Yes" Kiara cried, losing patience.

"We're a mile or so up into the hills, you need to go back out to the road"

She pushed herself away from the bed and stood, hunched with her hand clasped around her bandaged wound. She limped to the doorway.

The two men looked at each other. They were not to stop her leaving that place but they had assumed a duty of care when they saved her from bleeding to death in the scrapyard and nursed her in the safety of their hunting cabin. They had taken on the roles of her carers for the past few days and, just as she was awake, they could not forget their assumed responsibility to her.

"We'll come out with you" the man in the black t-shirt said, and the other man nodded his agreement.

She limped across the room without even listening.

The man in the shirt took her by the shoulder and stopped her and she spun around to him, her eyes deep red and her cheeks wet and blood beginning to drip from her side.

"Listen" he said, a little more sternly, "we'll come out there with you. It's some walk back down to the road and the ground is rocky, you'll fall down out there and most likely just die where you fall. We'll help you. We'll get you back to the road. OK?"

She nodded and took a breath.

"Just hold up, let me get my rifle"

She leaned sideways against the wall as the two men readied their hunting rifles and jackets and hats.

"We got your things here too lady" the man in the t-shirt called, turning out of the room into the hallway.

"It's Kiara", she said softly.

Her gunshot wound was starting to throb in a dull pain and her left leg wobbled. She wiped the tears from her eyes and took a deep breath.

The man came back into the room with the long red coat and carefully helped her put it on and held her as she stood upright.

"Here" he said, handing her the Colt. It's empty. We got some three fiftysevens though, we can spare a few, can't we Ritchie?"

Ritchie nodded.

"Sure we can".

He kicked his boot against the wooden wall and a hidden hatch fell open, disguised with timber to look part of the structure of the building. Inside was a small metal footlocker which he pulled out and dropped onto the floor with a crash.

He turned to her.

"Listen, don't you go telling nobody 'bout this place now will you? We been good to you, with the bed and such, I wouldn't want you to go turning on us now"

"Of course" she said, shaking her head.

"No coming back here looking to turn us over"

She shook her head again.

"No. You're helping me" she said ,"I've got nobody to come back here with, and nothing but this"

She held out the Python.

He nodded.

"Alright, I know it. Here you go"

He took a cardboard box of shells from the footlocker and flipped the lid closed. Fill it up"

He handed Kiara the box and she thumbed six of the shells into the cylinder and spun it closed. The man in the black t-shirt took the box from her and tipped a handful more of them into his palm and reached across and dropped them inside the pocket of her red coat.

He smiled at her and tossed the box back to his friend.

"Thanks" she said, "very much"

Ritchie lifted the footlocker back into the recess and closed the wooden hatch and pulled the cord above it and a fabric wall map fell into place over the top of the hatch to hide the joins in the timber.

The three of them left the room into the hallway beyond. A small kitchen with a steel sink and barrels of water was just off to the side and another small room or cupboard beside it with the door closed.

The man in the black t-shirt unbolted the four iron bolts across the front door and pulled it open. The wind rushed in and she shivered though it woke her and gave her feeling again.

They stepped out into the cold.

Two dogs barked and there was nothing to see but trees.

The cabin was built of split timber and stood on the side of a hillside in a small clearing amongst the pines. The door was secured on the outside with a steel beam that was padlocked at either end and the window to the room in which Kiara had been sleeping was barred with black iron.

Nothing was kept outside the building, no trash can, no tools, no barrels. Everything was enclosed within the building itself so that there would be nothing there to attract chancers and thieves. The cabin itself was as hidden as a small wooden cabin could be in that place, but it was not invisible. The timber of its construction was the timber of the surrounding trees and the wood had not been stripped or treated on the outside so that it camouflaged as best it could into its surroundings. There were even boughs of pine, still with their needles, laid across the roof of the place.

Two big mongrels were chained to a stake and they barked furiously at the three as they locked up the door.

Ritchie walked to them and they barked even as he reached in to unchain them.

"Hey, enough of that shit" he snapped and they both instantly ceased their noise.

He unclipped the chain from their thick leather collars and the two dogs immediately bolted into the trees and down the hill, disappearing out of sight in an instant.

The men did not appear to care and swung their rifles over the shoulders and began to head back out to the road.

"Will they come back?" Kiara asked as they walked.

The men laughed.

"Always. They ain't gone no place, they'll be chasing each other in damn circles down here somewhere. They dumb but they ain't so dumb to run off. You wait 'til I find 'em a rabbit and you see how quick they hustle back here and sit they asses down like puppydogs"

They walked through the trees as the land dropped away and they could see across the valley to the Teuhtli volcano beyond. Kiara limped and clutched at the throbbing pain in her side and refused to be held by the men as she insisted that she was strong enough to do every part of it herself.

After some time they saw the main roadway at the foot of the hill.

"You probably a half mile south right there, but up round that bend there the road straightens out. That scrapyard's up on the left"

She nodded and they walked.

The dogs were together on the dusty field before them, sniffing through the scrub.

"You mind me asking what happened out there?" the man in the black t-shirt asked as they pushed through the rough creosote bushes, the spidery stems pulling at the threads of their jackets and leaving little yellow petals in the fabric.

Kiara took a moment to answer.

She hadn't really thought back to the events which led to the shooting. She was solely focussed on getting back to her husband, dead or otherwise. Though she had no reason to doubt the men as to his fate, she would not accept fully what had happened there until she laid her own eyes on the scene herself.

"There were three men", she thought a moment, "four men. They wanted to rob us"

"You shoot all them men with that pistol?" Ritchie asked.

The memories flooded back to her, a blur of sound and colour, a few seconds that fell into a disjointed place which she struggled to understand. She remembered standing looking at the men over her husband's shoulders, she remembered seeing her husband fall forward and she remembered seeing the place quiet, sideways, darkened. She remembered their cart and then she remembered their secret tin which held the photos of her lost family.

"You missed New Years" he said, smiling.

They reached the road.

Kiara stopped and turned to them.

"Thank you. I can go from here"

The men shook their heads.

"No, it's no problem to us, we'll see you there"

"No. You've helped me enough, and I couldn't be more thankful to you. I'd surely be dead if not for you. But I've got to go do this on my own. I'll be ok"

The men were hesitant but Kiara insisted.

She turned from them and headed north along the road.

"Hey" the man in the t-shirt called.

She stopped and looked back.

"You wanna turn back, or you need to come back up here again, you can do it. See that white tree, the twisted one?"

Kiara looked to where the man pointed and nodded.

"That's us see. You know where to find us up there. Just holler, and don't let anybody follow you if you do"

"Thank you. Both of you. Thank you"

They nodded and stood and watched as she walked off along the dusty road, limping, the long red coat swinging behind her and the Colt Python hanging at her side.

As she walked between the piled remains of the rusted vehicles to the spot where the shootout had occurred, the sun was dropping behind the trees on the ridge to the west. The wind had settled and the place was quiet and white-collared swifts soared silently overhead and away to the south, silhouetted against the dying light.

Kiara limped across the rubble towards the office building. The wooden cart was still propped against the rusted schoolbus and beside it in the dirt were the two bodies, a man in a dusty brown poncho and her husband, laying face-down. Blackened bloodstains trickled away from his body in every direction and flies buzzed in a swarm.

She swatted them aside and fell onto his body in an explosion of tears. She buried her head into him and held his stiffened body and cried until she choked. There was no thought in her head at that time but for a purge of emotion so raw that she couldn't command it and which took her away like a great underwater current that spun her around and around beyond her control. When that current spat her out on to the shore beyond it she lifted her head, numbed entirely.

Her eyes burned. Despite not seeking the hand nor word of god for some time, she said a prayer in her head for him, in Spanish the way it was first taught to her. She rose to her knees and sat back on her heels beside him and caught her breath.

Thirty feet back across the rubble, another man lay in a patch of blackened thorn, his pale shirt browned and stuck to him with dried blood.

She remembered vaguely having fired the pistol, and she realised that she had killed both the men and remembered his leather jacket, though it had since been taken from him, as had his boots. The second man who had also been wearing a leather jacket was nowhere to be seen.

She pushed herself slowly and painfully to her feet and walked across to the cart. The tarpaulin that had covered it was gone, unclipped from the frame and either taken or blown away by the strong country winds. The cart had been ransacked. The rice and coffee and beans which were kept in sacks were gone, as were the two steel pans and the kettle. The three knives and the axe had been taken, though the long staff still hung from the cart edge. The blankets remained, folded into a neat pile and tied with twine, along with the timbers and the box of screws and hooks and nails, though it had been rifled through and was missing half its contents. The barrel of water sat untouched.

She heaved the pullshaft at the front of the cart and spun it into the open and reached underneath to where the tin of sacred possessions had been fixed. A great relief poured through her when her fingers touched the cold metal and she unclipped it and brought it onto the top of the cart.

She limped to Ryan's body and crouched next to it and reached in to his collar and found the thin chain on which the key was threaded and pulled it up over his head.

The tin's contents were as they had been. Eleven matchboxes of seeds which were preserved from the time that was, the jewellery that she had salvaged from the burning house which had belonged to her mother and her grandmother and the jewellery that had been scavenged on their journey, the old currency and the spare ammunition and the four photos of her smiling family which put tears back into her eyes when she saw them.

She took the photo of Ryan's parents and one of their family altogether, smiling gleefully and dropped them into the pocket of her coat along with some pesos and closed the tin and clipped it back under the frame of the cart.

She turned to face the bloody scene before her.

She knew she must bury the body to give her fallen husband a chance to pass rightly into the afterlife, should it exist in any form that she understood.

What tradition and ritual she knew of would be observed, and she would do so in keeping with that which was observed at the death of her beautiful Mia and her beloved parents. But hers was a rudimentary understanding of such things and she had nothing at hand but that which was already present there.

She searched the surrounding wastes for something suitable to act as a digging shovel and found a strong piece of metal, around two foot long and tapered slightly at one end allowing her to grip it well. She heeled the earth beside Ryan's body and couldn't break through the top layer of hardened, baked soil and set her metal digging tool back on the ground.

Bending next to him, she took Ryan by the shoulders and heaved with all the power she could muster to turn him onto his back and she screamed in pain at the muscles pulling in her side, and as Ryan's body fell on to his back, she practically fell down on top of him and some while to regain her composure and her breath.

She lifted him again by the shoulders and dragged him away from the scene to the edge of the yard where the dust and detritus and torn metal and rubble and broken stone gave way to the open grasses of the hillside and she laid him carefully down on the earth.

She reached inside her husband's coat and took out the dusty letter which had been written to Dylan and carefully put it into the pocket of her long red coat.

She pushed the metal shovel into the ground and picked away the hardened crust until she found softer soil beneath, and took out one small load at a time until the hole began to grow. The sweat poured from her and she stopped every few minutes to gather her strength and to catch her breath and to try to push through the pain which was screaming from her bandaged side. The earth was tough and there were rocks and stones which bent the metal tool and she frequently took it back to the stone wall beside the office building and hammered it with masonry until it reformed, and after some time it was shiny and silver where it had sharpened on the stone.

The sun fell behind the hill and she went on regardless, working faster in the cool of the evening.

She left the red coat on the grass and walked the distance between the grave and the water barrel more times than she put the shovel into the earth, and by the time the hole was two feet deep she had finished her own weight in fluid and the blood had darkened her bandages where it seeped from the fresh wound.

At times she fell backwards to the ground in tears but she knew that for everything that man had given her through her life, she owed him this.

Digging a hole would not be the end of her.

When the sky was black completely, without moon or stars, and with the last thread of strength from her burning arms, she reached a depth and dimension that would suitably bury her husband. She tossed the shovel to the side and sat back onto the grass.

The world around her swirled and the pain in her side had been so pervasive for so long that the idea of the pain itself had gone and she was again numbed by everything. She quickly drifted to sleep in the grass and dreamed of her children.

She wasn't asleep long before she woke, aware of a sound behind her, something moving in the undergrowth.

She listened for a moment and at once remembered the three lionesses and jumped to her feet quicker than she had moved for days, grabbing the pistol and pointing it in a wide-swinging arm into the dark. The bushes rustled again and she backed away, looking back over her shoulder for a place to run should she need to. It was a short distance to the office building, though the door didn't lock and she feared that enclosing herself in somewhere would not help at all if there were three hungry lionesses afoot.

She kept the pistol levelled at the rustling.

It did sound like a single animal and not three. She walked slowly backwards through the grass until, from the bushes, emerged a rough-looking black and white dog. It stepped out and stopped in front of her, its nose twitching in the air at the scent of the body laid on the ground before it.

The dog was tall at the shoulder, a crossbreed of crossbreeds. It was mostly black with flecks of white hair along its belly and nose and dotted on its toes. It stared at her, tail upright and ears straight into the wind, unflinching Its eyes glistened.

She had owned dogs as a girl and would go out of her way to care for them but she knew inside that the dog would die and not her should it come to that, and it would not have the chance to put tooth nor claw on her husband's body.

She waved the pistol at the dog and it flinched backwards.

"Go on" she shouted, trying to move it away. The pistol was cocked.

The dog took a couple of steps sideways and dropped its head.

She inched forward and the dog inched back.

She sensed her impending success and the nervousness of the dog and increased her waving at it, causing it to spin round and dart into the bushes again and she stood and watched as it hunched down beneath the branches and waited.

"Stay there" she called, "qué dese ahí"

Whether the dog understood was not to be known but it waited under the bush regardless.

After a moment, she set the pistol down on the ground and knelt by her husband's body. She reached under his arms and lifted him at the shoulders and felt blood pulse from the gunshot in her side, and in a single action she heaved the body forward to the edge of the dirt grave and let it drop off the edge. Ryan's body fell onto its side in the dirt and she jumped in after him to turn him into a position of comfort, laying him on his back and lifting his arms in front so that his hands lay over each other at the stomach and his head was settled in the soil.

She dusted the dirt from his face and looked at him.

His skin was pale and there was dried blood in the corner of his mouth and she wiped it away with her hand before carefully climbing back out of the hole.

The dog stood back, watching.

She pulled the coat back on over the bloodied bandages and winced again as she pushed her arm through the sleeve. She reached inside the pocket and pulled out the two photographs and stooped and gently tossed them down into the grave. They fluttered to a stop on his chest, almost out of view in the darkness of the grave. She said a short prayer and crossed her heart and tossed the pesos in too, for what little worth they had in that life or the next.

She was drained of energy but the job was not done and she knew that should she fall asleep she may sleep for many hours and did not want that scene left as it was, should anybody come to that place the following morning and find her there.

She pushed herself to her feet and took the deepest of breaths and felt the cold wind rush through her and took up the metal digging tool and stuck it into the ground.

She took a shovel at a time of the dusty soil and tipped them back into the hole over her dead husband until the body was lost to the earth.

Blood trickled through the bandages and she felt it on her legs and still she worked, panting and moaning through the pain as she piled load after load of dirt into the hole. The blood began to pour as she strained and she felt dizzy and stopped many times but refused to give in, until by the time the grave was full of the dirt which had come from it, there was a pool of her own blood on top of it and her boots were wet and warm. She threw the shovel into the grass and the dog, which had watched the ordeal unfold, flinched and watched and then inched forward, sniffing at it.

She limped across to the cart in a daze, her legs nearly giving way beneath her as she walked and her left arm completely numb. Her lungs burned from the depth of her breathing and she knew she was close to passing out for what felt like forever.

She unclipped the metal tin from under the cart and hoisted it on to the top of the wooden frame and flipped open the lid with her single working arm, the other limp at her side.

She reached in and took in her hand the first three matchboxes of seeds which cane to her grasp and clipped the box back under the cart and limped back to the gravesite and fell to the floor.

She pushed the matchboxes open with her thumb and scattered the seeds across the wet dirt of the grave and dusted the soil over the top of them as best she could.

There was no thought in her head as to whether or not she would return to that place, to pay respects to the grave of her fallen husband or otherwise, but she wanted his eternal resting place to show life to that desolate place. She wanted flowers to grow and to give his body one final purpose in fertilising the earth to life.

As the pain in her side became unbearable, she tossed the matchboxes into the long grass and crossed herself again with her thumb, and turned to the hills, dropped to her knees and passed out in the wet, bloody dirt.

Chapter Eleven

Mia ran through the orchard trees screaming loudly and Kiara's head shot around to watch.

"Mama" she wailed. Kiara stepped down from the window and walked into the yard.

The sun was hot and her eyes took a moment to adjust to the bright white light.

"Mama" Mia shouted again.

"Dylan" Kiara called, "stop chasing her around like that, one of you is going to get hurt.

She could hear the children still chasing around the trees and tossed the cleaning cloth onto the step and walked across to where they ran.

The breeze smelled of lemon blossom.

She walked up behind her son, and as he darted past her, she caught him in one hand and with the other removed the tree branch he was wielding.

"Give me that thing"

He spun around.

"Mama!" he wailed.

"No, what are you even doing? Stop chasing your sister around, you can hear she's not enjoying it. Why don't you go and help your grandfather in the barn and leave her in peace"

Dylan threw his hands to the side, his brow furrowed and the corners of his lips dipped in an exaggerated frown.

"It's too hot in there"

She let go of his shoulders.

A few feet further into the orchard, Mia was sitting on the grass with her stuffed panda, catching her breath. Her little white dress had been grass-stained at the knees.

"And you, up. Look what you've done to that pretty little dress. Run inside and give it to your grandmother and she'll help you clean it. You both need to be more careful out here"

"But mama" Mia called, "he was chasing me, I fell. I didn't do it"
Kiara nodded.

"I know, and I've told him to leave you alone. Now go on, run in and get yourself changed. And you" Kiara turned to Dylan, "go and busy yourself with something more useful will you, there's plenty that needs doing"

She pushed him gently away and he trudged miserably back into the yard to busy himself with something more useful or most probably to find somewhere else he could misbehave without being seen.

She tossed the branch he had been wielding as a sword into the bushes and plucked a guava from the tree and went back to her cleaning.

When she woke there was soil in her mouth and in her eyes.

She hurt but for a moment she couldn't remember why. With her thumb she picked the dirt from her lips and from her matted eyelashes and coughed and it hurt to do so.

She opened her eyes.

The sun was shining again, showing its white glow from behind the thin cloud and there was no wind.

In front of her, the sideways world was of dirt and she pushed herself to her knees. It was well into the next day. The side of her long red coat was covered in dried blood and there was dirt and soil stuck along the bandages. She pushed herself to her feet and dusted off the coat and kicked the mud from her boots and looked at the gravesite in front of her, as it had been the previous night, though illuminated there by the midday sun.

She looked around her, up into the hills to the west and to the raised roadway to the east, leading away to either horizon. The place was still. There were no birds and no people and she waited there for some time as the warm sun filtered into her skin and filled her with life again.

When she came back to the world she saw the dog, sniffing around in the scrapyard. It noticed her watching and stopped and looked at her for a long moment before going back to its business.

She tucked the pistol back into her belt and crossed to where the old cart stood.

She used one of the blankets to wipe herself clean and wrapped a second around her shoulders and unclipped the box from where it was housed. She reached in and took the remaining shells into her hand and put them, along with the two photographs of her children, into the inside pocket of the coat. She put the matchboxes of seeds into her outside pocket with the jewellery and left the empty metal box sitting open on the cart.

Ryan's black buffalo leather hat lay on the ground where it had fallen during the altercation and she bent and picked it up. Her hair had been tied behind in a long ponytail and she pulled the elastic tie out and let it fall, shaking it down across her shoulders before perching the hat atop her own head, adjusting it slightly over her hair.

She dipped a cup into the water barrel one final time and drank the whole thing down in one and tossed the cup into the dirt and set out along the road on foot.

As she reached the road, the dog followed behind her, walking at her pace without making ground on her, keeping its distance. She turned and looked at it and it stopped and only commenced again once she began to walk, interested enough in her to follow but not confident enough to approach.

She called it to her but it just stood and watched her, its ears to the air and its tongue hanging from its mouth.

She smiled very slightly to herself, even at that time of great mourning, and she turned and continued her walk south along the roadway.

East of San Pedro Atocpan, Kiara found where the road split and forked away onto highway 106 to Santa Martha. The road was shouldered with concrete balustrades which had been spraypainted in all colours, and camps were made in the surrounding foothills. The creosote that climbed from the roadside to the hilltop was blooming yellow and glowing in the sun, blossoming earlier than it should in the erratic seasons.

She walked slowly through the little neighbourhoods, dazed from the events of the past few days, the ever-pervasive tiredness and the pain still throbbing around her body.

No waterway found its route through that land and there was no stream or brook from which to drink and by the time she reached Milpa-Alta her throat was sore with thirst.

The dog had walked behind her the few miles south from the scrapyard, and had dropped in and out of view as it explored the surrounding lands. She would see it close behind her, trotting to keep up, and the next she would look the thing would be gone, silently slinking away to whatever ends, then a mile further it would be at her heel again.

She lost the dog once more as she passed through the town, off exploring whatever smells it found from cooking fires and waste piles, and when she stopped at a vendor selling corn snacks and water from the back of an open truck she actually looked back for the dog, hoping she would see it still.

The truck had no wheels, raised up on concrete cinder blocks and without doors or windows, and an elderly woman sat on the flatbed with a coal stove and a machine gun.

Kiara walked to her and stopped, looking up at her wrinkled face.

"Agua?" she asked and the woman nodded.

She reached a heavy ladle into the wooden barrel at her side and brought out water and tipped it carefully into a wooden bowl.

"Qué tiene?" the woman asked, enquiring as to the method of payment.

Kiara shrugged and reached into her pocket, bringing out a handful of pesos and the jewellery, hanging through her fingers.

The woman inspected it from her raised platform and leaned over to see it better and took a note from Kiara' hand.

Kiara smiled.

"Muchas gracias señora"

The woman nodded.

"Leave the bowl"

Kiara nodded and said that she would, and asked if it was ok to take it to the roadside to sit and the woman said that it was.

She sat on the kerbside and drank the water. It was warm and had been in the barrel for some time but it was clean and it was water nonetheless, in a place where such commodity was scarce at best.

She thought about the barrel of water that she had left with the cart at the scrapyard and for a moment questioned her decision to leave it there but it was heavy and could not be moved without the cart, and the cart itself had become cumbersome and broken and was not going to be of use on the next part of her quest. She did not need possessions, cooking utensils and pans, there was much to eat in that land if one was resourceful and she knew that she was. She carried a single blanket for warmth and a loaded pistol and knew that those two things were all that was needed to survive, along with a good amount of luck.

She remembered what the old lady in Xochimilco had said to her. She had lost and she would lose again, and to fear and to grieve were parts of that, but that the battle was hers.

She heard the old woman's voice in her head.

"These things do not make you. Fight, queen of cats"

"The old lady was wrong", she thought "these things, the losses, the failings, the heartbreak, they do indeed make me. They make me stronger. They test my resolve and they do not break me"

She resolved again in her head that she would find her son, that day or the next or in many years from then. She would go on. Regardless of what befell her she would go on, or she would die in the road trying, but she would not quit what she had set to do. She was a fighter and a survivor, but moreover she was still a mother. She was still a mother to Mia, who she knew was still with her, and she was still a mother to Dylan, whether he was with her or not. No mother would quit their children and sleep peacefully at night without regret and guilt, go on in peace knowing that she had not done all that she could to make things right, or died in the road trying.

In times past she knew Dylan would have ways to find her again, an address or a phone number, but that was no longer the case. Where was her son going to find her again should he go looking, the bridge over the river in Tehuetlán where they were last together? She knew that would of course not be the case, and the boy would not be foolish enough to consider it an option. Though there was no other alternative, no way of him finding her unless she somehow managed to get word to him and to arrange a rendezvous place or a method of reaching her again when the time came. The letter in her pocket instructed the boy that he could reach them again in Villahermosa, deep in the south of Mexico where the border to Guatemala was within a few days walk and where they would wait for as long as it took for him to reach them. Her aim, as was the plan with her husband, was to travel there to Villahermosa and start a life there, for the short or long term. If she were to grow old there, living day to day waiting for the boy to arrive, then that would be how her life would be. Until she either knew for certain that the boy would not find them, for whatever fate may have befallen him, or until she died there herself, that would be the plan.

Back along the road the way she had come she spotted the dog again, trotting casually along the centre of the road, its tongue lolling from its mouth.

She watched as it neared and it would have trotted past her should she not have whistled for it.

It glanced at first but seemed to recognise Kiara and stood and watched, its head slightly cocked.

She called again to it and it slowly edged a little closer and gathered its confidence before walking to her, its head bowed and its tail down as it neared and she reached out and stroked its head and it flinched but allowed her to do so.

Kiara and the dog looked each other in the eyes for a moment and the dog turned its head away, backing into her legs and sitting down on her feet in the road as though it were always hers.

She finished the bowl of water and put the hat back on her head from where it had been sitting on the kerb.

"Gracias" she said to the woman in the flatbed and the woman nodded to her.

"Chalco?" Kiara asked the woman, pointing along the road.

The woman's eyes narrowed slightly as she thought.

"Chalco de Diaz?" she asked.

Kiara shrugged.

The woman asked Kiara where exactly she was headed in Chalco and Kiara replied that she was looking for the military base south of the town.

The woman nodded.

She raised a finger to the air and made a stepping motion with it as she counted the towns on the route.

"San Antonio, San Nicolas"

She made a step with her finger as she named each place, indicating their order from the place they both stood.

"San Pablo, Los Reyes, y..." she said, landing her finger on the truck, "la base militar"

Kiara asked her how long the walk would be and the woman replied that it was dependant on how quickly one could walk. She said that if Kiara was quick of foot and made safe passage along the road, then there was no reason why she could not make it there by sundown of that day.

Kiara thanked her again and the woman wished her well and Kiara set out along the roadway once more, the dog at her heel.

The afternoon came and went and woman and dog walked together through the passing towns until, east of San Pablo the land opened up into sprawling countryside either side of the road and both of them were hungry.

"Can you hunt, dog?" she asked it as they walked.

The dog looked up at her as she spoke and panted onwards.

"You must have survived somehow. What are you, a scavenger? We could do with you scavenging something now"

The dog walked on.

The bandage around her side was itching and stiff with hardened blood and she felt as though she needed to immerse herself in water for hours to soak away the dirt though there was no river for many miles.

As they walked through Los Reyes there was no person in sight and the cars were torched and windows barred and boarded and the wind whistled across the open fields unrestricted.

There were simple homes behind simple stone walls and dead trees twisted around the stonework and reaching out across the road. The place seemed to no longer be home to any person and Kiara slowed to peer in the windows of those homes she could see into in the hope of finding something to eat or drink or indeed clean herself with.

Her searches were fruitless, and though she did not enter any of the buildings there she was confident that no person had inhabited that place for some time and that there was no reason to take the risk of breaking inside somewhere.

At the edge of town, Kiara stopped.

Across the field to the south, a brick-built structure sat like a sentry-box, nothing around it in any direction for a few hundred yards. It was no more than fifteen feet in width and in length and built three stories high, each plotted with little square windows of darkness and a simple steel door at the side. On the roof were two large satellite dishes, mounted on steel frames that occupied the entire surface of the roof and a small water tank, mostly hidden from view behind the communications equipment.

She stood and watched for a moment, determining whether the place was occupied. After some time, when there was no movement there and no light or firesmoke or otherwise, she began to set out across the field. The building was ringed with a high steel fence with twisted barbed wire along the top and a power box which had clearly once electrified the perimeter. The metal chainlink gate was locked with a bar on the inside and a rusted padlock that looked like it could possibly be smashed with enough force, though only from inside the fence. Kiara walked around the perimeter of the small compound to look for a weakness in the boundary, a loose connector in the fencing or a place where the chainlink was broken or rusted, but the thing was secure.

She watched again.

After a few moments she took her coat off and laid it on the ground with the blanket and carefully began to scale the metal fencing, poking the toe of her boot between the links in the chain and lifting herself upwards as the metal pulled into the skin on her fingers. She reached the top and carefully took hold of the barbed wire, holding between two of the barbs and pulling it downwards so that it was flat to the top of the fence. It scraped at her arms through her shirt and pulled threads from it, until eventually she managed to get her foot on to the top of the fence with a scream of pain. Fresh blood began to seep once again from her wound.

The dog paced anxiously around beneath her, half-jumping at the fence, wagging its tail and whimpering nervously. She swung her leg over the top and, in a single movement, swung herself over and dropped to the dusty ground on the far side, landing in a crumpled heap on her knees, her shirt torn and her arms stinging. She caught her breath and clutched at her bandages, warm and sticky with blood.

She knew that should she find water or food or more inside the old communications building that it would have indeed been worth it.

She rose to her feet as the dog lay at the gate, watching her with its ears pricked as it resigned itself to not following. She summoned her strength again and kicked at the steel door three times to break it from its hinges but it was locked well and the hinges remained intact. She took the pistol from her belt and turned it in her hand so that she held the muzzle and smashed the glass from the window with a single swing.

She stopped and listened.

There was no sound from inside and no sound from outside. The wind, which had ravaged that land for the past week had stopped that morning and the cloud had finally parted to allow a warm low sun to again heat the land. In the quiet countryside there were no birds and no people walking and no sound other than the panting of the dog as it waited for her.

"I won't be long, dog" she said to it and it paused its breath to listen as she spoke.

She hoisted herself in through the window frame and dropped onto the broken glass below, the pistol in her hand.

The room was dark and humid, the sunlight glistening against a billion particles of disturbed dust that swirled around in the burst of air coming through the newly opened window. It took a moment for her eyes to adjust to the dark.

Inside, the lower floor of the building was comprised of a single room, lined along the north wall with a bank of electrical equipment, computers and screens and communication devices, which in their day had powered and managed the substation. The equipment looked mostly intact, undamaged but for the inch of dust that blanketed everything there. A small table and chairs occupied the centre of the room with book cases of manuals and other old items along the opposite wall. At the west side of the room, a splintered wooden doorframe led out into the small hallway beyond and up the rotten staircase to the floor above. There were no footprints through the dust, though there were rat droppings and bird droppings across every surface.

Kiara carefully stepped up the old rickety staircase, supporting herself against the brick wall for the handrail was broken away entirely.

At the second floor were living quarters, a basic lounge and bedroom and a small bathroom that smelled of damp and rot. The lounge had two fabric armchairs and a coffee table positioned in front of a small box television that Kiara reckoned could have been from forty years prior. There were simple items of everyday use there, books, a lamp, some tools and writing equipment, and an old bottle of liquor with a paper label, covered in dust next to a single ornate drinking glass.

She took the liquor and blew off the covering of dust and swatted it away as it swirled in the air. She pulled the cork from the top, raised it to her nose and inhaled. She had not ever been a spirit drinker, preferring wine or the occasional beer, but she recognised it as a golden tequila. She took a sip, and though she didn't quite enjoy it, she did welcome the quick hit it gave her system and she popped the cork in and took it with her.

The bedroom was small, a single bed along one side and a dresser at the other with a pair of eyeglasses and a mirror and an old silver comb.

She opened the top drawer of the wooden dressing table. Inside were men's underwear, socks and pants and a flattened baseball cap. The drawer beneath had a few simple t-shirts and some overalls and the drawer beneath was full of greasy workwear, orange coveralls and heavy-duty gloves. She pulled a few t-shirts from the middle drawer and closed it again. She peered out of the window. The dog was still waiting at the gate, its head sitting on its outstretched paws and its tail dropped. Sad to be left there, or as sad as the dog understood.

She took the wooden steps to the top floor and found the kitchen and a storage space, piled with boxes of spare electrical cables and switches and bulbs and component parts for the satellite dishes on the roof.

The kitchen was sparse. There was a small gas stove for which the gas cylinder was missing, a short counter-top fridge that she dared not open and a sink. The single cupboard on the wall held two plates, two bowls, two cups and a small saucepan. There were no foodstuffs at all, anywhere in the kitchen.

She turned the tap, turning with force against the fused metal, and the pipes from the water tank creaked and squealed and eventually a slow trickle of water began to fall from the tap and disappear down the furry plughole. She quickly grabbed the pan from the cupboard and began to fill it for fear of using the last of the water. She had no way of telling whether the tank was full or as good as empty.

The water smelled stale, it had sat in that tank for many years and she hoped the thing was intact enough to stop anything from infesting the water. Whilst she was a little worried about the cleanliness of the water, it was at least clear in the pan and not brown and dirty and she filled the pan and turned off the tap. She sipped a little and it tasted old, as it was, but it would suffice for cleaning.

She pulled up her shirt to see the bandages below. They were blackened and had squeezed themselves together as she had walked and she searched for their end to try to unravel them. She carefully pulled the beginning of the bandage away and unwrapped it from around her body. As it pulled across the gunshot wound it sent shots of pain through her body but the release of pressure from the wrappings once it was done was welcomed. She put the heap of bloody bandages down onto the worktop, doing so slowly to limit the amount of dust that was disturbed with their movement, should she need to use them again, and then peeled the gauze away from her skin and cried out as she did.

She took one of the old t-shirts which had been taken from the drawer and dipped it into the water and began to slowly dab and wipe the dried blood around the wound, cleaning it gradually until the pan was red and the bloodied tank water poured across the floor like a massacre had taken place there.

Once she had cleared away most of the blood, she inspected the wound.

The entry hole for the bullet was small, no larger than a centimetre across, and the skin around it was bruised and swollen and the nerve endings tingled and stung to the touch. It seeped blood, and she wiped it gently away but within a moment it seeped again and she imagined it should need stitches or more though that was no option.

Medical care was rare, people died of afflictions that would otherwise be simple to cure. Scratches and cuts and abrasions to the skin which, if kept sterile and covered in clean wraps, may cure within a couple of days, were susceptible to infections that eventually took lives, even if the original wound was basic in nature.

Her gunshot wound was indeed not basic in nature.

The pistol had been low-calibre and the round small, though it was buried somewhere in her abdomen and there was no way of removing it or treating the wound the way it should be.

She popped the cork from the tequila bottle and took a swig and winced as it burned around her mouth and she threw some of it into her hand and splashed it against the wound.

She screamed as it singed her skin and it took her breath away.

She took another swig and poured some more onto the gauze and wiped it across the wound.

She screamed louder and kicked her boot against the kitchen unit so hard it splintered the wood.

She cursed in Spanish and sat panting through the pain.

Once she had caught her breath she placed the gauze, covered in mescal on one side and dried blood on the other, back against her wound, tequila-side down and wrapped the old bandage back around herself.

As she stood, the thing hurt more than it had done since she had first woken up, though she was at least sure by then that it was clean. Although she was unsure how sterile tequila could make an open wound, she reckoned it was better than nothing at all.

The dog had stood at her yelling and its nose was pressed against the chainlink, its tail wagging anxiously.

At the horizon the sun was dropping again, and though she knew she must only be a short walk from the military base, she had spent more time than she had intended in searching the substation and also needed to find food again before sundown.

She limped down the stairs to the ground floor, each step sending jolts of pain through her body from toe to shoulder. At the bottom, she stood in the hallway catching her breath again and steadying herself. As she stood, one hand against the old wall, a drifting smell floating past her and paused for a moment trying to place it.

Beside the stairs was a single cupboard door, slightly ajar and she wondered if something inside was rotting, a dead animal perhaps or some long-abandoned food. She could see from where she stood that the cupboard was shelved from top to bottom, with dusty boxes and a fusebox, and she carefully pulled open the door, apprehensive as to what may be inside.

There was nothing, nothing rotten and nothing dead, only the dusty boxes and the fuses.

As she turned to leave, her eyes fell to the floor.

Underneath the old staircase was a wooden hatch in the floor, a metre or so square with a thick iron latch and handle. The smell was emanating from below, underneath where she was standing.

She lifted the handle and heaved the heavy hatch open and let it crash backwards against the wall. The smell of rot poured out and she recoiled in the explosion of dust and stink. Inside, it was as dark as it could be, and she couldn't see further than the bottom of the wooden steps that led down there.

For a moment she considered turning away and returning to the dog and moving out to search for food, but she stopped. She knew that, regardless of the smell, there could be something in that cellar worth taking, perhaps food itself.

She took out the pistol and pointed it into the hole, pausing to prepare herself for what may be there.

She placed the bottle of tequila on the floor and stepped onto the first rung of rotten wood and it cracked under her weight though held. She tried to stoop to see down further but there was only blackness.

She took a few more steps until her head was inside the hole with her. Her eyes could not adjust to the utter blackness, and she feared to step further. She knew nothing could live down there, and she didn't fear rats and spiders.

She stopped at the bottom of the steps, the stink all around her, the pistol pointing at nothing in the dark.

She glanced up the steps and the light from above reset her vision so that when she looked back to the cellar she could again see nothing. She knew she had to focus entirely on the darkness in order to allow herself to see, and she waited at the bottom step, staring into nothingness, her eyes playing tricks of dancing movement as they adjusted once more.

The floor was concrete and the walls had been bricked, crumbling and damp. She put her palm against the wall and held the pistol in the other and edged into the darkness, kicking things on the floor that she couldn't see. The room was small, and as she neared the back wall, her shins clattered against something hard and she staggered to stop herself from falling. The sound scared her and she tried to quickly settle her breathing so that she could hear the silence again.

She crouched to see what she had hit, a wooden crate on the ground full of jars and empty bottles and old newspapers. She held a couple of the bottles up and the faintest fingers of light from the hatch showed them to be empty.

On the wall there was a hanging, old paper with a map.

Her mind raced as to what it may show, and her imagination filled with thoughts of treasure hunts or great conspiracies, but as she pressed her face close to see it better she realised it was mostly likely an engineering map, of a power grid or the locations of other substations or such.

She clattered on, turning along the far side of the basement into the darkest corner of the room where even the tiny amount of light from above could not reach.

She crashed her shins into something else, another box perhaps. As she stepped sideways to avoid it there was a crunching underfoot and she stopped walking entirely for fear of what she may be stepping on.

The silence was deafening around the place and she listened again, her heart racing fast enough for her to hear.

She stooped down again and reached into the black. Her fingers came against wood, another box and she dragged it carefully towards herself and reached inside, completely without vision of even her own hand. There were tins, aluminium cans of something. She lifted them out but could not see them, and as she rooted blindly through the box she scraped her hand on the exposed tops of tins which had been opened and she pulled some that were foul smelling and furry. Each time she lifted a can that she deemed unopened she placed it down carefully between her feet, counting them as she did.

She counted out seven of them, the rest rotten or bent or empty. She picked up the seven tins and dropped them into the bottom of her shirt so that she could hold them all together without them falling, and walked slowly back to the shaft of dull light at the opposite corner of the room.

In the centre of the room she kicked against something else and fell, her feet leaving the dusty ground and the cans tumbling forward across the concrete so that each was again out of view.

She pushed herself up with her hands, her feet still tangled in what she had fallen over, and she reached backwards to investigate it. She touched fabric, cotton, wrapped around something hard and as she moved her palms across it she brushed past a button and then onto the cold and sticky flesh of something long dead.

She pulled her hand away and gasped and shuffled backwards across the concrete floor like a desperate animal. She reached the wooden steps and clung to them, waving the pistol around aimlessly into the dark.

It took her a moment to calm.

Every impulse was to get out of that place, to scurry back up the steps into the light.

But she knew she had to get the tins back, whatever they were and wherever they had bounced to.

She took a moment and then crawled forward again, her arms sweeping the ground in front of her in the hope they would come into contact with the scattered tins.

She cursed again as she did it, the feeling of desperation coming over her like a blanket.

She would not panic. There was indeed somebody dead down there, who had perhaps been bunkered down there for some time, the operator of the building who had no power to go about his business and no place to flee to. His compound protected with fences and barbed wire, his food stored safely in the basement where it could be kept cool without refrigeration, but who had succumbed to something or to someone.

She did not care what. She pushed around on the floor, picking up and feeling in her hands the things she came across, two burned out candles, an empty jar, then one of the tins, an old book, a dead bird, two more of the tins against the wall, bones of something small, perhaps a rabbit, another tin. She found six of the seven and was happy enough with that and practically ran them back to the steps, climbing quickly out of the stinking hole onto the wooden floor above, falling forward to her knees and breathing heavily.

She was covered in dirt, the black jeans whitened with dust and her palms filthy and scratched.

She picked up the tins and set them on the ground in front of her. Four of them had paper labels and she read each one.

"Frijoles refritos, salsa verde de tomatillo, ready-to-use nacho cheese sauce, pork chilorio"

The other two were without labels, and she carried them all into the main room and set them all down on the desk with the computer screens.

The dog had spotted her through the smashed window and was stepping around excitedly outside, whimpering. She walked to the door and unbolted it from the inside and pushed it open.

"You've certainly taken a liking to me" she said smiling, and it jumped when she spoke, "hang on there a minute"

She crossed to the gate and studied the old padlock. She had not intended on finding a way for the dog to come inside with her, though she also did not want to scale the barbed wire fence again and she thought it better to eat some of the food and shelter in the safety of the building until the sun came back up.

She pulled the Colt from her belt and stood back, and with a single shot, blew the padlock off the gate in an explosion of sparks and sound.

The dog recoiled and spun on the spot.

She kicked open the gate.

"Come on in then, dog"

The dog sniffed the place from wall to wall, its tail upright like a mast as it sought out what memories lay in that place, and though there were nothing to see, there was to the dog much to smell.

She used the kitchen knife to open two of the tins, the salsa and the pork, and tipped them onto a plate from the kitchen, scraping a little of each into a bowl for the dog. The dog did not pause long enough at the bowl to take a single breath, devouring the contents in an instant before pushing the empty bowl around the floor on its muzzle. She filled a bowl with the tank water and the dog drank it in one and she refilled it seven times before the dog had drunk enough.

She sat in the old armchair and ate the food and steadily drank the golden tequila as the dog paced the room and came to rest at her feet, and the two of them soon slept there as the world turned dark around them.

She woke to the first light of the morning. For a moment she had no idea where she was, sitting sideways in the armchair in that dust-covered room.

The dog was gone again but she could hear it snuffling through things in another room.

She stood, pulled on the long red coat and pushed the pistol into her belt.

The dog appeared in the doorway, covered in white dust that hung from its fur.

She smiled.

"Ready, dusty? she asked and the dog panted, its tail waving slowly from side to side.

She bundled the remaining tins into her blanket and tied them into a bindle and pushed the tequila bottle into her pocket.

The warm morning air outside felt invigorating.

She had become used to the swirling dust of the substation, and the breeze out in the open countryside tasted sweet. They walked together, back through the crops to the road which they had left the previous day.

Within the hour they passed through the outskirts of the tiny village of Temematla and took the road south to Campo Militar 37-B.

At the end of the driveway, a green military speedboat was set up on a plinth in the centre of the road, with a mannequin soldier posed inside it and a pole which had once held a flag. The boat was emblazoned with the faded emblem of the *Cuerpo de Fuerzas Especiales*, the Mexican special forces.

Kiara stood and looked along the driveway, through the tall trees to the east. She began to walk it, the bundle of food over her shoulder and the dog at her heel.

She passed the running track and an old sentry point of crumbling stone before a group of soldiers approaching from the opposite direction spotted her and moved to slowly block her path.

They told her to stop where she was and she stopped.

"Esto es privado" one of the men called as they came to her, his palms up to signal her to halt.

She said that she knew the place was private and that she was there to seek information.

A young soldier, no older than eighteen with bright eyes and the faintest chalking of a stubbly moustache told her that they were not there to give information and that if she wanted to know anything then she must consult the central offices in the city.

She shook her head.

"No" she said, and the soldiers just watched her, their eyes widened by her brazen response.

They were all younger than her, teenagers themselves, likely untrained and inexperienced and following blindly what protocol they had been taught.

She stared them down, all five of them.

"Qué desea?" one of them asked, young enough to be her son himself.

Kiara told them that her son was enlisted in the army somewhere and that she had walked from Tehuetlán, through the city to every barracks and command post that there was, looking for him.

They listened.

"He must be somewhere" she said.

They nodded.

She said that she wanted to speak with somebody who could help her, that his name must be marked on a chart or a list and she wished to find it.

The soldiers looked between themselves. None had any authority to grant passage or access or otherwise, but nor did they wish to turn her away for they sympathised with her plight.

Kiara sensed their insecurity as their glances darted from one to the next.

"Find me somebody I can talk to or I'm going in there and finding them myself"

She didn't care how it sounded.

The young soldiers nodded and slowly turned and drifted back the way they had come, along the driveway towards the collection of buildings beyond the trees.

None of them instructed Kiara to follow, though none instructed her otherwise and she walked behind them at a short distance as they led her along the driveway to the compound, the dog a yard behind.

They stopped at the main yard, a vast space of dusty yellow earth marked in white paint where trucks and helicopters had once amassed and which swirled in the wind like a vortex, glistening in the white sun. Men in green ran around the place, left to right and right to left, calling and commanding as they went at their tasks. A group of tired-looking black horses, dusty to the knee from riding the open lands, were led in by a small platoon to be watered and fed before being despatched again. They kicked through the dirt and blew from their noses and jolted their heads in discomfort. The men leading them staggered sideways as they walked under the great power of the beasts, leading them away to the south.

The young soldiers stopped her outside the checkpoint building, a low white stone construction with a black roof and black door.

Two of the men went in whilst the others waited with Kiara in the yard, talking amongst themselves, none speaking to as she stood there, her coat a streak of red in their green and black world. A moment later the two men came back out, followed by an older officer in a military-issued shirt with the sleeves rolled up to the elbow and the end of a cigarette in his mouth.

He stared at her, confused and irritated at being interrupted from his work.

He frowned.

She told him what she had told the men and he listened and nodded and then, once she was finished, he shrugged and said he would not have any idea where to find a man in that country or anywhere else.

"Then find me somebody who can"

She stared at him and for a moment he stared back.

He flicked the end of the cigarette into the dust.

"What is his name, your son?" he asked.

"Dylan Beckett"

He nodded and watched away across the yard and sighed and then gestured for her to stay where she was and stepped back inside the building.

The younger soldiers had begun to disperse, not charged with watching the woman, unsure whether they were expected to stay whilst the exchange continued.

He appeared again.

"Come"

He waved her inside.

She closed the door on the dog, who stood watching with its ears up.

He took her to a small office with a simple wooden desk stacked with paper and thick with cigarette smoke.

"Sit" he said, pointing to the chair.

As she sat, she felt the cool metal press against the skin on her lower back and became aware that she still had the pistol in the back of her trousers. Nobody had taken it from her on her arrival, though she was keen to not have it seen should the soldiers suspect her of foul play. Though, she reckoned, there wasn't much that could be done with a single pistol in that place.

The officer returned, crashing a stack of papers down on to the desk and flopping into his chair with an exasperated sigh, resigned to helping.

"Dylan what?"

"Beckett. Dylan Beckett"

"Where?"

"Near Tehuetlán. November. The eighth, maybe. After Dia de Muertos"

The officer thumbed through the papers with his rough yellow thumbs and lit another rolled cigarette.

"Si si" he mumbled, pulling a sheet from the stack and holding it up to see it better in the light.

He read it.

"División veintiocho"

He handed the sheet across the table, handwritten lists and numbers and jargon she did not understand.

He looked at her as if she did.

"He's here?"

The man shook his head.

"División veintiocho. Oaxaca", he thought for a moment, "or some place near there"

Her heart lit up with the hope which she had longed for and dreamed of since the day they were parted.

She thanked him and asked how she would find him once she got there.

He shrugged and stubbed out the cigarette.

"There is no way to find him, you must simply look for him there"

She nodded.

They rose from their seats and he showed her back to the door and she stepped out again into the yard. The dog spotted her from where it was sniffing and ran across as though she were all it had, which indeed she was.

"Be careful down there" the officer called from the doorway.

She turned to him.

"It is not a safe place to be, watch where you walk. But you will find him there, I am quite sure"

For the first time since she met him he smiled very slightly through his straggly moustache and she thanked him again.

Chapter Twelve

There was nothing in that world that burned with quite the ferocity as the flame of eternal motherly love. A flame that kept its glow and its warmth in the gloomiest of times when there was no glow or warmth but itself. There was no weight to the love, nothing to burden or carry or be obligated by, no need for its reciprocation or even acceptance. It was there and it would be there regardless. Regardless of anything. From nothing she had brought her children to the world, conjured from only a dream and from love itself. Brought life from dust, and for Mia, returned her to the dust with her own hands. Buried the piece of her soul with her in that red dirt and scattered flower seeds and tears until the soil was blossoming and wet with her pain. That day there, kneeling in the dirt in the burning sun with her face raw, the allegiance in her heart to what still remained, grew in its intensity and she swore it unbreakable. Her man and her boy, the keystones of her survival and her existence and her ability to keep hope alive in a place where little hope prevailed and no future was promised to anybody. Her husband was under the flower seeds and tear-soaked soil with her daughter, running endlessly in the fields of beyond where the sun was ever-golden and the water sweet and the days endless. She smiled in her soul a solitary smile that they should be together again, the girl and her daddy, where they could remain together in a safety that no evil could ever reach. But where her boy walked he was not safe, as no man or woman or boy was. Their world was not one of golden sunshine and endless days. Their world was dark and terrifying and there was malice waiting to take a person by the hand wherever they were to walk and to put them into the soil with it. The boy was young. Not too young to understand survival, not too young to fight for himself, not too young to know the ways of the world he was forced to grow up in. But he was far too young, in the eyes of his mother, to be walking that land with a rifle in his hand, forced into conflicts that were not his where no other man truly cared for his welfare as much as their own. Nobody who would sacrifice like his mother. And with the flame burning in a place it could not be extinguished, despite what icy gloom may try, Kiara pushed herself relentlessly through the country. She knew she was unstoppable, the conviction of her quest blurring all else, the roaming nomad, the queen of cats.

The towns fell away behind her, Cuautla and Izúcar de Matamoros blurred. She slept rough, wherever she stopped walking and without caring for shelter or safety or true warmth. She wrapped the blanket around herself and over her head and pulled it tight like the wrappings of a mummy and pushed herself into whatever corner or hole or cave there was. She ate whatever she found. On occasion she traded money and jewellery for meat and rice, and on others she ate berries and nuts pulled from trees and on a dark night north of Tepexco when she had miscalculated her walking distance and was left on the open road, she pulled herself under a netleaf oak and ate the grass there.

The dog walked by her wherever she went. She questioned it as to where it had been, what life it lived before they came together, where its home was, or had once been. It would stare back, right through her as though it understood everything she asked of it but was merely unable to respond, and Kiara would laugh to herself for the dog did not understand a thing.

She tried to teach it to hunt down rabbits and birds but she got nowhere. The dog seemed to understand readily the concept of stalking its prey, stooping low and flat and quiet as it watched the grazing animals, but it would bolt too quickly, panting and yapping as it ran, allowing its quarry ample time to make the necessary escape and it would run mindlessly around in circles as Kiara stood shaking her head.

In a sideroad in Calmeca where Kiara sat drinking cold coffee the colour of groundwater, the dog managed to corner a milk snake against the back of an old restaurant and Kiara stood waiting with a knife for it. She had found a blade, a rosewood hunting knife with initials engraved into the handle. She fastened the knife to her thigh with a length of leather belt, angled so that the point of the blade hung just behind her as she walked to avoid injuring her own leg, though it frequently caught on the inside of her coat as she walked.

The dog pawed and yapped at the coiled snake, stepping around in excitement and hunger. Though for its troubles, the dog was bitten twice on the paw and the serpent disappeared into the stone wall.

At Guadelupe Allende, the streets were deserted but for makeshift camps of travellers, selling and trading what useless items they had found and scavenged along their ways.

Kiara passed slowly through the place, browsing what the people offered, and questioning in her head what value anybody could place in such things. Men and women, wrapped in dirty clothes and tending fires that had no flames, drinking water of questionable origin and picking at animal bones and dried grains. They had laid out on the ground, presented on blankets or in the dirt itself, items no person would need, paintbrushes without bristles, items that could only function with electricity, dirty children's toys and broken instruments and broken paintings taken from walls and fruit bowls and figurines missing limbs or heads.

They looked up to her at those who passed with big desperate eyes that they should trade coffee or food or clean water or medicines for such junk.

The poverty in that part of the land had been pervasive since long before the disaster and the place was cut-off from government intervention and aid, however rare that indeed was in other places. The people begged, as many always had, and Kiara shook her head to them for she had nothing to give, even if she wished. The desperate pleading from the helpless.

The desperate begging from the desperate.

A young girl came to her in ripped clothing and without shoes, white to the knee with dust, a wooden serving tray in her hands lined with stones that she had drawn faces and animals on and pleading with Kiara to purchase one. Her heart bled for them, but despite what pity and sympathy she may have felt there, she had nothing but the clothes she wore, the pistol in her hand and the dog at her heel. She blessed the girl and wished her success elsewhere and passed her by, her desperate mother watching from the shade of her hovel.

"You should not walk south alone" the woman called as Kiara had passed and the words grabbed her by the back of her hair and pinned her.

She turned.

"Why?"

"El Atoyac"

It meant nothing to her.

She walked slowly to the woman.

"What is that?"

"The river", she said, "is here"

She pointed south.

"It's not safe?"

The woman shook her head sharply, her eyes narrowed as though it were a foolish question to ask.

"Do not drink the water at the bridge, it will kill"

"The water from the river?"

"Sí. There is something in the water south of San Francisco de Asis", she pointed at Kiara with her withered finger and long dirty nail, "people like you walk this road, they stop at the river to drink and then they are gone. It is poison. The men in the hills are waiting there, they will know when you drink"

"The men in the hills?"

She nodded.

"The men in the hills. They have poisoned the water south of San Francisco. If you walk the road south then do not walk it alone, or be prepared, and do not drink from the river"

Kiara nodded.

She said she understood though she did not, and thanked the woman and the woman nodded.

Kiara needed to drink, though the prospect of trekking the open hills on the wrong course to find the place where the water was drinkable was not worth the effort to her. She had survived thus far, picking and scrapping and taking moisture from plants, and she had not accounted for the presence of a river regardless, so to pass the place without drinking would not be the end of her.

She adjusted the pistol in her belt, reassuring herself that it was indeed there. She whistled the dog onwards and set out on the road, walking alone against the instruction, the dog trotting beside her as her only companion and protection, though it was yet to prove itself of the latter.

The January afternoons were short and the sun was dropping again as the road wound the dusty scrubland to the gushing Atoyac. A white sandy track forked from the highway, leading up to the battered shacks and huts on the brow of the ridge, overlooking the water. The place was quiet, but there were smalls camps of travellers in pockets of land there, readying their camps and fires and making trips by foot down the rough bankside to the water and filling what containers they carried and bathing and splashing and washing their children.

Kiara watched from the edge of the road, her eyes darting around the surrounding hillside for sight of what men the old woman had warned of. The lowlands were bushy with white pine and cacti, and evening birds flocked silently and nothing out there moved. She hopped the metal barrier at the roadside and crossed through the scrub to the riverbank. She dropped to the water and called to a group of people in the river to their waists. They stopped and turned. She called to them that she had heard that the water was not safe and they waved her away and went on regardless and when she pressed her point to them they called her crazy and warned her away.

She shook her head and left them to their fate.

She sat on the hillside above the water and lay back between the thornbushes with the dog at her side and the pistol in her lap. The evening cool blew softly along the water and the sound of the current against the rocks and the bridge was calming. The sky turned to a deep indigo and the eternal night sky unfurled above her a canvas of stars and galaxies so infinite it was at once terrifying in its endlessness and comforting to her in its calm.

She lay on her back and watched, nothing and everything at the same time.

Her head was back on the ground and she had drifted away into a light sleep when she awoke in unease. She sat upright and felt around in the dark for the pistol. The dog was standing a few feet from her, staring into the darkness, unmoving.

She rose slowly to her feet, not kicking a stone for fear of making a sound that may betray her location.

She listened to the night, her ears pricked like the dog's.

In the scrub a few hundred feet from the roadbridge, shadows moved, black against black. She stooped and took the dog by the scruff to stop it barking or bolting and watched with only her eyes above the bushes.

A group of men, stooped as they walked, five or six strong, moved silently through the dark. She lost the shadows in the blackness, then saw them once more, three of them at the ridge, rifles glinting in the light of the moon. At the edge of the track a camp was made of blankets and tarpaulins and a metal cart, and the end of a wispy fire was dwindling. Travellers had come and gone across the evening, some taking water and others not, some making camps along the side of the road and others passing onwards to try to reach Tehuitzingo by twilight.

Kiara had paid to notice to those who had come and gone from that place over the evening, though she suspected the inhabitants of the camp to be the family she saw in the river.

She watched from her bolthole in the thorns.

The shadowmen dispersed through the low bushes, silently moving the terrain like a pack of wild bushdogs stealthily surrounding an unsuspecting reedbuck. Kiara watched their heads ducking and bobbing above the bushes as they took their places along the ridge and then all heads disappeared from view and, for a moment, there was nothing to be seen.

She held the dogs neck tight, its ears twitching.

"Leave it" she whispered.

Then the heads appeared again, rising out of the silhouetted landscape like gophers from their burrows, converging as one on the camp in a rapid sweep. There was little noise, the briefest of scuffles and muted cries and the thumping of a heavy instrument against something soft. Three of the men darted from the campsite, running across the ridge through the leatherstem and barrel cacti, carrying with them all manner of pillaged goods and staggering as they ran until they were gone from sight along the riverbank to the east. The canopy of blankets that had been pulled from cart to tree were whipped down so that all the men of the raiding party were visible to Kiara from where she hid. The items that remained in the camp were thrown quickly on to their cart and three men took up the front shaft to pull it away. They held it from the ground as more men appeared, another four or five that Kiara hadn't seen before, arriving in from the west from the ramshackle homes at the opposite side of the highway.

They lifted together the travellers' limp bodies onto the cart, and within a moment they scarpered again to the darkness from where they had come like roaches. The remaining men took up the cart and trotted it along the ridge into the night, leaving behind them no sign that a camp had been there at all.

No person, no goods or clothing or food or sleeping equipment, and no cart.

Kiara watched silently as the entire scene dispersed again before her, giving way to the peaceful night, only the distant rattle of the cart wheels to be heard as it was pulled away to the east, into the hills.

She stood, the pistol levelled at her hip, her eyes darting around the darkness.

To her right, the bush rustled loudly and she spun to see the tail of the dog disappearing through the thorns, giving chase to the raiding party.

She stood for a moment, locked to the ground as her heart and mind raced for a move, her eyes wide and glowing with panic in the moonlight.

Her first thought was to run for the dog, call for it, whistle it back, but she daren't make a single sound in that place. The raiding party were over the ridge of the first hill but the sound travelled across the countryside easily as she knew they would kill her in a moment if they found her there.

She paused still, her next instinct was to abandon the dog, leave it to run to whatever fate its mindless body was taking it to. Those few seconds that her mind rifled through her options, her legs swayed at the knees as she weighed up the two opposite decisions.

To run for the dog or to run for her life.

She knew she had come too far for it. She had shared water and warmth with the stupid dog for many a dry day and cold night. She owed it nothing, but she would not abandon it unless her life depended on such an action, and in that instant it did not.

She sighed loudly and cursed at the animal and adjusted the blade on her thigh and set off along the riverbank after the dog. She at least owed it a chance.

The river roared beside her as she ran, the crashing of the waves on the rocks drowning out the sound of the rattling cart ahead of her on the open land.

She clutched the pistol in one hand and the brim of her hat in the other, stopping it from flying backwards from her as she skipped over the desert.

The river meandered away and she could hear that she was gaining ground on them, able to move quicker than the men pulling the laden cart, even with the pain in her side still not numbed. The dog was nowhere to be seen and the omnipresent blackness of the desert night prevented her from picking out tracks in the dust, of neither cart nor men nor the dog.

As the river bent back to meet her, Kiara skipped across the scrub, kicking through rough thorns and cacti and scraping her shins as she ran. She could still hear the cart yet closer, though no sound of the dog.

She crossed onto a gravel roadway where the hulking bodies of rusted and torched cars lined the shoulder and nightbirds scattered as she ran. She could make out the silhouette of the men with the cart ahead of her, some few hundred yards along the road, and she slowed her pace.

She was there for the dog only, and intended to keep her cover at all costs, for the men she pursued had proven themselves a danger enough already and she was not prepared with a single pistol and knife and a bandaged gunshot wound for any level of combat.

Low buildings appeared either side of the road, rough adobe stone and sand and clay, and Kiara ducked from the road into the undergrowth at the river's edge and waited. The cart ahead slowed between the first two buildings and she could hear distant voices and laughing and a group of silhouettes appeared from the doorways and opened up a rough timber gate and the cart passed inside.

Kiara edged along the river bank, hoping the sound of the crashing current to her side would mask any noise she made on the ground, though she made little. The river turned east again, bending around the perimeter of the tiny village which had been repurposed into a compound for those malevolent men of the night, the raiders of good and killers every one of them. The place was small, no more than twenty little homes, a couple of barns and a small mill of sorts. It was fenced at the perimeter with old rusted wire, bent around rotting wood, nothing that could keep the evil secured inside or keep Kiara out.

She held her distance.

At a glance the place was rudimentary and defenceless, though she knew nothing of what eyes watched from the shadows. The wire fence was not substantial, but every man in that land was armed, some markedly so, and she would not risk her life against a countryman with a rifle who may be sitting at a sentry point or behind a well-positioned window. She watched and listened though there was nothing more to see nor hear.

The dog was nowhere to be seen and she cursed it again, questioning whether it had even gone after the men or whether it merely chased a groundfowl to the water, and for a few moments she crouched in the bushes there and considered aborting her quest to save it.

But she had nothing.

She had lost through her own fingers the things in her life that she cared most for. Both parents, both children. Ryan and their home. Both homes.

Her care and responsibility for the dog, which to her did not even have a name, was of no comparison to the things she once loved, but she had a duty nonetheless and she would not walk away without it.

Keeping to the edge of the black water, she moved north along the boundary of the wild little town until she saw commotion ahead of her. The fence stretched down to the water's edge, and at the beach there were a cluster of small timber buildings that reached the water. People swarmed around them and there were candlelights flickering inside so that they shone in that desert like nothing else.

From behind the cacti she watched, sitting on her heels with the pistol in her hand.

At the shoreline, men gathered, strobed by the dancing orange light.

The cart was pulled out from the village to the sandy riverbank.

The men laughed and bellowed, their sound all that there was there to hear in the eternal desert. They steadily pulled from the cart the items plundered from the camp and walked them to the river, stepping out through the current to drop them into the water. A man at the edge, a cigar glowing beneath a wide-brimmed hat, barked at them to move the things further into the water and the men did as they were instructed. When the cart was emptied, it was pulled back into the village and the men put out the candles from the glass lanterns and the place fell dark again, their commotion moving back inside the compound as the men went to their drinking and gambling and fighting.

Kiara waited.

"Where the hell is that stupid dog?" she muttered to herself.

She watched where the men had cast the items into the water, and the thought flooded her mind that should the dog have caught the cart early, it may well be laying there in the water too.

She knew she had to find out or risk searching the village for something that may already be lost.

She crawled forward through the scrubby land, her fingers in the sand and her face scratched with thorns, until she was sure her path to the waterline was safe

She rose to her feet and ran stooped to the water's edge.

As she neared the timber buildings where the fenceline met the river, there came into view before her a great pile of things which had been cast into the water, a dumping ground of items pillaged from the camps which the men did not want. The pile was high, damming half the river so that the white water pushed up the opposite riverbank and wore away the soil, carving a sweeping bend in the ground.

In the river to her side, she saw the little shoes sticking out from the water, still attached to the little legs and filthy brown kneesocks.

She stopped.

Looking closer into the darkness, the grotesque image presented itself to her. The river was piled, ten feet high and twice that wide, with bodies of men and women and children, tangled and pale and bloodied and broken. Their clothes were torn, some removed completely so that their wet and ghostly bodies shimmered in the moonlight and reflected the glow of the moon. Their eyes white, their hair thinning, gunshot and stabbed and battered and wounded and rotting.

Kiara fell backwards into the sand, her own eyes wide at the gruesome vision.

She understood why the water at the bridge was poisoned. It was poisoned with the rot and the blood and the souls of those who dared to drink from it. Those simple people who passed on the road in need of rest. The operation had been precise, a well-practised drill. They had dismantled the campsite in less than a minute, carrying away everything that was there, kicking sand over the fires and taking to the river its occupants.

There were shouts from inside the compound.

Calls of a woman or a girl, perhaps two. The shrill sound carried across the night, over the stone buildings from inside the village where Kiara couldn't see. There was a fire burning in the place, flicking orange light against the surrounding homes and casting long dark shadows of men over the dry land.

Kiara waited and listened.

The shouts continued, pleading for help, warbling and terrified. Men around her laughed loudly.

Kiara crept a little closer to the fenceline to try to see inside, past the stone homes into the village square, but it was obscured from view.

The crying woman was most likely taken from the camp alive, and Kiara feared the very worst for what she may have to endure. But she knew that there was nothing that she could do. She could not save the woman from her fate, whatever that was. She could not charge the compound, a single pistol and old blade, limping from a fresh wound. The men were all armed, each one of them. She knew she would barely make it over the fenceline before her fate joined that of the crying woman inside.

Her eyes glazed with tears, her heart throbbed with the helplessness, but that land was filled with horrific evil and she must survive, more importantly than anything. She must survive for her son. There could be no value put on a human life, but for what value there was, Dylan meant more to her than the woman who cried for help from inside that place, and it was a battle she could not enter, let alone triumph.

She cursed the lord she once gave her life to.

If there was a final judgement, a day of the lord, then surely it had been already and all those who still walked that dry earth were forgotten or not worthy and had been left there to fend for themselves without a divine hand.

"Lord of mercy, if you have anything to give, comfort us in our time of suffering, so that we might comfort those who need it now the most"

She looked up to the eternal blackness and knew she had been left.

There was nothing that would be offered to her, no solace from the torment, no agreement of reprieve.

She kept low, and moved back away into the dusty scrubland to the riverbank and headed back east to the road, resigning the poor woman to her destiny along with the dog.

She walked slowly, tears in her eyes. The white moonlight flicked against the thorns on the barrel cacti and within a moment there was nothing more to be heard but the flow of the Atoyac.

In the darkness at the water's edge she saw movement, the flick of a tail and the glinting of two white eyes in the night.

She stopped.

There were grey wolves and pumas wild there, and both roamed alone at night.

No sooner had she frozen herself to the spot and raised the pistol than the animal ran at her, bounding noisily up the dusty bank and across the scrubland and throwing itself at her legs, wet with riverwater.

"You're a stupid dog" she growled at it, relieved to see the thing alive and with her and free from the danger that surrounded them, but likewise angry at the thing for putting both of them in the situation that it did, and angry at herself for straying too close to the raiders' compound when the dog was likely at the river there the entire time.

She clipped the top of its head with her hand.

"I should have just left you. What's wrong with you, dammit? Next time that's it, I'm not coming after you"

It panted loudly and tried to lick her hand and she walked off into the darkness and the dog trotted behind her, oblivious as ever.

Chapter Thirteen

For eleven days Kiara walked south, unrelenting. The slow and steady and unstoppable walk of a migrating elephant, eyes fixed to the road as the sun arced above her time and again, lighting the horizon and then burning the day before falling away again to come around once more.

She walked the day and sheltered or did not shelter at all in the night, her feet numb in her leather boots. The dog grew skinny but it walked on with her. It took to eating the grasses and frequently brought them back up and she worried for its health.

Every few hours, another insignificant village or town would silently build up around them and then drip away as they passed. The places were nameless, faceless, nothing but something to look at on their trip. They were each battered by poverty and she frequently saw things she wished she had not. The dead were not buried, not hidden. They lay where they fell, no person there with the energy or tool or inclination to bury them or burn them or otherwise. What was left of the people's faiths had diminished. Crosses were worn, prayers uttered for the suffering, but the people knew they had missed the ascendance. They had missed what coming there had been, left in the dirt whilst their saviour walked on without them. They prayed regardless but the words were empty, as they feared they had always been.

As the road picked through the dry foothills of the sierra, bending from side to side like water searching for a route through drystone, the breeze brought with it the sweet smell of firesmoke from the south. It fluttered through the valley floor, and Kiara kept her eyes to the hills for sign of the camp, and though nothing showed itself the smell continued. The further along the road she walked, the more the smell blew across her, and as she were imagining what barn or home may be burning, the words of the officer from the military base spun through her head.

"The south of Mexico burns"

She pressed on regardless. She did not care what burned, it would not burn enough to prevent her finding her son.

At the northern edge of Oaxaca city, the sky grew dark, the wispy smoke trails blew across the horizon like climbing tornados from the desert floor, trunks of black smoke from individual fires that drifted away into the greater cloud of fumes above.

The neighbourhoods of Los Jimenez and Poblado Morelos were no more, levelled to blackness. Homes that stood there had burned long ago, and the flame and smoke long dispersed. There remained a charred carpet of impassable detritus, ash blowing across the place like awful snow.

Nothing there moved. The road had been cleared of what wreckage had once fallen on it, though her boots pushed through the black and white snowfall which fell around her ceaselessly.

Beyond, to the south, Oaxaca still stood, partly. It was there that the military had been relocated from far around to battle the blazes in the absence of any fire department.

Water had been drained from the Atoyac that flowed south with the road through the city, and carried by hand and by horse and by cart to where it was needed. Tanker lorries that had once carried water and milk and oil were recommissioned by the military and used for firefighting, each pulled by thirty horses or more. It had not been an entirely unsuccessful effort, though it had been long and men had been lost to the cause.

What remained was a city pock-marked with charred buildings where fire had been fought off, sporadic breakouts of flame from hidden places where ashes still smouldered and threatened to lick-up anything they could take hold of. The smoke swirled the paper-like ashes overhead.

The roadway was wide enough to have kept intact, passing straight through the blackened wreckage into the heart of the city. No tree lined its shoulder, the roadsigns that stood at the verge or hung overhead were scorched and bent, their place names obscured by the black as though a ghastly indication as to what lay ahead on that road.

Kiara and the dog walked south, the burned homes climbing the hills to the east and west, overlooking each other and nothing at all, until the sun dipped behind them and they were forced to stop once more.

As the road passed through Santa Rosa, the crumbled shell of a superstore was raised from the roadway, set back atop a concrete ramp that elevated it from the tarmac, the car park encircling its base. The raised elevation had prevented the front façade from succumbing entirely to the flame and the chips of red paint were still visible against the black. Kiara climbed the dog through the rubble, stepping over the charred remains of every thing that had once made up that town, fabrics turned to dust, glass and ceramics shattered into sand and metal bent and blackened and sharp enough at the point to cut through her boots.

She forced the dog to walk carefully, and it appeared to understand the peril, stepping slowly amongst the jagged ashes.

At the front of the store, which had largely fallen in on itself, they clambered over the front wall and took to shelter from the wind and the night. She pulled her coat around herself and wrapped up in the blanket, pulling the dog close to share one another's warmth, and simply waited there for the sun to rise.

They heard scavengers in the night, men with horses and ploughs, pulling methodically through the ashen sea, looking for what remained, though there was very little at all. Men covered in soot from top to toe like things of the underworld, eyes reddened, long blackened fingers poking around for gems in the dirt, their hacking coughs echoing around the land before them like the barks of dying dogs.

The night was still but for the gentle breeze coming off the hills, blowing the ash around in little cyclones, though the place was permeated with the smell of burned plastic and rubber and rot.

At first light they quickly climbed back down to the road to continue their progress into Oaxaca.

At Villa del Marquez, the road was clear to the west. Kiara stood and watched. The junction had been intentionally and purposefully cleared so as to allow passage to the Atoyac. The road there had once crossed a simple stone roadbridge painted with red, joining the main body of the city to the neighbourhoods of the west. The river had provided a natural fire barrier when the place was ablaze, and the districts of Azteca and Santa Cruz and Jacarandas had been allowed to burn away, a vast black desert passing away to the horizon where the dusky purple hills watched over it, untouched as they had always been.

The city to the east, where the government's assets lay, was beginning to look to Kiara more like the city it had once been. Entire roads of buildings stood. Greyed by smoke and with bolted windows and dead gardens, but standing nonetheless.

Kiara picked through the little sideroads past the stone homes to the river's edge. She cleaned herself in the water and the dog drank feverishly. Memories of what lay in that water to the north flooded back to her, and she considered not washing there, out of respect and trepidation as to the state of the water. But she was in no position to choose what water she washed with, or drank, or fed to her dog. Not in that dry land.

She took her coat and laid it at the water's edge and took off her boots and stood in the shallows and splashed the water through her hair, pulling pieces of tissue-like ash from it which dissolved in her fingers to the touch. She pulled it straight and wrung the water from the tips and let it fall against her back.

Three young boys watched her from the opposite bank. She smiled across to them and waved a hand, and they laughed and ran around in circles and disappeared into the black desert.

Gunfire rang out across the rooftops behind her and she took up her coat and hat and picked the boots from the ground, and walked the dog back to the road to redress herself.

She stood against the stone wall, facing the river, and pulling the red coat up around her shoulders.

More shots, from an automatic rifle, and shouting through the streets, the sound winding around the buildings and deceiving in its direction. Kiara pulled the pistol from her belt.

She crossed the dried scrubland to the road and at the end she passed along a spraypainted alleyway that slid behind a row of homes, keeping her head down as she walked. Gunfire rattled and her ears rung and the dog flinched and they quickened their pace. The alleyway took her to the main road, a row of old stores, their signs in red and black reading *Taceria* and *Consultorios Medicos* and *Auto Escuela*. They were smashed and looted and some burned but mostly the buildings there stood free of damage, salvaged at the time of the infernos and permitted to live on as remnants of what life there had once been there.

Though there was life no more.

No person walked idly along those streets, travelling or trading or passing by. The place was a warzone. Along the roadway, three men scrambled over a high wall and fell on to the concrete, staggering to get up, clutching rifles and rucksacks, the front man dragging the next by the scruff of his shirt to pull him faster from danger. The first two disappeared along the road and darted between the buildings, though the third hit the ground harder and took a moment to gather himself.

It was to be the final moment he had.

A group of armed military spun around the corner and two more appeared on the wall behind him and at the first instance he was gunned down in a spray of blood. He dropped to the dust and was left where he fell, the green-clad soldiers taking off along the road after his accomplices.

Kiara kept against the stone buildings, sitting on her heels and holding the dog around the neck. She could not trust it to keep itself from trouble, and she feared that the creature may get both of them killed before sundown. It had walked without a leash thus far, but it was not to be allowed such freedom in the confines of a city, especially one as obviously ravaged with ganglife as that one.

She found the highway again and followed it another half mile south towards the centre of the city, the imposing satellites and communication towers of the Observatorio Astronómico lining the hillside above her.

At the sweeping white steel arches of the auditorium, the highway gave way to the south and the panoramic vista of the city of Oaxaca spread out before her. She stood at the metal barricade at the edge of the road and looked out across the place. The twisters of fire smoke whipped around in the distance and huge swathes of the city had been swallowed by it already, blackened and levelled and turned back to the dust from which they came. Gunshots crackled in the distance in a place indeterminable, carried on the breeze with the ever-pervasive stink of burned metal and rubber.

The place was as uninviting as she could have imagined, but she would walk in the burning of any flame to find her son, she would kick what ash and cough what smoke was needed until she complete her quest. She would walk where fires still burned, until they burned the very boots from her feet, and she would walk where fire are to burn yet.

She resolved to search that place until she found the military, and she reckoned she may not have to look far, for the place was under-siege.

She climbed over the yellow barrier and scrambled down the dusty bank through the grama grass and the twisted skeletons of thorn, pulling long threads from her red coat as she went. The dog stepped nervously behind her, edging sideways through the grass, trying to pick out a clearer route which was not there.

At the bottom, she dropped to the ground behind a parking garage and gathered herself and straightened out her coat and repositioned the hat on her wet hair and listened for a moment.

She walked along the quiet street without any idea of a route, walking downhill without thinking about it. The buildings there were painted in deep yellows and dusky reds and pinks and graffitied from top to bottom, faceless names and logos and cryptic clues and signals and calling cards between the cartels of that place, messages passed silently between those who operated the underworld. The windows were boarded and barred and cars in the street were torched and dogs lay dead in the sun, their hair fading and their skin pulling tight around their bloated and baked bodies. Oaxaca's once significant feral dog problem had finally been remedied, to the sorry detriment of the dogs.

Shots rang out again and the dog flinched and Kiara stooped behind a wrecked truck and took the dog by the neck.

At the end of the road, a group of military personnel passed, rifles readied. They moved quietly and quickly, the lance corporal at the front wearing a black baseball cap and giving signals to his fireteam with his hands alone.

Kiara watched them, trying to see the faces of the passing soldiers, desperate to catch a glimpse of any boy who could be hers, but the soldiers were all young, even their commander, and they all looked alike from where she hid. She knew she had nothing to fear from the military themselves, they were indeed there to aid the security of the people, but she also knew that she could not trust anyone, and that military serviceman on active patrol were not likely to take well to her civilian requests for information. She decided to head to the centre of the city and find where the military were based there, to hopefully find an officer who had a little time to help her locate Dylan, or to give her any information towards that goal.

As she released the dog from her grip and headed south along the sideroad, four men rounded the bend before her and began to advance. They were young, dressed in black coats and hats and with torn shirts and dirty faces and pistols. They were a couple of hundred yards back and began running up the hill to her, and she found herself frozen to the spot as she watched them, unsure whether to run.

The dog watched, then barked. Whatever the men were doing there, whoever they were running from, whatever mischief they wanted in that place, Kiara reasoned that none of it involved her and that she had no cause to flee, and that moving out of the way of the advancing men would be sufficient to allow them to pass without incident. She whistled the dog backwards and stepped away from the road towards an open doorway into the shade of an old home, the pistol levelled at the hip regardless.

As the men advanced closer, she saw the fire in their eyes and the blackened gritted teeth, men who fought without the need to. They were gang members of old, survivors of the apocalypse, men who had got thus far by whatever means necessary. Taking without guilt and killing without mercy. What caused them to run was not clear, but Kiara realised with a jolt that they were indeed running for her, and by the time she reasoned to act the men had halved the distance between them.

One fired at her and she felt the shell slam into the stonework. The dog crouched in against her legs as she raised the Colt Python and the charging group and began to run up the road. She volleyed shots back along the road at her pursuers, her arm backwards at the shoulder as she ran. One of the men cried out and staggered and dropped slowly to the ground, clutching his thigh where the round had struck him. The men glanced backwards and faltered in their running and the man at the back of the pack stopped to tend to his fallen accomplice.

The front two ran on.

Kiara ran for her life, the dog sprinted ahead, for once very aware of the danger.

Her eyes scanned the dusty sideroads ahead of her for a place to duck into or jump down or climb up, but she had no idea where she was, a city as alien to her as any she had walked and she didn't know if to duck down an alleyway may trap her there completely. Though she also knew that she could not outrun the men on foot. Another two shots whistled past her and she threw herself from the road through a break in a chainlink fence and headed to the bank of the highway which she had scrambled down earlier. The dog hopped through the hole and stuck close to her. She pushed through the undergrowth, tripping on the dry earth until the white stone retaining boundary wall appeared before her through the high grasses, supporting the weight of the land behind it.

She was trapped against it. There would be no way she could climb the incline at the speed required to evade the men, and she had now lost herself in the roughlands behind the road which were fenced in by the metal chainlink she had squeezed through.

She cursed herself. She had trapped herself by trying to be clever, and now she would pay. She sat back on her heels against the stone and held the pistol out in front of her at arm's length at the high grass, waiting for her pursuers to burst through. She approximated a head-height and trained the pistol at it, hoping that if her reflexes were good enough she may drop the men before they realised what was happening.

She held the dog by the neck and waited.

The rustling of the grasses approached.

But she had miscalculated.

The men were not directly behind her. They had followed her through the metal fencing but they had headed along the edge of the roughland and appeared suddenly off to her right. She spun the pistol and fired and the men ducked back into the grasses until she heard the pistol clicking.

The cylinder was empty.

She froze. There was nothing more to do.

The dog growled through its teeth, set back on its haunches as though it were to pounce, tail and ears upright and eyes white.

The men slowly stepped out from the grasses, both carrying revolvers.

They smiled at her and walked to her, their battered old boots kicking through the dry earth at the foot of the high stone wall.

A bird sang a happy whistling song from the bushes beyond.

The front man glanced at the snarling dog and lifted his pistol and pointed it at the dog's head and smiled again.

A single rifle shot rang out, a thundering sound against all else which hung in the air and a single spot of red exploded from the man's forehead. His eyes stopped and he faltered in his step and his knees gave way and he dropped on the spot.

The man behind him had the briefest of moments to panic. He watched his accomplice fall, glanced at Kiara where she sat wide-eyed, and glanced upwards to the bushes beyond before a second shot rang out, and a spot of red exploded from his head. He tried to bring his hand up to it but it didn't pass his waist before he fell, landing down on top of the other man.

Kiara spun around on her heels.

Behind her in the bushes, a small opening had been made into the wall, the large white stones removed and a tunnel made, perhaps an old service tunnel or an entrance to sewers. From it stepped a tall man in a long and dusty white priest's robe and a brown suede fedora, a long hunting rifle at his side.

"Come with me"

The tunnel disappeared into the raised hillside, black as pitch within twenty feet and not lit by anything more than the lantern the priest carried. He walked ahead of Kiara, the flame swinging in his hand and casting the dim orange light up the dirt walls. The tunnel had been dug through the dirt and braced where necessary with timbers and bricks. There was no floor but for the earth itself and the place smelled of the damp and the musty soil through which it passed.

Once they had walked some fifty feet or so into the tunnel, past the young sentry in the cloth cap who stood guarding the opening, and the priest was satisfied they were hidden, he stopped, turning to Kiara. She had thumbed more rounds into the pistol as they had walked, her distrust in all people extending even to those in the clergy. For all she knew, the robe could be stolen, a ruse, a con to elicit trust.

He spun and watched her.

"What do you know of those men?"

His voice was low and deep and rumbled around the enclosed space. His accent was not one Kiara recognised, his English immaculately worded but not from that land.

"Those men chasing me? Nothing"

The man nodded, he watched her eyes glinting in the light of the single flame that swung in his hand.

"What did they want with you?"

She shrugged in the dark.

"I have no idea, to rob me most likely"

"Do you have something they want?"

"What? Like what? My gun, my boots. The hat? How should I know?"

The man thought about this.

"You do not know who they are?"

"Listen, I've told you I don't. I'm looking for my son. I've just come here from the north. They appeared from nowhere, those men, probably trying to rob me. Then you were there. Thank you. Thank you so much"

The man nodded, his trust in her growing.

His tone softened.

"Those men are Hoja Negra"

"What's that?"

"They are a gang, a cartel. An army. They started small, in the north, now they are everywhere. They run many parts of this poor nation. They have their hands on the government, control parts of the border to the south and the entire west coast up to Baja"

"What did they want with me?"

"Who knows. You are a beautiful woman and I imagine that is all they wanted"

"Well I'm lucky you were there"

He nodded.

"You were. No woman should walk alone here. No man can truly do so safely either"

For a moment Kiara began to rebut the man's comment, argue her own strength and survival skills, show to him the handgun and tell him what she had fought to make it to that place. But she could also not deny that the man had indeed saved her in that moment and his warning was genuine and not prejudiced.

She looked around, what little she could see. They stood in a void of nothingness, her eyes unable to penetrate anything beyond the spherical glow of the lantern. She could barely see her own boots and could most certainly not see the dog, though it panted in the dark.

"What is this, a sewer or something?" she asked.

The man shook his head.

"Come, I will show you"

As they walked along the tunnel, the priest called back to her to mind the low beams and she clutched the hat to her chest and kept close to him.

"These are the tunnels of Santo Domingo. They are a very well-kept secret that you have stumbled upon. We fight to protect them, they are a lifeline that we could not operate without. A network which runs beneath this city, allowing us to move freely"

"Us?"

"Los Conservacionistas de San Pablo. Preservationists. We ensure that the rich history of this nation is not lost to the villainy which has taken this world in its own hand. From the sixteenth century this land has been filled with the sacred relics of the testament, a devoutly catholic place where the lord has made his presence known time and again. The artefacts that adorn the beautiful churches and palaces and basilicas should be fought for, as they have been fought for in the past. They should not fall into the hands of petty criminals, cartels looking for selfish gain. El Hoja Negra.

He began to walk, the lantern moving away along the tunnel. Kiara followed and the dog followed her.

"So we protect this place, we find the sacred icons and we protect them. In this city and in many others. Our group is huge, we are everywhere you can not see. And we will not stop until history itself is preserved in time as it should be, for when the light comes and the world begins again, there will be a reckoning of those who did not keep the faith to fight in his name"

"Militant preservationists" Kiara said, smiling to him.

He nodded as he walked.

"Exactly"

They turned a sharp corner and the priest disappeared briefly from view.

"It is the only way now"

"Where does this tunnel go?"

"The tunnels are a means to an end. We work very hard to expand them as much as we can. There are parts of our group digging around the clock, pushing the fingers of our reach further across the city"

"Where do they go?"

"This one joins to the main line between the templo and the convent, the original line, the secure part"

"The original line?"

"There was always an underground passageway between the Templo de Santo Domingo and the Convento de San Pablo. A secret route, under the old streets"

They rounded another corner, the low ceiling brushing the top of their hair and releasing little clouds of dirt which dropped without being seen.

"The temple is secure, it's a fortress there. It always was like this, barred windows, high walls. It was a military barracks for many, many years, and we have secured it yet further. It is impenetrable"

The priest moved quickly through the darkness and Kiara skipped along behind him to keep up. From what she had seen there had been no junctions in the tunnel at which to turn, though she feared if she were to lose the priest down there she may be lost beneath the ground forever.

"Impenetrable thus far at least. What is your name?"

"Kiara"

"Kiara, hmm. Kiara mind your head there"

She ducked and staggered forward, into the back of priest.

"I am Gerard"

In the blackness she sensed the tunnel opening out, the claustrophobic energy of the ratline dispersed and her breathing eased, although there was still only blackness. The priest stopped ahead of her, the glow of his simple lantern dimmed as the light cast from it spread across the place.

"The tunnels lead from this one. This is the historic route to Santo Domingo. You see the wall here?"

He passed his outstretched arm across to the wall, the lantern swinging from his hand. It bathed the wall of the tunnel in the orange glow.

"See the stone? Look, here"

The walls were built from sandy white and red stone, carved ornately with figures and birds and words in Latin.

"How old is this place?"

"The tunnel?" Gerard asked

Kiara nodded.

"The temple was completed in the seventeen hundreds, it took maybe two hundred years to build the entire compound. The tunnel was put in in this time, I could not tell you when. We have expanded the tunnel system now. We have pushed out to Oaxaca cathedral and the Zócalo to the south, and to the basilicas of the east"

"Are they safe?"

Gerard nodded.

"Ah very. How would one go about getting down here? These tunnels took months and months to construct. We have sentries at each entrance, if one is breached then word will come to us and the entrance will be destroyed. There are explosives built into the walls, the design is faultless"

"I'm glad the sentry there saw me in time today"

"You were unlucky and also lucky today. I would say there was more luck on your side, should you not have taken the hole through the fencing. I'm presuming you did?"

She nodded.

"Well, then you would not have come across the entrance there in the grasses, and, well, who knows"

He began to walk along the tunnel and Kiara and the dog followed, for they had no alternative.

He stopped and spun around in the dark and looked her keenly in the eyes.

"You are trusted with this information, you understand?"

She nodded.

"I know you are good, I know that, but these tunnels and our work are difficult to defend. You must not pass the words I speak to anybody. The conservacionistas can protect you in this city, help you find your son, but if you deceive us or betray the trust I have afforded you then I will shoot you in the head and you will be buried in the desert. I hope I am clear"

His eyes glowed orange in the dark and they were all that Kiara could see

"Don't let the cassock fool you"

She nodded quickly, like a reprimanded child.

"Of course. You saved my life back there. All I want is to find my son. I need to find the military command and find him and we will be gone. It's not safe here, obviously. I would appreciate your shelter, and you have my word, to god, I won't betray your trust"

He watched her for a moment and then nodded.

"Good. Come"

As they moved along the tunnel, there appeared in the dark little spots of orange glow like the eyes of dogs in the night. Candles burned in ornate stone sconces along the walls, illuminating their way north to the Templo de Santo Domingo de Guzmán.

"What happened to your son?" the priest asked.

"He was drafted"

Gerard nodded.

"Ah, a difficult time for any mother"

"He's twelve. He'll be thirteen this month, on the twenty fourth", she shrugged and cast up her hands, "I don't know today's date"

Gerard laughed dryly.

"Nor I"

They walked.

"What is your son's name?"

"Dylan"

"Very nice. When I was a taking my seminary training in Avignon, a very long time ago now, I shared accommodation for many months with a wonderful man named Dylan, Dylan Malloy, I remember him well. He went on to do fantastic work with Catholic aid in some developing countries. A name I am fond of"

Kiara smiled softly.

Another tunnel branched away to the east, arched at the entrance with large square stones to support its weight as it disappeared into the darkness beyond, somewhere out underneath the city. The air underground was still, there was no breeze and no smell of the burning metal that swirled around the city. It was an ancient calm, a subterranean burrow under the feet that ran above and the flames that towered atop the derelict remains of what once was. It was clandestine and protective.

"The military is a very disingenuous and corrupting place for a young man" Gerard said, "For an old man even. We see them here, running around these streets in their never-ending battle of bad versus evil. Many mean well, you know, in their hearts? They have helped tremendously with the fires, but they are children, they are not trained to deal with the issues they face here. They hold rifles but they can not shoot. They outnumber the cartels here by three men to one yet the cartels win any battle they enter. The cartels are outnumbered and outgunned, but yet it is the young men of this place who are piled in the streets, heads shaved and green uniforms covered with the blood of the fallen"

He saw the impact of his words of Kiara.

"But yet you should have faith. I speak too freely, do not put stock in my words. The military personnel here are yet tens of thousands strong", he thought for a moment, "you know he is here, in Oaxaca?"

The tunnel began to incline and the walls closed back in, a spiral of white light ahead of them in the darkness.

"I don't really, no. I got word from a camp south of Mexico City that they had sent all their groups down here, but I don't know"

"Do you know what you feel, in your heart?"

Kiara shrugged.

"I don't know"

The priest stopped in the light and turned to her. Behind him, a stone staircase led from the dark tunnels to the brightness of the daytime above. There were voices in the distance, a calm energy flowing through them.

"You do. You do know what you feel in your heart. That is why it is in your heart, and not in your head. When it is in your head it is clouded, there is too much for a person to think about for the thoughts to be pure of form. But in your heart you know the truths"

He pointed his finger against her chest.

"Do you know you will find him?"

She nodded.

"I know I will. I don't know if he is here, in this city, or if he was here, but I know I will find him. If he had died I would be able to feel it"

Gerard nodded and smiled at her.

"Exactly"

The stone staircase spiralled into the blinding white light as though it were the ascension into the glow of heaven itself. The underground walkway continued onwards, past the staircase and rose in a gentle incline to some other place in the compound where horses could be led into the warren of tunnels and out to the river or to the hills.

Above ground, the high walls of the sandstone courtyard towered over them, the sun perfectly placed in the space above as though it were painted on a glass ceiling. Three grand oaks pushed themselves from the stone tiled floor and wound up to the light, their bows showing the signs of new life, budded with green. Birds sat atop them, whistling as though it were the tree of life. People passed all around them on the cloisters raising three stories high.

Kiara stood and stared.

"Beautiful, yes?" Gerard said, noticing her awe.

She nodded.

"Very. It's amazing to see such life in a place where nothing else lives"

Gerard nodded.

"The curates take phenomenal care of these trees, and the gardens here"

Kiara's brow furrowed.

"You've kept gardens?"

"Ah yes, there were once monastery gardens, sanctuaries for the friars of Santo Domingo. After the war, when the place was given back to the church, the gardens were turned into a biological conservation area. We have over two acres of some of the finest plants that grow in this country, used for foods and medicines too, you know? There were once nearly a thousand species of plant growing here, but we have sadly lost some of them to the weather"

He shook his head, a look more of frustration at allowing such an event than the sadness of its passing.

"Though, that said, we do hold one of the largest seed banks on the American continent, so, you know, when the time comes, we will rebuild this beautiful world in the glory it once enjoyed. Now, come with me, I will show you inside. Are you hungry?"

He began to walk.

"Yes, very. Thank you"

Gerard waved over a young man in civilian clothing, who skipped to him keenly and smiled at both Gerard and Kiara.

"Please, can you take the dog for me. He will be happy in the garden. Please show him where to find water. And don't let him eat the plants though, no? Get him something"

The young man nodded and whistled to the dog and it did not hesitate in going with him, waving its tail around wildly and trotting away through a grand stone archway to the land beyond.

They walked across the courtyard and through an arched doorway into the ancient enclave. There was a bustle inside the place as men and women came and went about their business, some dressed in the traditional clothing of the church, others in plain clothing and some in military coveralls with automatic rifles.

Gerard waved her through the crowds and through the network of corridors within, past artwork that hung in ornate frames, paintings of the saints and the scenes of the gospel. He led her into a stonebuilt room, square and with vaulted ceilings so high that the ornate carvings that adorned them were out of clear sight. The masonry was worn, crumbling around the perimeter, and birds sat high on the arches.

Along the centre of the room were four oak tables, thirty feet long each and immovable by even a hundred men, set in their place forever by their weight alone. White ceramic plates and mugs and sparkling clean drinking glasses and glistening silver cutlery were all laid out on the back table, stacked high. The other three tables were empty but some dirty crockery that was yet to be cleared, but Kiara knew that come meal time those tables would be lined with the hungry workers of that place. The men who had spent their days digging by hand the tunnels that stretched beneath the city like fingers of a great hidden hand. The women who brought water by cart from the Atoyac to feed and maintain the plantlife and the glorious gardens and to keep the building in the state of cleanliness that it enjoyed. The men who lined the high stone walls of the temple perimeter, watching vigilantly through the scopes of rifles to protect what was vital to protect. Those men and women who made up the bands of preservationists who fought with knife and pistol through the streets to salvage the priceless fragments of history. Each man and each woman was given food and drink and simple board and protection for their part in supporting the greater cause.

The preservation of the nation. The preservation of the lord himself.

Gerard took a plate from the top of the stack and took a drinking glass and walked to the end of the tables and poked his head inside the arched doorway.

"Buenas tardes, Margerite" he called with a smile.

From inside a woman spoke back to him.

"Buenas tardes, padre"

"Esta la comida lista?"

The woman appeared in the doorway with a washcloth and batted Gerard with it, telling him to get out and that they were busy

He laughed and recoiled from the doorway, playfully.

From outside he called her again.

"Margarite"

She appeared in the doorway.

"Esto es Kiara"

She saw Kiara and smiled to her and nodded gently.

"Hola señora, bienvenida"

Kiara smiled and thanked her.

"Espere" she said, holding a finger up to them, and disappeared back into the kitchen. She reappeared a moment later and beckoned them forwards to the door.

"Here. We don't have the fish cooked yet, I like to make with the skin, er, crisp, you know. But here, is vegetable and rice for you, if is ok?"

"Of course, gracias Margarite. Qué dios le bendiga"

She took the two plates from them and approached where the pans were cooking on the fire and put a ladle of cooked vegetables onto each followed by a heap of brown rice.

"Is coffee here, and water, but water is from, er, this morning"

Her accent was eastern European, her Spanish and English both tainted heavily with intonation.

They thanked her again and took their plates to the long oak table and sat opposite each other.

Kiara had to restrain herself from devouring her plate of food as quickly as she could in such company. She took a fork and tried to eat politely, though her stomach bubbled with hunger and the mere smell of the food was overcoming her.

Gerard took her glass and returned a moment later with it full of clean drinking water.

Kiara did not know what to say. She ate the food as her head swirled.

"How have you done this?" she asked, finally.

Gerard looked up from his plate.

"Done what?" he asked.

"This. All of this" she said, passing her hand around the room, "you have cooked fish? Beautifully steamed brown rice, manicured gardens and seed banks and clean drinking water. The place is clean, the people are happy. You have created Eden"

Gerard laughed.

"We have what every person could have, nothing more. Life is simple, very simple. The rice is grown and harvested and the vegetables are our own. They are the same vegetables every day, the same rice. It is not glorious. The people are happy because the people are safe. We do simply what we must to survive. Surely we all do"

"But how can you possibly fund all of this?"

She finished the plate of food and placed her fork down gently.

"It is not funded. There is no money here, these people are not paid in material goods, there are no jewels or gold. Everyone here is safe, and the protection that we provide for each and every person is the justification they require to work towards our cause"

He motioned with his fork to the kitchen door.

"Margarite, she is not paid money for her work, nor does she want such a thing. Margarite came to us a couple of years ago like yourself, lost, looking for help. She too lost her family, three girls I believe. Now you see how happy she is? She cooks food here with some others, and in turn she gets to eat the food, sleep under this roof, be safe. You understand?"

Kiara nodded.

"I do"

She was impressed and her heart warmed again for the first time in many months. It made perfect sense to her, the rebuilding of a society as it once was. The people in that place could not offer anything more than the people of the country deserved and which they had always enjoyed, simple food, clean water and protection. Nothing more. And for those simple privileges there was nothing asked. Nothing but their allegiance to the greater good which was being realised and achieved in that place.

"Tell me, Kiara, you have religion in your life?"

Kiara nodded instinctively, though Gerard read her clearly.

"You doubt him?"

Kiara tried not to shrug, to seem definitive in her faith. She was sitting, after all, in the house of the lord and eating from his bounty.

Gerard nodded.

"It is ok to have reservation, to be uncertain as to what guides you"

"I am from a very strong Catholic upbringing, I just, you know..."

She tried to pick her words.

Gerard interrupted.

"You don't see him too often these days, no?"

"I lost my daughter and both of my parents on the same day, at the hands of savages. There was no cause for it. Robbery, spite, evil. They could have easily been spared, life was ok. We left, my husband and son, we left after that. To leave Mexico to the south, find a place where we can restart again. Then Dylan was taken, pulled, physically, away from me and taken away for this awful government to use as fodder in this horrible, horrible place"

She was not going to allow herself to cry, though she knew no shame in it.

She looked at Gerard through glazed eyes, her fingers fiddling with the brim of the hat on the table next to her.

"I'm sorry", Gerard said, holding a hand across the table and touching hers.

"And then my husband too"

Gerard nodded.

Kiara said no more of the details and she did not need to. Gerard understood what was to be understood.

After a moment of quiet he spoke again.

"There is sometimes very little here to be thankful for. Our faith is tested by the things we see. How can he create such a world, you ask?"

She nodded.

"Your faith will revive. You will see there is light for you yet"

She nodded again and sniffed and sat upright.

"I see now. Look at this place you have. Look at what people can achieve when they trust in the good"

Gerard smiled.

"Revelations, Kiara" he said, holding a finger up to her with a smile, "be faithful unto death and I will give you the crown of life"

She smiled.

Gerard took the plates from the table and walked them to the kitchen and thanked Margarite once more and came back to Kiara's side.

"We do not ask for your faith. We do not judge your worth by your trust in any Abrahamic text. The judgement is not ours to make. Do right by yourself and by those around you, that is all we require for your being here. A good tree bringeth forth good fruit"

She smiled.

"Come, Kiara, I will show you to a place where you can rest, and clean, and then we will go about the mission to find your son"

Chapter Fourteen

"We have, like, four matches left in this box Ryan, you'll have to light the rest of the candles from the ones already lit"

Ryan nodded.

The store at the corner was less than a mile, and he could walk it, but he'd much rather not if it could be avoided. Mia was asleep against her mother's chest, limiting what Kiara could do to tame the relentless energy of Dylan, who was at that time head-first in the television cabinet, pulling out old video cassettes whilst looking for the toy aeroplane that was absolutely not in there.

"Come on, you" Ryan said, taking hold of the back of Dylan's jeans at the waist and pulling him backwards, "out of there fella, you come help daddy"

Dylan wailed and swung his hand backwards at his father.

"Hey hey hey" Ryan said, sterner, "don't start that with me"

The place was dimmed though it was the middle of the day, the sun barely showing light nor warmth through the veil of snow cloud. Candles were lined along the mantle and the top of the television and the windowsill, little spots of yellow warmth against the dull afternoon light. The lounge and the kitchen were the only places lit, the walls dancing with the flickering flame and throwing tiny shadows around the room.

Dylan came backwards out of the cabinet clutching the box of an old animated movie. He got to his feet and handed it to his father.

"Daddy" he said, a smile on his face.

Ryan bent down to him and held him at the waist.

"Sweetheart listen, there's no power, so the tv doesn't work, but when it's back on we'll watch all of these movies yeah? I promise"

Dylan just looked at him.

"I promise. Do you want to help daddy?" he said in a cheery tone, aiming to snap the boy's attention away from the movie and on to something else.

"No" he said, chirpily.

Kiara smiled.

"Well, you kinda have to. Come on, leave mummy with Mia, while she's asleep, yeah?"

At two, there was not much reasoning to be done with the boy. The way to achieve anything with him was largely bribery and distraction.

Ryan stood, and turned for the door, his hand trailing behind him waiting for Dylan's to take hold of it.

"Come on, champ"

Dylan snapped out of it and trotted after him, though ignored his hand.

"I'll take him out back and we can get some more wood for the fire while we're there. You warm enough in here for a while?"

Kiara nodded and smiled.

She was wrapped in a blanket and big furry slippers, cuddled around her baby. The tin of cookies left from the Christmas party were firmly wedged onto the sofa next to her, the cushion in front of them to keep them from the prying eyes and wandering hands of the two year old.

"You want to put on your new boots that Santa brought you?" Ryan asked.

"No" Dylan replied again, and again Kiara laughed.

"Well, er, you need to. It's snowing out there, isn't it? You don't want to get those feet cold do you?"

"No"

"OK champ, well let's get your boots on"

Dylan cheered a little cheer to himself, and ran from the room into the darkened hallway where his boots and hat were waiting by the door.

"We won't be too long out there. We've got a fridge full of stuff that needs eating before it spoils"

"Mmm, cold meat for dinner again", Kiara said.

"Hopefully this won't go on too much longer. Kathy over there said she saw the vans at the bottom of the hill working on the boxes down there, they said hopefully by morning"

Kiara cocked her head, untrusting of any timeframe given by local council workers.

"Well, we can hope. See you in a bit sweetie" Ryan said, moving through the doorway.

"Love you" Kiara called after him.

"You better" came the reply from the dark.

Kiara sat on the end of the steel bunk. Her boots were on the floor in front of her, torn and faded and the laces frayed. Ryan's hat sat on top of the long red coat, laid out across the bed behind her, the pistol tucked underneath.

She held the letter to Dylan in her hand with the photographs, turning the soft paper around in her fingers.

Three sisters came past her and nodded and smiled to her gently, though their long blue tunics were dirtied and one blood-splattered and they wore black work boots which were worn and dusted with ash.

Despite what safety was offered by the temple and by those who lived and worked there, she felt overcome by the grief of loss. In the open country she had no time to reflect. Despite many long hours of walking, alone or with only the dog for company, she had little time to think. Such focus was given at all times to surveying the landscape for movement and keeping her wits about her in the ongoing quest to simply live another day. She had, of course, missed her family dearly, such was her drive onwards, but she had not grieved properly, certainly not for the loss of her husband. From that day she had awoken in the bed in the hunting cabin, she had filled herself with the desire to push on from one point in time to the next, and whilst tears had indeed been shed, she was yet to expel the full emotion she harboured inside.

She felt such sadness sitting there in that safety. A place where she did not have to listen to the sound of the winds for danger or to pick out the smell of distant camp smoke, or question where next she may find water. She had stopped, for that moment, looking over her shoulder. She put the photographs and the letter down on the bed and stood and stretched. She was exhausted and felt that she could sleep for a lifetime should it be afforded to her.

But it was not, despite there being no time-limit placed on her welcome there. Gerard had told her to make herself comfortable and had gone to great lengths to find her clean underwear and a hairbrush and a toothbrush, and showed her to a bunk in a room full of others where she could take her time to recuperate. He would, in time, expect her to work for such luxuries, but for that time she was a welcomed guest.

But that was not how Kiara viewed it.

She would clean, eat, sleep what she could. But then she was onwards. Whilst her son was out there in the country in the eternal danger placed on him by the very nature of his company, she would not rest. She was thankful, greatly so, to Gerard and her hosts, and her unwillingness to join their cause was not routed in a place of ingratitude or greed. She would happily decline all the luxuries offered to her should she have to, for she had something greater to achieve.

Gerard understood. He had told her that the passion and anger of a mother separated from her baby was one that echoed throughout the natural order, and that no person would, or indeed could, stand in the way of that. He told her that she was welcome to stay for as long or as little as she wished, or indeed to return there one day in the future, should she find her son and have no further place to go.

Once she had cleaned herself and redressed, she left the vestry where the bunks were arranged and passed along the long dark stone tunnel towards the bright white light beyond. The ceilings were arched and the white stone cladding was cracked and crumbling, though there were ornate carvings and paintings adorning every foot of wall. In the grand courtyard beyond, where the afternoon sun fell warmly against the sandstone, the operations of the Conservacionistas de San Pablo were laid out to see.

Men unloaded paintings in golden frames from boxes on the cart, bridled to the back of two great black horses which stood at nearly twice the height of the men, kicking in the dirt and snorting loudly at each other, swinging their heads in the heat. Younger workers were tasked with carrying them away under strict instruction to take as much care as they could, to a place where they would be locked away and preserved in the extensive underground crypts which had been converted into the securest of vaults, and which were guarded fiercely. An older man in a long blue cassock marched keenly out from one of the stone archways, flanked by men with rifles leaning in to him and listening carefully as he gave commands and waving them on to men in the cloisters with hand signals, and they passed quickly and away into the building as they had come.

All about her was activity, the courtyard a central hub to the vast operation and a thoroughfare to all areas of the sprawling compound. Kiara felt that she had nothing to offer to them, but she also felt that she could easily make that place a home, should the opportunity arise.

Yet she would not allow it, it was not her plan, not her quest.

As she stepped again from the bright sun into the dim interior of the old monastery, her eyes took a moment to adjust, and she found herself standing in the doorway of the grand hall. Her feet froze and her breath momentarily fell from her as she took in what was before her.

She had not in her life seen anything so stunning. The temple towered some hundred feet or more above her to the most intricately carved gold ceiling, covered in statuettes of the saints. The flowing glow from the sea of flickering candles that adorned the place spun flicks of white and shadows of black across the dome so that it moved before her eyes. Great pillars, clad in the highest quality gold leaf, climbed to the eaves, each one towering over the nave below. The altar remained in the chancel on the end wall but the pews had been removed to allow passage and other uses but for that of prayer.

Kiara walked slowly along the centre of the grand room, her eyes wandering slowly around the seemingly-endless display of stunningly crafted gilding.

As her mind wandered away with her eyes, the silence in the room was broken. A soft voice from across the hall, amplified ten-fold through the acoustics of the great building.

"It's very striking indeed isn't it?"

Gerard walked slowly from a doorway, the low orange glow flashing across his smile.

"I've never seen anything like it"

"It is, I would say, on a par with the beautifully crafted churches of Spain and France. The work on this place has not really stopped, the restoration, since it was built. There is always something with a crack or a crease. It takes much work"

"It's incredible"

Gerard cocked his head sideways.

"We do not have the attention to detail these days. There is not the time there once was. The ceiling here", he pointed his finger to the vaulted dome, "this has not even been cleaned for some time, many months. We try"

"It's amazing to me that you've kept this, as it was. Most of this city had burned to the ground, and what hasn't has been pillaged and destroyed. Yet look"

Gerard smiled and nodded softly.

"I know. We are blessed. This is why we must fight. You think when I took my training and swore my oath to god that I imagined myself walking around the kingdom of our lord with a rifle? I shot and killed two men this morning, for you. They are by no means the first. Is that what god asks of me? To kill? To take another man's life? Am I a false prophet? Of course not, but we must fight for what we have. Like the Order of Solomon, we fight hand to hand"

He looked Kiara straight in the eyes and she felt the conviction of his belief.

"This will not, Kiara, will not be the end of this beautiful world of ours. There will again be a time when we can walk through fields of gold. A time when our children can play as we did. This world is in turmoil but it is not terminal. And so we must not lose what we treasure. We must not lose these pieces of history around us. And you, Kiara, you must not lose your son"

Kiara nodded slowly.

"I will not"

"Come, I will take you to meet those who walk out with us tonight"

"Tonight?"

Gerard smiled.

"Of course. Did you think you were to set out from here alone?"

"I guessed so. I'm ready to"

"You are strong indeed, my friend"

"I have to be"

"Of course. But we will escort you, unless you mind?"

Kiara shook her head.

"Of course not. Thank you"

"Five of us, and yourself, will leave tonight. We will get you to the military base, hopefully they can help you locate your son. They can hopefully give us some idea where he may be. From there the decision is yours, of course. You can continue onwards, or you can return here for as long as you need. But you won't be going out of here alone, we know the streets of this place well, how to move quietly"

Gerard put a hand on her shoulder and began to lead her to the doorway. She walked next to him.

"And", he said, turning to her with a slight grin, "should our stealth fail, then you will at least have more firepower"

"What about the dog?" Kiara asked.

Gerard thought.

"It would not be right to bring it. It is not safe for the dog or for us. You can return for it, we'll keep it here. There are many dogs here, they have a great life running around the land"

Kiara nodded.

She cared for the animal, but there were priorities again, and the dog would be safe and happy regardless.

She smiled and thanked him.

At the back of the Templo de Santo Domingo de Guzmán, overlooking the vast gardens, Gerard and Kiara reached the auditorium. As they walked into the huge room, decorated beautifully with grand pieces of artwork from across the centuries, a museum itself to the history of Catholicism in the area, the rest of their group were already waiting.

Three men and a woman were readying their packs and loading their weapons and chatting idly to each other in the dim light. The tall windows looked out across the dark allotment and across the dark city beyond, little specks of white flickering in the sky above, vague hints of the infinite sea of stars that existed up there, somewhere off behind the veil of cloud and firesmoke. Candles were lit in three of the iron sconces that lined the wall, their glow illuminating nothing more than it needed to.

They all looked up as Gerard and Kiara approached.

"Buenas noches mis queridos amigos" Gerard called across the hall, his voice strong and resonating around the high walls.

They nodded and greeted him.

"This is Kiara"

Kiara smiled and held up a single palm in a nervous attempt at a wave.

"Kiara", Gerard said, placing one hand on her shoulder and passing the other across the group, person to person, as he spoke, "This is Alejandro"

Alejandro nodded, without a smile. He was short and dark, his wide-brimmed leather hat already on his head and casting much of his face into near-darkness.

"Alejandro has been a great comrade to los conservacionistas for many years, he is a very trusted man. A man whose heart is very much dedicated to Oaxaca. He will be leading us tonight, you should listen to him above all else"

Kiara nodded and smiled.

"And here", Gerard continued, "this is Matteo, from beautiful Genoa. Have you been to Italy, Kiara?"

"No, I haven't been to Europe. I would love to. Or, would have loved to"

"Oh you would love it very much" Matteo said, smiling to her.

"Matteo and myself have known each other a very, very long time. I don't even want to try to count the years" Gerard said,shaking his head.

"Nice to meet you" Kiara said.

"E tu" Matteo said back to her, tipping the brim of his black cap.

He had big blue eyes and wispy blonde hair nearly at this shoulders, a blue shirt and ripped blue jeans and high brown leather cowboy boots.

"Here", Gerard said, moving around the group, "this is William. He is a fantastic priest, you should hear his sermons. And an even better shot with that rifle"

"Will", he said, reaching in to shake Kiara's hand, "where you from?"

"Originally, near Santa Fe, New Mexico, my parents are Mexican"

"Ah, I've been up there a tonne. I'm from Payson, Arizona"

Kiara shrugged.

"I don't think I know it"

"North of Phoenix. There's nothing there to know. You're a long ways south ain't you?"

"Just as well though, eh?" Kiara said, smiling back to him.

Will laughed.

Kiara liked the warmth she felt from him, and was comforted by the accent of somebody from the world she knew well, the world that she had once regarded as her own. He was tall with a deep tan and the rough beard of an outdoorsman.

"Ain't that right" he said, "good to meet you"

"And finally" Gerard said, moving his hand across to the only other female of their group.

"Ariela", she said, cutting Gerard off and leaning in to shake Kiara's hand, her own in black leather gloves, "I'm the muscle" she said, winking.

Her accent was Mexican, though she was pale skinned, her dark brown hair dyed bright red at the tips, much of it pulled up into a ponytail and the rest falling around her face.

"Do you have everything ready to go?" Gerard asked.

The group nodded.

"Kiara?"

"I have nothing to get ready. This coat and this pistol. It's all I got"

Gerard nodded.

"That a Python?" Will asked.

Kiara nodded.

"Here"

He reached inside his pack and took out a small white box of rounds and passed them across to her.

"Thank you. Very much. Are you sure you can spare them?"

"Oh yeah, I doubt I'll use them really. I got a pistol as a back-up weapon, a twenty-two though, I'm relying on Carla over there"

Against the side wall, barely visible in the dim light of the candle flames stood a Barrett REC7 Carbine rifle with a long black scope, the lens glistening.

"You're happy with the pistol, Kiara?" Matteo said to her, swinging his pack on to his back and straightening it between his shoulders.

Kiara turned the Colt around in her hand, as though inspecting it or weighing its quality or worth.

"Yes" she said.

"We have many weapons here if you would prefer to take a rifle or something instead?"

"No, I've fired this for many years, practically nothing else. I trust it, and I trust myself with it. It's quick"

"Good" Gerard said, swinging the strap of his old wooden hunting rifle up over his shoulder, "let's do this then"

Alejandro led the group through the near-dark hallways and they emerged out into the cool night in the courtyard with the towering oaks and descended the stone steps, down into the underbelly of the monastery and of the city itself.

"We will move underground as far as las canteras, then we must take the streets from there. The old canteras there have been flooded to make a lake. That is the furthest east that our underground network goes, at least since the military filled in the tunnel which led into their compound. We would have like that one tonight, eh?"

Kiara smiled.

Once in the tunnels, Will and Ariela walked at the front, each holding their automatic rifle across their chest as the army are taught, despite neither having ever served time. Gerard and Kiara walked together behind them with Matteo, a long scoped Winchester across his back, and Alejandro walked some distance behind. He walked with a long staff in his hand, tapping on the stone floor of the tunnel as he walked, two long-muzzled pistols hanging in a double chest harness. He walked silently, his hat low, emanating an air of either mystery or suspicion, though the group's trust in him was absolute.

The air was still in the main tunnel, the warmth of the day and the cool of the night kept out entirely, deeming it impossible to determine the time of the day or night at all.

After a few minutes of walking, they came to the first tunnel which led from the main artery, a dark descent away to the east. Matteo swung his lantern up in front of him and waited in the entrance. It was supported along the length with thick timbers and long metal screws which supported the weight of what world sat above it. The floor was paved with sheets of reformed wooden board, overlapped on the dirt and which wobbled underfoot when walked on.

Matteo held the lantern there until the entire party had reached the entrance.

"Mind your hat on the wires" he said as Kiara passed him into the tunnel.

Kiara took the hat from her head so that she could see better.

All around the circumference of the high doorway were black wires, looped around the timber braces and dropping to the darkened ground, running away along the tunnel towards the monastery.

"What are they?" Kiara asked, stepping forward along the dirt tunnel.

The visibility had dropped considerably and she could only see Ariela in front of her as they walked single file. The ceiling was high, much higher than Kiara thought necessary, though the tunnel was rudimentary at best, dirt walls and ceiling and not wide enough to walk aside one-another.

"Our protection", came Will's voice from behind her as they walked, "the entire network is rigged with explosives. Every doorway, every entrance. Tonnes of the stuff. If we're breached, we can bring the house down"

Kiara nodded though nobody could see.

"Smart" she said.

"Tunnel warfare is nothing new" Gerard said.

She could see the swinging arc of light from the lantern he carried, careering up one wall and then the other in rhythmic motion with his footsteps, "the tactic was used by the ancients of Greece and Rome, dug, like ours, by hand alone. Tunnels were used throughout history from that time, in the Crimean war and to devastating effect on the western front in the first world war. We only copy what has been tried and tested over hundreds of years. This is why we know it works"

"They might look a bit rough but they're built well, and seriously well protected" Will said.

"They are" agreed Gerard, "we have airtight doors at both the monastery and at the convent should there be a chemical attack, or a gas leak or such. History tells us that enough dry woodsmoke in one end of the tunnel can soon cause problems throughout the network, and smoke-out anyone inside"

"The gangs here don't know they exist?" Kiara asked.

"Oh, most do" said Will, "they stumble across the entrances occasionally, we've had bands of the Hoja Negra get in. We're more than able to keep them out like that though. A man on horseback can ride the tunnels, extinguish the candles where they burn, cave in the doorways and entrances and the place is a deathtrap. We know the routes, well, and they're mapped out. These idiots, these street gangs, however well-armed they may be, they're stupid, and they don't have the faintest idea what we're doing beneath their feet"

"I think they know more than you think they do" Ariela said, "you can't assume they're all stupid"

"Sure" replied Will, "I'm not saying they're all stupid. You haven't been around here as long as I have. There have been all sorts of attempts to get in. They've tried to storm the monastery from the outside, there were two hundred or more of them that day, and not one single man made it through the walls. We've brought the tunnels in more times than I can remember, pulled bodies out of here by the cartload once they get lost in the dark. Sure, we've lost men, way more than I'd like, but I tell you Ariela it isn't because of these tunnels"

Ariela said nothing.

The arc of light from Gerard's lantern swung away to the right, momentarily out of view around a corner. The group snaked along behind him like linked carriages behind a train.

"So how'd you get this far south of Santa Fe, Kiara?" Will asked.

Kiara scoffed at the absurdity of her answer.

"Walked"

There was a moment where the group considered her response.

"You must have sore feet" Matteo called from the back, laughing.

"It's all about having the right boots" Kiara replied.

"That's a long-ass way" said Will.

"Well I didn't quite walk from Santa Fe. We lived in Monterrey back when the blast happened, and then we spent a few years at my family's farm south of there, out in the country. But I walked from there I guess"

"What is that, a thousand miles?" called Matteo.

"Probably not quite. It feels like it though"

She thought back momentarily to the green grasses of her farm, the lemon trees and the laughter of her family. She couldn't have come further, geographically and within herself. Where she walked at that point was dark as pitch, crumbling with dirt, alone.

She pushed the thought immediately from her head. It was no time to grieve.

"We are here. Wait and I will go first" called Alejandro.

There was yet nothing more to see in the tunnel than the tunnel itself, though the group clearly knew, by some clue, their location, a marker perhaps on one of the timber supports.

Alejandro stepped past Gerard and disappeared away into the blackness alone.

The group waited in the light of the two lanterns, Gerard's at the front and Matteo's behind.

There was a gathered silence, ears listening to what little sound drifted underground. There was no light from the entrance, and the sun was long down above ground regardless, and they waited together where they stood.

After a few moments there was a sharp whistle along the tunnel.

"Let's go" said Ariela, and the group silently walked forward.

Gerard blew the flame from his lantern and Matteo did the same and they were plunged into an absolute blackness for a few moments, shapes dancing in the corners of their eyes as they adjusted. Kiara staggered forward and took hold of whoever it was that walked in front of her and steadied herself, and within a minute they had reached the entrance to the tunnel. The cool breeze wisped in to the opening and they all took deep breaths in and dusted themselves of what dirt had dropped over them on their passage.

"Don't step too far out" Will said to Kiara, holding the back of her long red coat, "there's quite a drop"

Kiara's vision settled and she saw before her.

The tunnel had brought them out onto the side of a cliff-face. At the mouth of the tunnel there was ten feet or less of rocky ground and beyond it a drop down to a lake of black water, still and glistening in the pale moonlight, reflecting back to them the stars that hung above. Either side of them climbed up the craggy rock, not quite sheer but spotted with overhangs and places where rocks had fallen and exposed earth of different colours

and small shoots of grass and thorn that had found life there on the precipice.

"Help me with this please, William" called Gerard, taking hold of a thick trunk of twisted brown greasewood, long-dead and brittle.

Will took hold of the other side of the bush and together they lifted it from where it lay, not rooted into anything at all, and placed it over the entrance to the tunnel, adjusting it slightly so as to better aid the illusion of it growing there.

Kiara smiled.

"You got it all covered"

Gerard nodded.

"There is no alternative. Now let us be quick before anybody sees us down here and the ruse is futile"

Kiara looked about the cliff-face, behind her and down away to the east ahead of her. She was considering their route away from that ledge, considering the climb down to the water or the jump, when behind her Alejandro and Ariela had quickly gone about enacting their exit.

When she turned, Alejandro was ten or more feet up the rocks to the side of her, Ariela just behind him, seemingly climbing sideways as though walking on invisible steps that were built into the cliff, moving swiftly upwards towards the top.

"Here" Will said, leading Kiara towards the side of the ledge behind them, "there are pins in the rock, they will take your weight but make sure your feet are well placed before you transfer your weight"

Kiara looked. She couldn't see any pins, nothing there in which she could put the trust of her life. She turned to Will.

"You're kidding?"

Will smiled.

"Watch"

Beside her, Matteo stepped up onto the first pin, a four inch bolt of steel which had been drilled a foot back into the rock. He held the bare stone and pushed himself upwards, dropping his foot down onto the next pin, as though it were dropped onto nothing at all.

Kiara's heart raced watching.

She looked again at Will, and then at Gerard. She didn't know what else to say but to repeat what she had previously said.

"You're kidding?", her tone the second time more desperate.

"Or you can go back up the tunnel" said Gerard, following Matteo up the rock, "we're doing this for you"

Kiara added guilt to the terror that she already felt.

She shook her head.

"Well, ok", she mumbled, watching the group disappear up the grey rock.

Alejandro had already reached the top and was helping Ariela over the edge.

She placed her foot down on the pin and bounced her foot on it to test its strength, despite having seen it comfortably take the group before her. It didn't move in the rock. She held the rock and took a breath and lifted her back foot from the ground so that her weight was entirely on the one pin.

"There you go" said Will from behind her, "now just use them as stairs"

She took another big breath and let it blow long from her nostrils, calming herself slightly.

She reached her leg up and out to the next pin, and then lifted the back foot and stretched it to the third pin, much as one would climb a simple staircase. A staircase, though, with a seventy foot drop beneath each step to the angled rocks and stagnant water of the lake below.

She steadied her breathing and tried to ignore the terror, the risk of the fall, the distrust that the pin could come free from the rock at any moment, or her clothes snag and pull her backwards. There was no handrail, no safety harness, no carabiner and rope to catch her with a swing if she missed her footing. She focussed simply on getting her hands in the right places on the rock, tucking her fingers in behind them where she could, and ensuring that her front foot was as well-placed as she could get it before lifting her trailing foot.

She watched the pin ahead with intense focus and breathed slowly as Will muttered encouragement from behind her that she couldn't even hear, until before she knew it, she had reached the top of the cliff and she fell sideways to the ground with a deep sigh and smiled and then laughed.

Matteo and Gerard were standing waiting and they laughed with her.

Gerard turned and swung his rifle down from his shoulder and cocked it.

"That's the first part of many. Now the real danger begins. Get up"

Chapter Fifteen

The land at the top of the cliff opened out into a vast parkland, scrubby and dry where dust billowed in circles and swirled the dead leaves and ash with it. The ornate stone tiled walkway was as it had always been, neatly laid with white and red stone and not tainted by time nor the elements, and transporting the group backwards in time as they walked it.

The vast black lake of the flooded quarry was crossed by a high white stone bridge with decorative construction, stretching across the abyss to the eastern part of the city where a dull orange glow lay over the horizon.

To the west, directly over the tunnel, sat the great open-topped sports ground, low concrete bleachers stretched around its perimeter, the grass of the pitch dead and brown.

The group convened in the trees and Alejandro stood before them, shuffling the bō staff around in his gloved palms, his hat pulled low to his brow so that his eyes were shadowed to the night.

"It is maybe two miles to the base"

The group nodded.

"We move fast, and we move silent. You do not fire until you must. You do not call out unless you must. We are not here to engage in any stupid battle"

The group said nothing.

"Sí?" Alejandro asked sharply, expecting more assurance from the group.

They all agreed and said that they understood.

"Padre" he said, turning to Gerard, his thick south-Mexican accent rumbling low in the stillness of the city night, "I go in the front. Matteo, you are here, behind me, twenty feet, no more, you watch my hands and watch your fire. Stop when I tell you to stop"

Matteo said that he understood.

"Will, Gerard, you move with Kiara, watch the sides. If you stop, you tell Matteo. Understood?"

They said that they did.

"Chica" he said turning to Ariela.

She cocked her chin up to him. She was shorter than the rest of their group but her shadowy eyes and red-flecked hair gave her the look of something otherworldly and Kiara could tell that the diminutive warrior was accustomed to the death that surrounded them.

"Chico" she replied, smiling.

"Esta en el seis" said Alejandro, thumbing over his shoulder as though he were hitch-hiking.

She winked and brought the rifle up to her chest.

Alejandro nodded.

"Then we go"

He spun on the spot and moved purposefully away along the stone pathway to the north, and his group filed in behind him in the agreed formation.

They crossed silently over the stone bridge that separated the two vast black lakes beneath them, walking in a line like camels in a caravan, their eyes darting from side to side and ears pricked as they surveyed, with all senses, the city around them for what signs or sounds of danger there may be.

The outskirts of the city at that place were a rabbit-warren of narrow streets, walled and enclosed with stone homes and high gates and twisted power lines that hung from old poles like dead vines across a lost jungle temple. The place was silent but the silence was disarming. What may, in other circumstances, have been a warm evening in a quiet area of the city, was to those who passed there a deathtrap of blind turns and dead-end streets with sentries in windows with rifles and grenades who were looking to rob those ill-prepared or ill-defended.

Their group was neither ill-prepared nor ill-defended though the threat remained regardless.

Gerard had removed all of the religious clothing that he had previously been wearing, and the rest of their party was not marked as such either. The sight of a cassock or Roman collar would attribute them to the Conservacionistas de San Pablo, reveal their identity and allegiance at a glance. The Templo de Santo Domingo was a fortress, impenetrable at wall and gate, but its underbelly was weakened by the existence of the tunnel system beneath it. Single lines of entry that led straight to its heart. Whilst they were protected fiercely, hidden well from view, rigged with explosives and full of labyrinthine passageways that led miles through the dark, many deliberately to nothing but dead ends, their existence itself was a vital secret that should not be lost or fall into the hands of those who could exploit it. A group such as theirs, passing armed through the city in the depths of the night, was not an easy target for mere theft, they were clearly well armed and it would take a number of men, well drilled and well positioned, to take them on in a firefight for little cause. All manner of passers-by crossed through that city, as with any in that country or otherwise. For the men and women of the south heading north into the country, Oaxaca was one of the first major sites that would be encountered and word of its widespread destruction had not reached every ear. Regardless, it was still a place to scavenge, irrespective of its state. For those bands of thieves and gangs and cartels of the Hoja Negra and others like them, there were plenty of opportunities to exploit those roamers and ramblers who crossed that city looking for salvation or wealth or simply food with which to survive.

The presence of obvious religious clothing that connected them to the Conservacionistas, however, changed that dynamic. Should they be captured there may be opportunity to learn valuable information on the entry points to the tunnel system, and ultimately to the unprecedented amounts of wealth that sat locked beyond the high stone walls of the temple. It was, very simply, a life or death existence for their group to keep their true identities hidden and their rifles fully-loaded.

There was a sharp whistle ahead in the dark and Will's hand clasped Kiara's shoulder from behind, snapping her to a halt.

Just ahead of them, Matteo was stooped, his knees bent and rifle up to minimise his chances of being hit by gunfire, stepping quickly along the street to catch Alejandro.

They waited, crouched behind the shell of a car.

Kiara tried to stay calm, steady her breathing and not show panic to her guides, but her heart was beating a hole through her chest and the moonlight lit up the whites of her eyes.

Ariela stood some distance back, scanning the street ahead and behind through the rifle scope.

Two hundred feet or so along the quiet road, a group of figures, black against the night, silhouetted in what little glow fell from the clear sky, moved slowly together. They walked calmly, seemingly without purpose. Men of the night.

Their group waited. The men ahead had not seen them there, hiding in shadow, so much was yet apparent.

A few moments passed before another whistle, different from the first, wavering in pitch like a songthrush. The signal to move on.

They quickly trotted along the street to where Matteo was waiting at the corner. He nodded as they approached and gave a quick hand gesture to Gerard, who simply nodded in return.

The information passed went entirely over Kiara's head but she didn't care, she knew her escorts were well trained and that she was in the very best hands.

At the end of the road they stopped again.

The low houses and yellow stone walls dropped away to the highway, crossing east to west through the middle of the city.

"There" said Will, pointing, "you see the brown wall there, with the black metal bars?"

Kiara nodded.

At the far side of the multi-lane road was a barricaded perimeter wall, tall dead trees twisting out from beyond it like a cartoon graveyard.

"That's the military zone. The gate is up that street next to it"

From the central reservation of the highway, a hidden Alejandro again whistled, three little bursts of shrill sound like a solitary morningbird breaking the dawn.

From behind, Ariela replied with a whistle of her own.

"Go" said Gerard, pushing Kiara in the back.

She darted across the street, her red coat swinging behind her in the moonlight.

Will and Gerard ran behind her and the group reconvened against the stone wall that enclosed the military compound. Ariela stood back at the far side of the road. She raised her hand high above her head and signalled with a finger and a circling motion. Once more, the signal's meaning was lost on Kiara but the group understood and Matteo nodded and waved them onwards, leaving Ariela to ensure their safety from the rear.

The low brick wall ran the length of the road, atop it high black steel bars tipped with points like medieval spears. It was not an impassable barrier at all, but the people who knew that city knew also that, whilst the perimeter to the compound was not in itself able to keep out trespassers, it was indeed protected further by the scopes of many rifles that were shrouded in the darkness of the trees beyond.

They walked freely along the road there, the residual protection of the compound itself enough to deter any gang member with sense. At the far end, the road turned west and in front of them the guarded entrance to the barracks of military zone 28.

"Raise your rifles" Gerard said, lifting his own above his head with one hand and holding the other hand open as though surrendering to an enemy. The group all did the same.

As they neared the gate, a flood of soldiers in green and black emerged from everywhere, assault rifles readied and aimed head-height at the group.

"Ponlos en el suelo", one of the soldiers called loudly, a deep growl in his voice, "en el suelo"

They slowly lowered their weapons to the ground and placed them down as though they were fragile and stood again slowly, hands still raised.

"Slowly", Gerard instructed his group, "wait here"

He stepped slowly towards the gate and the horde of raised rifle barrels. The group murmured and stepped around on the spot.

"Soy el padre Gerard , del temple de Santo Domingo" he said softly, "Me gustaría hablar con el Mayor Salamanca"

The soldiers at the gate looked between one another, their rifle barrels wavering from their aim, unsure what protocol to follow. One stepped forward from the back, a squat man with a beard wider than his face and the deep tan of one who had worked extensively in the desert. As he walked through the raised rifles, they dropped one by one until he stood before Gerard.

He stood for a moment watching Gerard, as though trying better to recognise him in the night. He nodded once, and waved him inside.

"My group?" Gerard said as he stepped forwards to the barrier.

The squat man turned to see them, standing in the dark, and thought for a moment.

He nodded and pointed his hand to the small white checkpoint cabin beside the entrance barrier.

"Leave your weapons with this man in the office here"

He led them along a grand avenue of trees that ran north from the gate where the air was quiet and insects chirped and occasional servicemen passed and nodded and saluted the officer when they saw him. They passed white apartment blocks with red tiled roofs which housed the vast number of workers and servicemen who operated there, each built in the image of the last, curtains drawn to the rooms inside but for the odd flickering candlelight of a soldier reading. The place was calm, but it had the functions and capabilities for war. Sentry towers were positioned amongst the trees, silent men watching like owls, the moon flickering from the lenses of their rifle scopes.

The avenue turned gradually west and the land before them opened onto playing fields and training yard, painted roughly with the markings of a football pitch and a basketball court. A black dog lay out flat in the penalty box, sleeping carelessly beneath the stars.

They rounded the corner of a grand white building, lines of windows showing barely a glimpse of the blackened offices inside. They entered a central yard and the squat officer led them in through a tall doorway and picked a lantern from the low shelf inside the door and took the candle from it and lit it from the already burning sconce on the wall and placed it back inside.

"Here"

He handed the lantern to Gerard and led them through a wooden door into a room set up like a boardroom. They slowly filtered in and took seats at the table and removed their hats.

"You can light here", he pointed to the sconce on the wall holding three thick and mostly burned-out candles, "and here, on the back wall also. Major Salamanca is sleeping, he will not rise easily for you I am sure, but I will go to see him now. You may have to wait some time"

Gerard nodded.

"Of course"

"I would offer you water to drink, but, you know, I don't have any to offer"

He left sharply and closed the door behind him, clicking the lock from the outside.

There was no way for them to know what time had elapsed whilst they sat there, though they were safe and relaxed nonetheless and they talked quietly about everything and nothing at once and Alejandro lay out across the carpeted floor with his hat over his face. There was no sound from inside or outside, but for the faint footsteps of servicemen occasionally passing by the window. There were paintings and posters on the wall and a hanging in an ornate gold frame and the orange flickering from the candles lit each of them one moment and then cast it again into darkness the next.

After some time, they heard the main door to the building open and a moment later the door to the room.

A young officer held the door and a huge man in a black tracksuit stepped into the doorway, a towering silhouette with no features to his darkened face but for the outline of a beard. The group in the room sat and stared at the doorway, none speaking a word. His head barely cleared the doorframe.

"Padre" the man's voice boomed, loud and deep and warm.

Gerard rose and walked to the doorway. The man stepped into the room and the two shook hands.

"Major Salamanca, thank you for seeing us so late"

"Ah, do not worry, I was not sleeping. If I was, you may not have woken me", his voice softened and he looked Gerard closely as though relaying a secret, "I am tired Gerard, the years are not as kind as they were. Some days all I want to do is rest"

"Of course" Gerard replied, smiling, "as we all do. But the war goes on, major"

"So it does. And I will not rest a moment until the time comes for me to step down. But Gerard I tell you, I will need good reason to do so"

"Well you do a superb job, señor"

The major walked to the boardroom table and pulled out the end chair and sat. The floor of the room seemed to shake under his weight.

"Major Salamanca, my team" Gerard said, stepping beside the army commander's chair and passing his open palm across the room where the group were all sitting.

He nodded and they all greeted him.

"Ah, Teniente Alejandro, I didn't recognise you there. Take off your hat inside, will you?"

Alejandro was sitting in the dull rear of the room and he slowly took off his hat and tossed it onto the table.

The major turned to Gerard.

"You have the problems with this boy that I did too, do you?"

Gerard laughed.

"Alejandro is the best we have, and as a result of the training he received here from you major"

The major laughed and nodded.

"Are you still boxing, Alejandro?"

Alejandro shrugged.

"I have not boxed for many years. I train in other arts now. You know bōjutsu?"

The major furrowed his brow.

"With the, er", he thought of the word, "palo?"

"Bō" Alejandro corrected.

The major nodded and smiled dryly. He was not one to openly accept correction.

"So, what has brought you out from the tunnels then, padre?"

Gerard sat.

"We are looking for someone. This is Kiara"

Kiara nodded and smiled.

"Her son joined one of the travelling squadrons up in the mountains of Hidalgo, some time ago now, and she has reason to believe that he was here at some time in the past few weeks. We hoped you could help"

"Gerard, you see, we do not keep record of the names of every boy who passes through here, and many do not even give us their real names. How would we check?"

"This is why we came to you directly. I know that your men, for all their qualities señor, would not be able to help us themselves"

Major Salamanca nodded and thought.

He turned to Kiara.

"What is the boy's name?"

"Dylan Beckett. He joined them at the end of November, near Tehuetlán in Hidalgo. Thank you"

The major nodded.

"OK, ok", he rubbed his face with his huge palm and sighed, "give me some time. I will see what I can do"

They thanked him and he rose and left the room and they were again left in the silence of the old building.

It was some time before he returned.

The door opened sharply and the hulking major entered the room with a handful of papers and dropped them onto the table.

Kiara stood.

"I don't know if you have this, Gerard, but you just can not recruit competence any more, can you? How many times must a simple question be asked? They waste my damned time"

"We should be lucky there are people still here at all, major"

"Oh Gerard, I should know your response before I speak. Always the diplomat"

He began to approach the table, and then as though the thought came to him, he turned to Gerard and spoke again,

"You know, we have chemical-powered searchlights here now? You know this?"

Gerard looked puzzled.

"You have what?"

"Strontium. We have to mine it. Jesus Gerard, it is difficult. But I can make batteries from it and power the lights. Can you imagine that? Lights Gerard. Do you know what that means for us, for everybody? Batteries, Gerard, power. We can rebuild the damned world again"

Gerard was stunned.

"Then, I open a letter this afternoon, brought here by a horseman like we are medieval. You know what now? I am instructed to remove it due to safety concerns. Two years of development into this technology. All the mining, by hand no less"

He sat.

"It is pyrophoric, Gerard, you understand"

Gerard nodded, untruthfully.

"We store it in paraffin or it will, you know, ignite. But it needs removed from use, they say. They are coming here with men to remove everything that has been mined", his voice raised, angrily, its resonance nearly shaking the paintings from their hooks, "what am I to do now, Gerard? I lost men in those mines, for what? Damn them, I will continue regardless, what the hell do they know? They understand nothing, sitting in their high towers"

He thumped his fist on the table.

"And now, I am in there, looking through the files myself to find what information I need, because this damn idiot running my night shift in administration is an imbecile"

He shook his head slowly.

"Maybe I will step down without a fight after all"

He picked up the papers and tossed them across the table to Kiara.

"There is your son"

Kiara's eyes widened and she audibly gasped.

She grabbed the papers towards herself, long lists and hand-written charts and scribbles. She could make no sense of it at all as she turned through the documents.

She looked up to the major who saw her confusion.

"He was here, your son, he left back on the twenty second"

"What is the date today?" Will asked from next to her.

"Today is the second of February", he paused, "or is it after midnight? The third now"

"So not two weeks ago? That's it?"

Kiara turned to Will, the smile across her face from ear to ear and unbreakable and true. He was smiling too. He put his hand up on her shoulder.

"You are hot on his heels, Kiara"

She spun back to the major.

"Do you know where he went from here?"

"Salina Cruz. Though there is nothing left of that place now"

"Where is that?"

"Salina Cruz? It is nowhere now. It was a coastal town, south of here. It flooded years ago. Your son is part of a division tasked with policing the roads to the border in Chiapas and Tobasco. They do not report to me here, they were simply passing through. If you follow the road south to the coast you will find trace of them. They do not move quietly, those platoons, you will hear word of their route as you go"

He rose from the seat.

"Now, conservacionistas, this war will not wait for me to rise late. I must retire, and I must ask you all to kindly leave"

"Of course" said Gerard, rising and shaking the major's hand

"Thank you so much, you don't know how much it means to me, I've been searching for a long time" Kiara said, the emotion evident on her face.

Major Salamanca cocked his head to her and smiled.

"Good luck"

He left, and two guards who had been waiting outside the room, escorted the group back to the front gates of the military compound. They reclaimed their weaponry from the gatekeeper's office and thanked the men and passed out again into the dark street.

As they gathered themselves and checked their rifles and reloaded and recocked, a sharp whistle came from the darkness, followed shortly by the darkened figure of Ariela, the moonlight flicking from the red tips of her hair as it swung around her shoulders.

"You found the kid?" she asked.

"We know where he went" said Will, positioning the hat atop his head. Gerard stepped forward.

"The boy went south to the coast. Eleven days ago. Kiara, I wish we could take you there, I truly do, but we can not spare the men to go on such a venture"

"Of course" Kiara said, "I would never expect that. You have given me so much, more than I could ever ask, and for no reason other than the good of your soul. You saved my life, padre. But the quest is mine. I know now that I am right behind him. Like the major said, I will quickly find trace of where they have been and I can move far quicker than a platoon can. Far quicker. Hopefully I will be with him again in a matter of days. And I have you, all of you, to thank. Can you tell me how to get out of the city to the south?"

"Just here, the main road. Turn left there and the highway will take you south to the coast" said Matteo, pointing back along the shadowy road, the way they had come.

Alejandro shook his head.

"The road there is not safe to walk, not alone" he interjected, "the road goes to the south east, but you should pass first, into the mountains, and find the road again far from here, far from this city"

"The mountains to the north are no place to be either" said Will.

Alejandro shrugged and thought.

Ariela spoke.

"I know a place"

They turned to her and listened.

"South from here. Through the barrio. You cross the river at El Rosario, you can get into the hills from there. You can stay in the countryside for some time. You should walk more than a day before you find this road again. San Sebastian Abasolo is ok, if you make it that far"

"Thank you" Kiara said.

"No" said Will.

Ariela looked puzzled.

"Qué?"

"You want to send her through the barrio?", Will asked.

"Come back to the temple, Kiara" Gerard offered, "wait until the light of the morning. You can travel safer during the day"

Kiara shook her head.

"No way. The chase is on now, I can't waste another moment. Whilst they sleep, I can make up hours of distance on them. I must go"

"You must also sleep, Kiara"

She shrugged.

"Don't worry about that. Take care of that dog for me, please"

"Well then, I will take you there" said Alejandro, hitting the end of his staff on the ground, "I know the roads to El Rosario, I will take you out of the city"

Will nodded.

"As will I"

Kiara thanked them.

"Then we all go" said Gerard, "the tactics needed to move through this city are well drilled, and they are not possible with two men only. We move as a group, the way it always is"

The group agreed and Kiara again and thanked them.

"You are all ready to go once more? Same drill?" Gerard asked.

The group affirmed.

"Then Alejandro my dear friend, I believe you are out in front"

Chapter Sixteen

They moved into the dark of the city, Alejandro leading the pack, stooped and alert, the bō staff neatly held along the back of his arm so that its tip rose up behind his head. The two pistols which he wore in the chest harness glinted in the moonlight, polished and silver and cocked to fire. His eyes scanned the dark before him, listening like a wildcat to the noises that came from the web of streets, assessing what danger may be to come.

Behind him, Matteo walked with his rifle raised at all times, switching his view between the scope and his own vision as he crossed it left to right and back again, over and over. The two conversed in low fluttering whistles that were barely audible over the sounds of the night though the two understood them fluently and needed nothing more.

As before, Kiara was flanked by Will and Gerard a short distance behind, watching Matteo for signals to move or to stop, weapons levelled and readied.

Ariela walked off behind, at times disappearing from view entirely as she scanned the backstreets and sideroads to ensure that they were not spotted nor followed at any time. They paid no attention to where she was, whether they could see her or not, whether she had dropped behind or taken a side route. The trust in her abilities to survive and to take care of herself in such an environment were apparent, her diminutive stature bursting at the edges with an unbridled confidence and power, like Artemisia she walked the city and knew the authority of her own hand.

They moved quickly through the little streets, an implementation of rehearsed methods and tactics which they carried out with the precision of a military unit. The short whistles they passed along their line told the next what moves were being made as they ducked through the low residential areas of eastern Oaxaca, past the blackened shells of homes and stores which still smouldered with wisps of smoke into the sky.

There was occasional gunfire over the rooftops, gangland battlefields where wars of mindless causes were fought out for pathetic commodities.

Rice and corn were to kill for. Cartels who once shipped coca in all its forms throughout south and central America, had lost their business and their crops and their money. Their need to remain as indoctrinated members of some underground and illicit network remained, and drove them to trade in the production and transport of simple wines and once-legal medications and goods that had been salvaged and which were now rarities in that world, and whose values had now increased substantially. Pesos were of no use to any person there, they commanded no power. The power was in owning arsenals and high wired fences and horses and drinking tequila and eating fresh fruit. That was the man who was envied, and that was the ambition of the streetrats who still fought, tooth and nail, pistols in hand, through the dusty and smoke-filled streets of cities such as that.

The conservationists pitied them.

As in the previous life, their goal of power was flawed.

Where once the need for cars and jewellery had driven most to imprisonment or death, their wars for grains and rusted tools were more pitiful than ever before.

"They still go to their knees and offer prayer to god", Matteo told Kiara, "but god has no space in his kingdom for those who kill for selfish needs. Theirs is not a holy war, or one of survival, theirs is a selfish quest for pathetic power in a world where power means not a thing. They are animals without leashes, and they will know one day the fury of the lord. Their time will come"

They crossed Avenue Ferrocarril and Alejandro stopped them at the corner.

The streets before them were intact, not reached by the fires, dark and quiet.

"We need to cross Calicanto to the river. This place will be crawling with people, we travel close from here. Watch the next man, do not get split up"

"And do not fire unless you have to" Gerard added, "a rifle shot in the barrio will have the same effect as flooding water into a termite mound"

Alejandro spun the bō across his back.

"Keep close"

The streets through Calicanto were full of whispers and the smell of cigar smoke. They kept low and to the shadows of cars and trucks. The streets were narrow, some barely wide enough for a vehicle, overlooked by darkened windows which could easily have hidden watching eyes. There was no way for the group to ensure safe passage, but simply they had to stay low and quiet and pray for luck to be on their side.

The place had suffered great poverty, even in times of economic stability, where the rest of the city had thrived and when beautiful buildings and bridges and parks had been built. Unemployment and crime thrived there for as far back as any person could remember, and the place was as derelict and dangerous as ever. There was no wealth, no food, no prospects and no faith. Rubbish and waste piled high in the streets, a city uncaring and unable to help, a governmental blindspot which had not seen aid for many years. There was barely the wealth or strength to even maintain true crime, pistols were empty and blades were rusted. A people hanging on to the final fraying threads of a society, snapping one by one so that those who held on there would eventually fall to their fate, dead where they lay, helpless and forgotten. Most with sense had left years prior, travelling on foot, into the country, forced out in search of anything that would allow them another day. The majority of others had followed once the fires begun, smoked out of their own existence, walking without hope for there was nothing else.

But some remained. The infirm, the sick, the old and the crippled. The city turned into an abandoned memory, rife for the Hoja Negra and others to turn into a battlefield, a nightmarish and unpoliced playground.

The conservacionistas declared war, refusing to allow the history of the ancient city to be torn from its roots, the priceless artifacts of the Maya and Toltec and Aztec peoples plundered inanely for no good, the gems pawned and the gold melted and the rifleshot bodies piled in the streets. They were not peacekeepers nor saviours, but they were armed and they were led by what almighty hand they believed guided them, and to that end they toed the line of battle.

To aid the good. To pull light through the dark.

Kiara was thankful. She knew she stood little chance without them. She would most likely have sensed the danger and fled from the city altogether, without having made it nearly that far, and would have not gained what information she had from major Salamanca. She owed them everything but they did not see it that way. That was their duty, and the duty of good did not require praise or gratitude.

Alejandro whistled the group to a halt.

He and Matteo advanced slowly while the group waited, Matteo's rifle trained along the narrow road.

There were voices ahead in the dark, laughing loudly and shouting and the barks of a dog. Whoever was there knew nothing of their advance, carefree were their calls and laughs.

Alejandro closed in on the voices, gathered a short distance along the street in a concrete yard where a basketball hoop hung from the crumbling stonework, and where a fire burned in a metal trashcan.

He approached cautiously, waving Matteo to stay back.

He stopped at the edge of the building and removed his hat and peered around the edge of the stone home for a moment and then returned to the shadow. He waved Matteo onwards and Matteo quickly crept along the far side of the road, keeping low behind a parked truck before jumping quickly to the next vehicle and ducking safely beyond the sightline of the men in the yard.

He took up a crouched position and raised his rifle, covering the rest of the group for them to pass.

Alejandro raised his hand and beckoned the rest of the group forward, pointing to the parked truck as the safest method to cross. The group hurried silently forwards and jumped in behind the truck, crouched as they moved along its length as the men in the yard still called and shouted and laughed.

Will jumped to the car and into the safety of the shadows beyond.

Beneath the chassis of the truck they could see in plain view the men in the yard, and Kiara and Ariela watched them from where they hid.

There were five men, dressed in black coats and robes with gas masks covering their faces, dusty and blackened and their hair long and matted and ashen. They jumped around each other, laughing and shouting and one held a length of rough wood, burning with flame at one end. Tied by chain to the brickwork was a dog, black and white with long hair and wide eyes. For a moment the thing looked fierce, a dog of hell, blood in its mouth and fire in its eyes but as they watched they saw the thing trembling with fear, hunched on its back haunches, snarling not for the men but at them as the man with the fire poked at it, singeing its hair and its flesh and causing the men to roar again with laughter.

"Come on" Gerard whispered loudly, calling the two women from their vantage point as he leapt to the safety of the shadow beyond.

The dog squealed again and one man kicked it and it snapped at his foot and thrashed on its chain, unable to escape the torment as it bucked from side to side in a desperate attempt to pull its head from the collar.

The man kicked it again and it spun and shrunk back against the wall, burned and bloody.

"Fuck this" Ariela said, standing up above the truck and pointing the rifle into the yard at the men.

Kiara grabbed at her coat and tried to deter her from taking the shot but she shrugged her off and kicked her backwards, steadying her aim.

To the side, each man's eyes were wide and their breath held as they watched, unable to intervene.

"Ariela, no" called Alejandro from the wall, causing the men in the yard to each turn and face the road, just as Ariela squeezed the rifle trigger and put a single shot into the dog's head.

It fell to the floor, finally out of what torturous misery it had been subjected to.

The men in the gas masks took a moment, watching the dog fall. In the first instance they had no idea where the shot had come from, deep in their own territory in the small hours of the night, but they each pulled their weapons and moved to the road.

The moment Ariela had pulled the trigger, the group had prepared their weapons, ready for the inevitable.

Alejandro was waiting at the edge of the building, the closest of their group to the yard, and as the first man stepped out to the road, he brought his staff around, stepping forward with force and bringing the bottom of the bō up into the man's stomach.

The man yelped and as he buckled in two, Alejandro stepped forward onto his other foot and slammed the top of the staff down onto the back of the man's neck, putting him flat to the ground without another sound.

As soon as the man was down, Alejandro spun backwards from the opening to the yard and took place behind a pile of rubbish bags on the street. Kiara grabbed Ariela by the arm and the two swiftly moved out from behind the truck so that the group was split in two, Will, Gerard and Matteo on the far side of the opening.

The men in the gasmasks got into formation inside the yard, stepping slowly to the opening, aware of the risk of putting themselves in a firing line. They were not soldiers, not trained by any elite, but they were wild and they knew how to fight and how to fire with precision.

"We have to move" Kiara called to Ariela as they hid behind the car.

Ariela thought and said nothing.

Alejandro whistled sharply.

He was stooped a few feet to their side against the wall, circling his finger in the air to call the girls to turn around. He pointed back the way they had come and Ariela nodded.

"Matteo" he called loudly.

From the dark Matteo called back.

"Sí?"

"Go around. We will meet you again"

Matteo called that he understood, and in the shadows on the other side of the yard, the three of them quietly ran into the dark. A trail of rifle fire followed them along the road as the men in the gas masks took position, sparks jumping from the road and the homes and the parked cars as the rounds scattered behind them.

"Go" Ariela called, pulling Kiara's red coat.

Ariela stood, her rifle raised and volleyed shots into the yard, one round thumping into the chest of one of the men and causing him to recoil backwards and fall to the ground clutching himself.

In the cover of her fire, Kiara used the opportunity to run, ducking along the street until she fell around the next corner and caught her breath. A moment behind her, Alejandro spun around the corner, grabbing her by the collar as he passed.

"Don't stop" he screamed, heaving her back to running again, "keep going, go right up here and we will get back around. We have to get out of here now"

"Ariela..." Kiara started to call to him as they ran, but Alejandro interrupted her.

"She will come. Don't worry about her"

The two ran along the dark street, gunfire echoing around them and shaking the stone buildings. The sound of the riflefire and their pounding boots on the road and her own heavy breathing flooded Kiara's head and she was unsure in the panic whether they were being followed closely and fired upon directly or whether they were in safety but she did not dare look around for fear of slowing herself down.

Alejandro had proved himself on that night to be amongst the most fearless of their group, and possibly of all men, and the urgency in his voice as he cried at her to run had left Kiara in no doubt as to the importance of getting away as fast as was possible. They threw themselves around the next turn and ran through the dark. Ahead in the road Will was standing with his rifle raised and he raised a hand to indicate his presence there and to ensure that he wasn't fired on. As Alejandro and Kiara neared him, he turned and ran with them.

Gunshots sparked around them.

"Down" the voice came from ahead of them.

Matteo and Gerard were standing side by side behind a car, their rifles steadied on its roof.

Will pulled Kiara to the ground and they fell together into the dust as Matteo and Gerard rained fire back along the road above them at their pursuers.

It bought them just enough time to regroup at the corner, momentarily catching their breath and reloading their rifles.

"Where is Ariela?" asked Will as they steadied themselves.

"She was giving cover fire" Alejandro said, pointing back along the street.

"She nearly got us all killed" bellowed Gerard.

"And she might yet" cried Matteo, resuming fire into the dark as the men behind them appeared to double in number.

Others appeared in darkened windows, the flashing of their rifles illuminating their battered homes in bursts of white and orange light. Two men in gasmasks made progress along the street and Matteo found his aim and put a rifle shot through the leading man's head so that he spun backwards to the dirt.

"Go" he cried.

The group darted through the network of tiny streets, overlapping their runs whilst the front group covered their progress, pushing back the men who chased them and watching ahead for signs of more.

"Which way?" Gerard called out as they reached an intersection.

"South to the river" Matteo called back, pointing across the rooftops.

Alejandro jumped into cover beside them, breathing heavily. His staff was strapped to his back and he held a shiny silver revolver in each hand like a bandit.

"South?" Gerard asked him over the gunfire.

"This way" he called, rising and running east past a ruined convenience store which had been burned to black inside.

"Al" Matteo called after him, "the river is just here, where are you going?"

Alejandro turned as he ran, firing back over their heads.

"The damn bridge" he cried.

Matteo rose from his cover and followed him along the road.

"No Matteo" Gerard screamed as he ran, and Matteo turned to see Gerard pointing to the upstairs window of the store.

A boy no older than fourteen, a red baseball cap pulled low over his shadowed face, leaned through the filthy blind with an old pistol and aimed it at Matteo and, just as he turned his head to follow Gerard's finger, the boy squeezed the trigger and put a single shot into his arm.

Matteo staggered sideways in the open street as the boy reloaded and he managed to stumble against the storefront and fell backwards into the blackened charred glass.

Gerard filled the window with riflefire and ran forward, taking the stunned Matteo under the arms and thrusting him forwards to Alejandro.

"Go now" cried Will, as he and Kiara left their cover of a doorway.

The noise around them was deafening.

Shrapnel sparked from the buildings, blocks of concrete popping from the walls, windows shattering and all around the screaming of their group and of their pursuers.

As they ran, Kiara clutched her hat, that of her fallen husband, in her fist and ran low, her flowing red coat thick with dust.

Will faltered in his stride and Kiara turned her head to him.

His eyes were wide as he staggered, momentarily paused and stunted and unable to run as his knees buckled, his mouth open in a silent gasp.

He dropped to one knee, and in that moment Kiara realised he had been shot. She spun around and ducked low, crawling quickly back to him, but before she reached him he rose again to his feet.

"Don't stop" he cried to her, limping forward as Alejandro and Gerard fired back along the street.

Kiara took Will by the arm and the two ran, Alejandro heaving Matteo along with them until, by the end of the road where the buildings stopped, the chasing men appeared to have gone and the echo of gunfire rang out of their ears.

They ran to the edge of the barrio with only the sound of their own breath and boots.

The road bridge crossed the river beside them.

"See? The bridge" Alejandro said, pointing.

The river was overgrown, twisted bushes crawling across the road so that what water ran beneath them was obscured from view. Beyond, the landscape opened up as the city streets dwindled into farmland and the purple hills rose in the distance, the very faintest glow of dawn lining the horizon at the east like a single fibre of spun silver thread.

They took cover in the abandoned gas station and propped Matteo and Will against the wall and Gerard began tending to their wounds, removing his coat and wrapping the gunshots tightly.

"What the fuck happened there?" he growled backwards over his shoulder, his hands red with blood.

"Ari shot the dog" Alejandro said calmly, taking a cigarette from his pocket and lighting it with a match.

Gerard shook his head.

"The dog is more important than two of our men?"

Alejandro did not respond.

After a moment he spoke.

"She is wild Gerard. We have spoken about her"

"We need to get these two back to the temple immediately. Where is the nearest tunnel?"

"Back at the quarry" Will croaked.

"There is a hospital just here" Alejandro said, pointing into the dark.

Gerard looked around.

"A hospital? Where?"

"Here. Across the fields. I am sure there is nothing left there now, but we have no choice. Or we make back north to the lakes"

There was gunfire again in the barrio and shouting and Alejandro and Kiara raised their pistols to the road.

The sound stopped and there was running in the street, approaching their position.

Gerard stood and took up his rifle.

The running approached the corner of the street and then, from the shadow, the glinting red tails of Ariela's hair rounded the corner, her coat flowing behind her like a cape.

She ran to the group.

"Why have you stopped?" she cried, the adrenaline squeaking her voice.

"Will and Matteo are shot" Gerard replied angrily, the blame in his voice obvious.

Ariela looked over her shoulder.

"Get them into the hospital. I will go back for a medic"

She didn't wait for confirmation, and she did not need it.

She saluted with a finger and spun on her heels and took off back along the roadway to the north, into the heart of the barrio, the scoped assault rifle swinging at her side.

"OK let's get you up" Gerard said to the two injured men, "we have to keep moving. Ari has probably led every man in that place right to us"

"Kiara" Alejandro said, turning to speak to her, "you have been put in enough danger. Now is a good time for you to make your exit. Cross the water here, take the road along the riverbank on the far side and you will leave the city into the fields. The foothills will be before you after a short distance. Hide yourself, rest, take up the road again many miles away"

Kiara nodded and looked to the dusky hills, lit every moment more and more with the glow of dawn.

"The danger you are in is only because of me. I don't even know what to say to you all for what you have done. I owe you my life, ten times over. And when I find Dylan, his life will be owed to you too"

"We are preservationists Kiara, we preserve" Gerard said, walking to her, "life and soul. I hope to see you again when the time is right"

Kiara nodded.

"I will be back here. One day"

Gerard smiled.

"God bless you"

She could not stop herself from leaning in to embrace him and he wrapped a single arm around her like a father and then pushed her away gently.

"Now go, before there is no time"

She smiled to them all and they waved and wished her well and she turned and in a moment was alone on the dusty path at the riverbank, silent and throbbing with pain and dirty and stumbling with exhaustion.

The road was featureless, dusty and bare and lined with tall thin grasses which grew from blue to grey to brown as the sun found its way above the horizon and cast its arms across a new day. A mile along the road, with the sounds and smells and acrid fumes of the tortured city fading away behind her, she took a track south into the foothills and stopped at the small wire fence of a homestead.

She entered through the broken wooden gate into the front yard, overgrown beds of plants and a broken metal bench and terracotta plantpots on the sides, spilling out dried soil onto the cracked paving. The building was silent, its windows long smashed from their frames and the roof tiles removed and the kitchen taken apart for its piping. There was nothing there to take or to use but she was not there to scavenge. She did not bother going up the wooden stairs to the top floor, content with the spot she chose in the back room to lay on the floor and allow herself to pass out into a black and dreamless sleep.

When she woke again, she did so into a wild panic, not remembering at all where she lay or indeed how she had got there and her mind swirled with flashing images of gunfire and the tortured dog and the blood on Gerard's hands.

She gathered herself and looked around the basic old home, and was, after a few moments, flooded with the warmth of the realisation of her situation.

She remember what major Salamanca had told her, remembered that she knew the route of her son, only a few days ahead of her on the road, and remembered that she had indeed survived the ordeal of crossing Oaxaca, escaping with her life. If only just.

She knew that she had to begin her progress south as soon as she could, to move fast and without mercy as she chased down the platoon which had taken her boy. But she allowed herself some time to clean in the water gathered in the animal trough, drinking the rain water and eating fruits from a tree that she didn't recognise which tasted sweet at first but left a bitter tang behind her teeth and her tongue numb.

It was later than she had hoped it to be by the time she took back to the road.

The track led up through the foothills and deep into the nearly impassable spread of cacti and scrub which led to the pines beyond.

She crossed south east, keeping far enough away from the homes and buildings below to ensure her safe passage, but low enough in the hills to ensure she did not lose herself and her way. The hills there were not expansive, but they were dangerous to cross alone, the rocks sharp and red and which dropped away to would-be graves where snakes and scorpions reigned and from where, should she twist an ankle or worse, she would almost certainly not return.

She crossed the hills in a day, sleeping that night on an outcrop with the pistol in her hand, listening to the bats go about their hunt.

A day later she was in San Francisco Lachigoló, where she traded the last of her jewellery for dried fish and tequila and ate in the street, and a day more she had already reached San Pedro Totolapa, battered and blistered and defying any expected walking time between the two places. She rested light and travelled fast, taking water from the ground where it ran from the hills and eating what grasses and berries she found on her route.

A group at Quiechapa met her at the roadside, twenty strong with mules and carts and rifles, offering her company on the way south. They carried buttes of clean filtered water and sacks of grain and corn and the women had made tortillas and stewed beans and they welcomed her and offered her what she needed.

She quickly declined without consideration.

"You will travel too slowly for me" she told them succinctly, thanking them regardless.

The women smiled when she told them her need for haste, and one rolled some tortillas in paper and handed them to her and held her by the hand while she drank a cup of water there, before saying a prayer for her and allowing her to go, relentlessly onwards into the country along the open road where the birds soared silently and where no wind blew.

With her eyes on the road and her mind focussed, she walked.

The soles on her boots were worn and on the third day she left the road at San Juan Lajarcia and followed the dirt track to the collection of old homes where stovefires burned and elderly women wove reeds and grasses into hats on the ground.

She walked to them and went to her knees before them and asked for water and they obliged her with a small tin cup of warm water from a tank which tasted terrible but which she finished in a single motion.

"Necesito botas. Por favor" she said to the old woman who sat on the ground before her, her dark weathered face showing the lines of her age.

She peered up with thin eyes from under her wide-brimmed straw hat.

The woman watched Kiara for a moment then looked down at her feet.

She turned and spoke to the woman seated across from her, quiet and thick with the accent of the south. Her friend looked at Kiara's boots too and nodded and spoke back to her.

"De qué tamaño?"

Kiara thought.

"Veinticuatro"

The woman sat for a moment as though she didn't understand, then eventually called out across the yard to the quiet stone home opposite.

A young boy, ten or so years of age, poked his head around the door and the woman waved him over and asked him if he could find any boots of Kiara's size and the boy shrugged. The old woman waved him away, telling him to go and look.

Kiara thanked the woman and she nodded but said nothing, returning to her weaving.

A few moments later, the boy trotted back across the yard with a tall pair of men's workboots, black leather with thick laces.

Kiara asked the lady what she wanted for the boots.

The woman thought.

"No tiene nada" the woman said.

Kiara shrugged and smiled. The woman was correct, she truly had not a thing to offer.

She took Ryan's hat from her head. It was not a cheap hat, made of well-tanned buffalo leather.

The woman smiled and passed her open hand around the grasses that lay on the ground around them, ready to be woven.

"Tenemos muchos sombreros" she said, smiling.

Kiara smiled. Hats were the last thing the people in that village needed.

Other than the hat and the coat, the only things on her person were the Colt Python, which she would not part with, the rosewood knife strapped around her leg, which was also of such an array of uses that its worth to her was high, and the letter in her pocket for Dylan.

Kiara pointed at the knife, offering it as payment.

The woman waved her away.

"Tome las botas" she said.

Kiara bowed graciously and thanked the woman and then thanked the boy and took the boots. She pulled her own off and pushed her feet inside the workboots. They were a little big and a little wide but they felt tough and well made and they were better by some margin than her own.

She thanked them again and the women smiled only slightly and Kiara took the dirt track back out to the highway.

Early on the morning of the fifth day, she passed three men moving north along the road, leading an old pony which walked on its last legs.

"Buenos días" she called, and the men stopped in the road.

Two smoked cigarillos and they each looked more ragged than the next, their clothes torn and sunbleached and battered by sand and their beards and nails long.

Men of the road. True roamers, without destination or purpose, scavenging their way from place to place in a vain attempt to live another day until their number one day be called.

"Hola señora" said one, his voice gruff and deep.

"Have you seen military on this road?"

They looked about between them and shrugged.

"No, not here" the man said.

"Anywhere? Maybe in the past few days?"

The man behind him spoke. He was taller than the others with high cheekbones that pushed on his skin where all fat had long gone.

"Sí, two days", he thought, "or three. North of the floodland"

Kiara smiled. Her eyes widened and she felt yet closer.

"Where is that, I don't know these parts?"

"The floodland?" the man asked.

"Yes"

The front man spoke again.

"Everywhere señora. Ten kilometres from every coast"

Kiara nodded.

"I understand. Where did you see the military?"

The man thought. He looked at his comrade, though the man only shrugged back at him.

"North of Juchitán"

"How far from here?"

The man shrugged again.

"Two days walk"

Kiara thanked them. The man had claimed to see military on the road two days prior, but she was yet two days' walk from that place, and they had surely moved on. If she kept her pace, she knew she may be four days from catching them where they travelled. She also knew that the man could be wrong, and also that the military convoy that he had seen, may well not be the one her son walked with.

The hope flooded her heart regardless.

It was yet the best lead she had for finding him, and she would track them down like a lone wolf stalking the herd until she held her son again. She thanked the gods of fate that her son was heading south, closer and closer to the Guatemalan border. Her escape route. The beginning of the next phase, the route south into pastures new and fresh where they could find salvation.

She hoped. There was no alternative but to.

"Thank you. Good day"

She moved on.

By night, she had reached Jalapa and the vast cerulean lake of El Marqués. The town was vibrant, thriving on the trade and passage of those who came from miles through the desert for the fresh water of the lake. Music played and campfires were lit along the main street. Villagers still occupied most of the homes there and the gas station forecourt had been transformed into a night-market where women sold woven goods and glass bottles of tequila and homemade wines, and a man toasted nuts in sugar and the children ran.

It was, at a glance, a beautiful melting pot of travellers from across that land, each bringing stories and goods to swap with others. They told of places where fish could be found and books could be read and where the crops grew and the flowers blossomed and where the safest places were to make camp and where children could play openly.

Thought there were layers to the place. Deeper currents that ran beneath the veneer which not all eyes could see.

Kiara was not fooled.

She walked slowly through the place, and while the people went about their evening, carefree in the streets, Kiara watched the rooftops and the shadows.

There was more there to be seen.

Dark men in dark clothes with rusty knives and old pistols lingered in darkness, marking the vulnerable and plotting night raids on the surrounding camps. The women of the night-market were complicit. They traded with travellers with broad smiles but, upon seeing a person flaunt too much of their wealth, gave discreet nods and whistles into the dark and the travellers were tailed quietly away into the night.

The place was a con.

A smart traveller, moving alone as Kiara was, would be able to briefly acquire goods and information and move briskly onwards, but if one were to linger too long or speak to the wrong person in the wrong way, they would likely themselves become a target for theft or worse.

Kiara took up a place on the outskirts of town where she unrolled the tortillas from the paper and put inside them the last of the smoked fish and ate it quickly and sat with the small quart of tequila and drank from the bottle with the pistol in her lap.

Voices floated across the rooftops and drifted out across the sprawling black lake, the reflecting stars still in the quiet water as they were in the sky above it. Silhouetted birds gathered at the edge and darted in and out of the blackness and scattered again and Kiara rose and walked into the still lively town.

A stone archway crossed over the road and men had hung from it flags and ribbons in all colours, and beneath it two men dressed in shirts played ranchera on a guitar and trumpet. The guitarist led the tune, skipping around in the road in an exaggerated manner and calling to passers-by, whilst his heavily inebriated colleague blew awful notes on the horn and staggered between the stone pillars. Their noise could be heard blocks away, and a crowd had gathered, not so much to dance and enjoy the music but to laugh at the spectacle, a notion which had indeed gone over the heads of both oblivious musicians.

Kiara approached and slowed and listened, a smile on her face.

As she watched, three military personnel crossed the road behind her in their green combat fatigues and black t-shirts, one holding a bottle of wine by the neck.

She ran to them.

"Perdone" she called as she crossed the street, "perdone, señores"

The men slowed and turned.

"Can I speak to you? Please"

The men nodded.

"I am looking for someone, in the military"

They said nothing.

"My son. He left the barracks north of here, Oaxaca, I don't know more than that. Two weeks ago, maybe, heading south to Salina Cruz"

The men looked between themselves, shrugging.

They were young, teenagers still.

"Sorry" one said, "there are many people here, in the military, we don't know most of them"

"Please" Kiara pleaded, "you must know something"

Another spoke.

"I can tell you one thing, there is no place by the name Salina Cruz any more, it is under ten feet of water"

"The major in Oaxaca told me that they were heading that way. If not there, then where would they go?"

"The military flood relief in Salina Cruz ended years ago, it is nothing now. The road continues north of there, just follow the water. Will you leave in the morning?"

Kiara nodded.

"Yes, early"

"If you walk without a break you will see the Pacific by noon. Take the road north from there and the highway will take you in a curve around the floodland. I don't know where your son and his group are, but there is nothing there to keep any military busy for long, so they are surely passing through. If you reach Chiapas Nuevo, go north. No man will go to the border from there, and no military captain will make him do so"

"Why not?" Kiara asked.

The man scoffed and the others chuckled, in on a joke that Kiara was not party to.

"El Sepultura?" the man asked, "nobody goes there"

Kiara looked confused.

"What is that?"

"The fog forest. It is too dark to enter, and you will not live to tell. There are many legends of what lives there, and I tell you, I don't care to find out if they're true"

Kiara furrowed her brow.

"Well I won't go there, but honestly, what could live there that is so bad, eh?"

She smiled slightly at the thought.

The soldier was not smiling.

"Men forgotten by time. Men who eat other men. Even the jaguars and the tapirs and the monkeys left the forest there. That is all I will say"

Kiara nodded.

"I think that is all you need to say. Thank you for your help"

The men nodded and wished her well and went again into the night.

Chapter Seventeen

The flooded Pacific coastline was immense.

It stretched from horizon to horizon, vast and white and shimmering with sparks, engulfing the towns which had once lined the shore. The artificial harbour that enclosed Laguna Superior had long gone, spreading water inland for more than five miles and destroying everything in its path.

Years of cleaning and clearing had been attempted, plucking and sieving the flotsam so that the water could not spread disease, but all attempts had ultimately failed and for mile after mile the place was in ruin. No birds swooped down on the water there for no fish swam, and no person of sanity bothered stopping in that place for any longer than needed for the place served no purpose to man nor beast.

In what was left of Tehuantepec, Kiara took the highway north through Puente Madera, an open and featureless desert road through a vast arid plateau of nothingness. There were no plants there to eat and no clean water to drink and no tree to cast shadow for rest and she walked onwards, straight and focussed, for there was no alternative.

The sun fell away behind her as her shadow stretched further and further until it went completely and she walked in darkness, a complete darkness that covered everything there was there.

It was well into the night when she reached the first sign of life at the outskirts of Juchitán de Zaragoza. An old gas station that was crumbling into nothing, a restaurant hung in coloured ribbons and pocked with bullet-holes, an old tanker, a hole splintered in its side and its contents long drained.

Kiara took shelter from the night in a stone shed, the original purpose of which had been lost to time. She ate the last of the tortillas from the paper, though it had dried and left her with more thirst than before and which plagued her through the rest of the night until the light found her again the following day.

When she emerged from the hovel the sky was grey, great billowing clouds hung ominously overhead. She followed the road into the town as the wind began to whistle through smashed windows and the doors creaked on hinges and signs that hung above the road rattled and swung on their fixings.

She found the Rio Los Perros where it intersected the city and climbed down from the roadbridge through the rough scrub to the water's edge where she washed in the cold current and drank all she could.

An old man watched from the road.

She nodded and he smiled, watching her there as though she were out of sorts with the town, which indeed she may have been.

When she had pulled the water from her hair, she put the leather hat back on top of her head and tipped the brim of it to the old man again and he bowed to her very slightly as though tipping the brim of his own hat, though there was no hat there to tip.

"Have you seen the military come through here?" she called to him up the bank.

He took a moment to respond and smiled inanely as though he had not understood the question.

He pointed along the road, into the town.

She scrambled up the bank to the road and approached him.

"Really? The military passed here?"

He nodded.

"Sí"

"This way?" she asked, confirming the way the man's finger was pointing.

He nodded.

"Sí"

"Recently?"

"Sí"

She began to question the validity of his responses, watching his eyes closely for any hint of senselessness.

She straightened her long red coat out behind her.

"You're sure?" she asked.

The man nodded.

"Sí. I am sure. You don't need to keep asking me. They are in the town now. Camped in the grounds of the Instituto Tecnologico"

Her heart raced.

"Thank you, thank you" she gasped, turning from him to run along the road, "this way?"

He nodded and she turned and went.

The man smiled again and waved behind her as she ran.

It wasn't more than a mile and she did not stop.

As she ran along the centre of the road with the long red coat flowing behind her like a cape, the grey clouds above opened up and the rain fell on her for the first time in weeks. It dripped from her eyes and the tip of her nose and dripped from the brim of the hat and she didn't care and let it pour over her. It grew heavier, pooling in the road and chasing the people there, of whom there were few regardless, into the shelter of the buildings until she was the only thing in the street that moved, a streak of red tearing through the rain.

She followed the road, not knowing the distance nor time nor direction of the institute but for the instructions of the old man at the river, and as she ran the thought rattled around her head that she may be trusting the word of a fool. The man had no reason to lie but he may well have been wrong or delusional and as she approached a road junction her eyes scanned the signposts for any indication of where the place may be.

She spotted it, written in yellow on the blue sign, the letters faded and behind graffiti and she ran around the corner in the direction indicated.

To her left was a low white stone wall, no more than three feet from the ground and smashed in places and beyond it a grove of trees, great oaks planted with purpose to shield the extensive garden beyond.

She saw them. The horses first, kicking and stepping in the rain as the water dripped over them. Twenty horses or more, tethered to one another and pulling left to right on their chain. Then the men, dressed in the customary green trousers and caps, running frantically as they tried to construct their shelter to keep the rain out, pulling sheeting between them and roping it to the trees, others dragging their boxes and crates underneath it.

She stopped at the wall and caught her breath.

She was excited and relieved and tired and desperate to hurdle the wall and find her son, but it was clear from what she saw that the men were going nowhere quickly, and she had at least time to gather herself.

She pulled the water from her hair and tucked the letter for her son deeper inside her pocket where it could not get wet and shook the water from the hat and put it back on her head.

She climbed over the low wall and stood under the trees, enjoying for a moment the shelter from the downpour.

She watched the soldiers in the grounds of the institute, hastily going about their business, trying to catch a glimpse of her son. But the times had changed those young boys, they each had shaved heads which took from them their identity, they were tanned, tattooed, weather-worn and dressed identically to the next.

She righted her hat and walked out of the cover of the treeline and into the dusty open scrubland in front of the buildings.

For a few moments nobody saw her, so busy were they with building their rain shelter and stopping the horses from pulling themselves free from their stakes. She covered half the lawn before any man looked up, and when one did and saw the bright red figure walking purposefully through the rain as though it were not there, he sharply whistled and brought her to the attention of the others.

A couple grabbed rifles and they cut her off on the outside of the camp. She slowly raised her hands as they neared.

"Détente ahí" one soldier barker and she stopped walking and stood calmly in the rain.

"I am looking for someone" she said, her voice low so as not to spook any young soldier who may be more trigger-happy than was required.

They walked to her.

"There is no business here for you"

She cocked her head.

"There is. I am looking for my son. I believe he is here"

The soldiers were unsure how to respond, taught and trained to repel outsiders and keep civilians well clear of their camp and operations, yet sympathetic for they surely all had mothers of their own and no man there was older than twenty-five.

Protocol came first.

"You cannot come in here" the man spoke, his tone more understanding than before and a softness in his voice.

"Do you know him? Dylan Beckett? Please"

The man shrugged, though the younger soldier behind him looked briefly to his comrade and Kiara could see in his eyes that the man did indeed know where her son was, or at least where he had been. There would not be many soldiers with American names that far south in the country, Kiara reckoned, and the young soldier could not hide it well.

"Please" she said again.

"I will speak to the captain and pass on your request. If he knows where your son is then the decision will be his"

Kiara nodded.

"Do you know him, have you heard his name?"

"Señora, I have to ask you to move on, you cannot be here"

Kiara stood for a moment, watching the men, saying nothing more. Her eyes scanned the troops behind him but the rain blew into her face and the soldiers obscured her view and most of them had by that time taken shelter under the canopies.

She turned slowly and walked back to the treeline and shook the water from herself and sat. She was still inside the grounds of the technology institute though she was far enough away from the camp so as to be out of sight, and she sat on the wet grass and waited because she had nothing else to do.

She had walked the length of that country, from Monterrey in the very north to her parents' farm, and then slowly down the length of the land in search of salvation and safety and, ultimately, an escape over the border from that diseased and broken land to a place to start anew. She would not cross that border, or any other, without her son by her side for he was the only thing that she had. She knew he was alive, there was no doubt in her soul of that, and though she did not know whether or not he was camping there before her, she did know that she was as close as ever to finding him and was not going to move on until she was sure.

The rain fell harder and the trees shook and thunder cracked from horizon to horizon. The trees did little to shelter her as she wrapped her coat around herself and hid under the brim of the hat, and after some time she felt forced to move back over the wall to the road and seek temporary shelter in one of the many abandoned buildings there.

On the far side of the road, she ducked inside a small stone apartment, painted in bright orange paint that was crumbling from the masonry. There were still windows in the place but little else. In the front room an oil painting of religious iconography hung above an empty fireplace that was thick with dust and a broken wooden rocking chair stood in three pieces against the side wall. The place smelled of rats and rot but it was safe, and for the time being it was dry also.

She took off her coat and hung it on the corner of the door between the front room and what had once been a kitchen and kicked some of the detritus from the ground and the dust billowed and blew in circles, and when it had settled she sat down by the front window so that she could see across the road to the military camp.

There was little to see.

She did have a sightline on the camp, but through the driving rain against the window and the rain bouncing on the road and pouring from the trees, she could see nothing.

She took the assumption that as long as she could see that the camp was indeed still there, there was little chance of any of the soldiers moving on without it, and should she see them begin to break it down, she would have plenty of time to get over to them. If they wouldn't talk to her, wouldn't give her word of her son, then she would follow them relentlessly on their tour of that country until they did, or until she saw her son with her own eyes or saw him buried in the ground.

Time dripped slowly away, swirls of nothingness as the hours of the day disappeared and bled one into the next. She sat and watched through the window almost without pause, but for brief forays into the rest of the old home in futile attempts to source food.

The rain did not cease and the soldiers did not move on and she sat.

As her head spun, weakened by hunger, the black clouded sky above her slowly lost more of its light until the place was cast again into night and her view of the camp beyond diminished entirely. She took her coat from the door and checked the pocket for the letter to her son and went to the front door of the house and stood just inside from the rain. She had to find food. She stepped out into the rain and followed the road south along the perimeter of the institute, the little orange glows of the campfires within still visible. She knew they would have food at the military camp, but her chances of finding a way to infiltrate their camp were minute and she knew that should she get caught she would simply be executed on the spot. The brutality of the military had been evident to her on many occasions before and she knew even her own good fortune could not extend that far. She stooped in a doorway and took off her hat and turned it upside down to catch rainwater from a dripping tile roof and she filled it and drank a few times, subsiding her hunger very slightly. She understood that water was required far more than food and that she could survive a long time indeed provided she had something to drink, but she also felt like she may pass out in the street if she did not find food soon.

She sat in the covered doorway of an old electronics store.

The thunder cracked again and the water gushed in torrents along the road and she sat there for some time before snapping awake in a panic.

She had no idea how long she'd been asleep and through the rain she could see that the campfires beyond the trees had been extinguished, though the camp itself still stood. It was deep in the night and nothing moved. The rain echoed in the silence and her neck was twisted and sore and her trousers were wet and sticking to her legs where the water had poured into the doorway.

She stood and staggered back along the road to the bright orange apartment and fell back inside and pulled her boots off and stood them upside down to dry and wrapped the coat around herself and dropped to the dusty floor.

Her dreams spun around her head, repeating themselves in delirium. Nonsensical and strange. Visions of faces from her past, faces she knew well and faces she did not know at all. Snapshots of places she had stood, both in that world and in the world preceding it when life was different. She stood again at her daughter and parents' graveside, looking down on the three mounds of red earth from above, tears flowing down her cheek and her eyes stinging and each tear burning into her face and falling to the ground in a microcosmic explosion of red. A voice spoke over the scene, as though behind her and she could not make out the words and then she saw again the bodies in the school kitchen and then a faded memory of their first home after getting married, swirled together as though in a cauldron of her life. She saw her husband's face, distorted by memory, but his nonetheless. It smiled to her. She remembered the warmth of it but then it was lost again and she saw the firelight flickering from the old lady's face as she read the tarot cards.

"You have lost, and you will lose again, but the battle is yours" she said, her voice ethereal and echoing.

"Mom"

Her son's voice, jumpy and stuttered and warped. Her head swirled again and she saw him standing by the river with tears in his eyes as the soldiers fought back her husband. She saw the back of his head as they pulled him away, a single black bird effortlessly circling against the blue sky as she lay on the dusty ground.

"Mom"

The image disappeared to white.

"Mom"

Her eyes snapped open.

"Mom"

Her heart nearly jumped from her chest.

In the doorway stood Dylan, silhouetted against the morning light but unmistakably him.

She scrambled to her feet and threw herself at him, clutching the back of his head in to her neck.

She couldn't speak and tears fell from her eyes and she gasped for breath.

He wrapped his arms around her body and squeezed her tight.

"How on earth did you find me?" he asked, crying with her.

She sputtered her response to him.

"I... I followed... you. I asked at, the military, in Mexico City and, er, Oaxaca, there was a commander there, a major"

She caught her breath,

"It wasn't easy"

She looked into his eyes and her world became right. Nothing more mattered but that.

"I would never give up on you"

She wiped the tears from her eyes and stood back and looked at him, her smile pushing the limits of its breadth.

"Look at you. What have they done with your beautiful hair?"
She stroked his shaved head.
He smiled.
"It will always grow back, mom, it grows quick. They have to shave it a lot. They always cut my head though, here, see?"
He pointed to a small scab on his head and she hugged him again.
"Well I've found you now, finally. I love you so much Dylan"
"Where's dad?"
She hadn't thought of it and it took her breath away and the shine faded.
She just looked at him. There were no words ready inside her.
He nodded.
"What happened?"
"We... we were coming down south of Mexico City and we were, he..."
Her eyes filled.
He held her hand.
"It's ok mom"
She stopped herself from crying and took a deep breath.
"Do you remember where it was?" he asked, calmly.
His service had numbed him, such was his experience there in the brutality of survival in that place.
She nodded.
"Of course I do"
He looked at her. His eyes were glassy but his gaze was firm.
"I'd like to go there. Some day, you know. To see him"
She smiled.
"Of course. Of course"
She looked out of the dirty window to the street outside.
"How did you know I was in here?"
"I saw you last night. I saw you when you were in the camp but I couldn't get to you. I watched you all night from in there. I like your coat"
She smiled.
"I missed your birthday, sorry son"
He shook his head.
"Who cares mom?"

"Come" she said, "let's go from here. We're still going to the border. Unless of course you wish to go to see, you know, where your father, er...?"

He shook his head.

"Mom there is no chance"

"Huh?"

"I can't just leave"

"What? Of course you can, we just need to go now. Are you worried they'll see you? We can sneak out, there's a back door from the kitchen there"

"They know I'm here mom. The guy you spoke to over there told our squad leader you were looking for me, and he let me come here to speak to you but they are waiting for me. They're probably even watching"

She turned to the window. There was nobody in sight but that did not mean there were not men waiting and watching. To fight parents and force their children from them, enlisting boys far younger than the national conscription age, they were clearly ready to fight to keep them too.

She fumbled for words.

"I'll leave mom. I'll come with you, of course, I hate it here, we work all day and all night and nothing we do is good. I don't want to be here doing this, I want to be with you", he held her, "but I can't leave them today. Not here. Not now"

Kiara nodded. She understood.

She reached inside her pocket and pulled out the old letter. The envelope was battered and brown and curling at the corners and ruffled from getting wet and dry, time and again. In pencil on the front the word *Dylan* was still visible in her husband's handwriting.

"Here"

She handed it to him.

"This explains everything. It tells you where I will be waiting for you"

He nodded.

"Where?"

"Villahermosa. It's east, north east maybe, across the forest. A week perhaps. Can you get there?"

He nodded.

"Yes"

"Are you sure? I can wait here instead. Or somewhere else?"

"Mom I can get there. We're moving out of here this morning, now in fact. We're going that way I think"

"East?"

"I don't know mom. They don't tell us much. Round the coast I think, for today at least, but I think north east. I'll do it, I'll meet you. Of course I will"

"I'll wait there"

"I'll have to wait for the right time, mom, if they see me go they'll bury me alive in the desert, I've seen it happen"

She had no words.

She nodded.

"I'll wait there as long as it takes. Be so careful Dylan"

"I love you mom"

She began to cry again.

"I love you so much. I am so proud of you"

"I have to go mom. They're waiting for me"

She nodded through the tears and hugged him again and could barely let go and he pulled himself slowly from her and stepped back again into the light from where he had come and out into the slowing rain and away.

She fell to the floor again and cried into her hands, but inside she felt relief at seeing his face once more and that he was well and that their plan would, eventually, come to some fruition.

Chapter Eighteen

The cashier was bagging the goods when the phone vibrated in Ryan's pocket.

"Thanks" he said, swinging the bags down in one hand and fishing the phone out with the other.

It was the photo of Kiara's smiling face on the screen.

He pushed the green button.

"Hey"

"Hey. How far away are you?"

"Just leaving now, ten minutes. I've paid. You ok?"

"Yeah. They're coming, like, every eight minutes now"

"Are you ok?"

"Yeah I'm fine, but can you just..." she paused and groaned down the phone, "can you just hurry?"

"Do they hurt?"

"Do they hurt? Yes dammit. Hurry up, I need you here"

"Ok, ten minutes max, I'm getting in the car now. Just sit tight"

"Sit tight?"

She sounded frustrated. He never knew the right thing to say.

"I love you" he managed, an attempt at something more likely to succeed.

She hung up.

He raced home, faster than he should. The bag was already in the car, complete with all the items that they would need for a few days in hospital, though they both hoped that would not be the case.

He was excited, his heart was racing and he wanted to call his family to tell them that his wife was starting to go into labour and that, all being well, there would be a beautiful little boy with them before dawn.

He calmed himself. He had promised Kiara he wouldn't tell anybody when it began, their parents worried and that the last thing either of them needed. It would be a surprise. He would call them once he was born, it would be nicer that way.

The drive home blurred. He knew the roads well and didn't need too much thought at the turns and stop signs and before he knew it he was frantically opening the front door to the house.

Kiara was leaning against the steps in the hallway.

"Are you ok? Are you ready to go?"

She nodded, breathing through another contraction.

"The bag's in the car. Do you want to get your boots on?"

"You'll have to do it" she smiled.

He nodded, grabbing her boots from by the door and pulling them onto her feet.

"Have you got the seat?"

"Yes, I've got everything"

She went to the door, swinging her handbag over her shoulder and holding the wall.

"Did you put my slippers in the bag, I hate those ones you get there?"

"I've got everything, come on. The car's unlocked. Are you ok walking out there?"

She nodded.

"Can you please remember my lip balm?"

"It's in the bag Kiara, stop worrying about this stuff. There are stores at the hospital if we've forgotten anything, now go on"

She buckled against the wall again and clenched and moaned.

"Don't hold your breath through it"

He held her shoulders and she panted and caught her breath again.

"It'll be so worth it" he said, guiding her out of the door into the evening cool.

"I know. I know it will"

He pulled the door closed behind him and the two of them got into the car and drove away from their home for the final time as a family of two.

Kiara stood in the doorway of the old apartment and watched as they soldiers swiftly broke down their camp and packed the canopies and the fire pits into the crates and loaded them onto the trailer. They hitched twelve horses to the front of it and moved them onto the road and the troops fell in behind them in loose formation. When the platoon was gathered in the road, the captain and his lieutenants arrived at the front and called out orders and the group set off slowly east.

At the front of their convoy, twelve men walked with assault rifles and long rifles, some with scopes and some without, a short distance ahead, ready to clear the way for the rest. Behind them came the body of the group, twenty men on twenty horses of all colours and breeds, laden with saddlebags and satchels and the men atop them holding pistols and rifles. Swarmed around them were the infantry, of which Dylan was one. The youngest of their group, the recruits, teenagers at best, moving on foot, each with a weapon of varying type and origin.

Dylan smiled and nodded to her as they passed and she crossed her heart to him and smiled an empty smile with tears in her eyes.

Behind them came their load. The twelve horses were bridled and chained in three banks of four and each tied to the next and to the horse behind it, and the back four tied to the trailer, four wheels along each side. Two men sat at the front with the huge reins to the horses and called out across the group like conductors of the great show. At the rear of the convoy, another small band of troops with assault rifles, watching behind themselves as they moved.

The group travelled slowly and their sound signalled its coming from some distance. The sound of the boots and hooves on the road like a distant train and the bellowed calls from the captain and from the lieutenant on the trailer and the rattling of the axels under the weight of its load and the clanging of chains and cracking of whips.

Kiara stood and watched for all the time it took the group to move out of sight along the road, and then watched the nothingness.

She thought of following them, moving slowly and quietly behind the convoy where it went, staying to the shadows and keeping check on her son's safety. That way, she reckoned, when he does make a break from the group, she can be there. She decided against it as quickly as the thought had arrived. If she were spotted then it would jeopardise their plan, and she knew that some of their group had already seen her face. Indeed, the captain himself was aware of her presence there, and she knew little or nothing about their daily routine. Those soldiers were not simply walking the country with no purpose, and they surely separated into splinter groups with different tasks and there was no way of hiding from all of them.

She would stick to the plan.

She would make the walk to Villahermosa and she would stay there and she would wait.

As was the plan.

She walked north out of Juchitan, the open road as dead as the towns through which it snaked. The rain fell for three days without stopping, flowing in currents along the rough roads and dragging with it rubbish and waste and all the diseases that a person can catch and more, and pooled yellow and foaming in the road where homes stood. The people of that land collected the falling rain in all manner of items, haggard people with thinning hair and worn clothes, their faces gaunt and clinging to their cheekbones and who watched Kiara pass with dead and desperate eyes. They were ghosts, forgotten as living souls and left there to their fate where they clung on needlessly in a painful attempt to survive that apocalypse and to see salvation beyond it. Their existence itself was futile, they struggled to eat and drink there, and did not have the strength nor perseverance nor wits to find their way out. Many had walked from other lands, staggered across the country and across other countries and seen great struggle to find themselves there. They had walked in hope, searching for places where crops could be grown and where the water was clear and where they could survive in safety.

No place such as that seemed to exist in that ghost world. There was only shadow.

People were intrinsically good natured and helpful to one another and Kiara had witnessed it first-hand. There was hope in that world. But one had to fight, tooth and nail, and crawl on their knees and hold a light in the darkest of darks to succeed.

Kiara realised that her dreams of finding a promised land in the arms of Amatique Bay were as futile.

She held a vision in her mind of lush and vibrant farmlands near the coast, where they could make a small boat and fish every morning and grow crops to feed their family, and where she could grow old watching children play.

She felt foolish for ever having believed it.

She imagined what lay there in the floodlands of Guatemala.

The flooded coast at Salina Cruz was a wasteland. There were no people there, thriving on the sea air and the bountiful oceanlife. There were no communities of like-minded folk in hand-built homes who spent their days tending crops and weaving and painting and watching their young play idly in the sea.

There was despair. Vast areas of extreme damage, entire towns beyond recognition, smashed and splintered and lost. The land around, such as that where she walked, had not thrived. There was sun and there was rain and the land was decent and the soil soft and fertile, but there were no crops. There was no chance for the people who lived there, indeed they were barely living at all. Such opportunity to rebuild, to take timber from the woodlands and construct again the great towns of before, such opportunity was there as it was anywhere, but it was not an opportunity that had been taken.

Kiara felt like screaming to the people of that entire nation that there was need for community, a need for togetherness and co-operation. It was not beyond the capabilities of even the lowliest man to take up a tool and work with his neighbour to rebuild, but the hearts of those people were lost, their souls crushed and withered and diminished to nothing. They could, at any time, join together and build again and prosper, grow and tend good land and raise animals and filter water.

But instead they fought. They stole from one another and they turned readily on their neighbour and everywhere there was disease.

Any funds the national and state government acquired, in whatever form that took, were funnelled into military funding and increasingly into the pockets of the already wealthy. Theirs was always a corrupt government, a pyramid of financial greed, where those sitting at the top held every card and every decision and walked, to that day, in expensive boots and smoked expensive cigars. All whilst the population crawled around below in poverty. Abject poverty, a nation of traders at best and thieves at worst. Those with land protected it with assault weapons and struggled regardless.

Kiara felt a despondency and a misery and an intense depression at the prospects of their future and the future of the generations to follow, and in a sad way took solace that her beautiful Mia would never have to suffer in that place.

But Dylan was there. His future would be there, and for the short time being, it was yet hers to shape.

What use there may be of trekking through jungleland to Amatique Bay was questionable at the very best, but she had witnessed beneath her own feet the spectre of the nation which she once cherished and its gradual yet pronounced death at the fingertips of its own people.

They could stay. They could stay there in the south of the country, or they could work their way gradually back north. They could return to the capital again where goods were easily traded and where opportunities were more frequent, or they could return to the Templo de Santo Domingo and reignite their faith.

But there had to be more.

There had to be a place where people did things the right way. This would not be her apocalypse, she reasoned. Not hers and not her son's.

They would go south, go across the border and go to Amatique Bay. And if there was nothing there for them then they would continue onwards and they would walk until they reached the Amazon basin if that was what it took.

There may be no safe place, there may be no place any better than the road which she walked on that very day. But she knew that whatever situation dictated for them, whatever lay ahead of them of their path, lurking around the corners and creeping up behind them, she knew that she would not allow them to turn into those people who lingered behind the shadowy doorways of the towns of that country, thin and helpless ghouls of nothingness.

There would always be more. Always a reason to keep going.

She was a mere woman. Not trained nor well-equipped in any skill beyond maternal love and she would need nothing more. It was love which would drive her through the dark, hold her by the hand as she walked blindly into fate, negotiated her way through the endless trials and tests.

Though in the same breath she was indeed trained and also well-equipped in many, many skills which had allowed her to survive as long as she had done, and she knew she had her father and her husband to thank for it.

Her home was gone, torched to the earth from which it had been built. Her parents taken in horrific circumstance. Her daughter, her beautiful daughter with her boundless joy, put into the dark by her own hand to pass over into the light, her husband to follow her to the place where they would play together forevermore.

Yet she went on.

And still she would. She would walk through the fires that burned around her and through the pain and through the loss and through the grief, for she knew them all but temporarily.

There would be joy again.

There had to be more.

There had to be. She would find it, she swore it to herself and she would swear it to her son when again she held him.

She smiled and the brightness of that smile lit the dark ahead of her and she walked on with her head high for she knew the battle was hers. The queen of cats.

At Boca del Monte she left the road and took the trail into the woodlands.

There was little left of what world had been there, swallowed again by the natural order where the greenery spread across the roads and where the birds flew freely, and when she crossed the river into Veracruz she was at once very lost and entirely free.

She wavered with hunger, the grasses and leaves she had been surviving on thus far turning her stomach around on itself, and she staggered at times with a deep weakness.

At the river she stopped and sat in the shallows and let her mind wander in the silence of the place. The rain had ceased and the place glistened.

She fell into sleep there on the bankside and woke and struggled to stand and went again to sleep.

There was no time and no place. A drifting, floating peace overcame her and for a moment she felt like the warm hand of her death in that place would not be a bad thing.

But she fought again. It was what she did.

She sat up and gathered herself.

A white-tailed deer stood a short distance upriver, drinking from the water, its ears twitching as it listened for its life.

It raised its head, ears and nose to the wind and waved its little tail and drank again.

Kiara watched without moving.

There had been nothing driving her to kill beautiful wild animals for food, not even rabbits or birds. She had not been a vegetarian or had any real issues around the consumption of meat, beyond certain production methods, but she had seen such beauty in the innocence of beasts that whilst she could survive on berries and fruits and grains, she would do so.

But that time had passed and she held in her hand a powerful pistol and the deer was not thirty yards from her, oblivious of its fate.

She watched.

The pistol was loaded and cocked as it always was and she carefully thumbed the safety off to avoid it clicking.

It shook in her hand. She pushed herself up from sitting to a stooped position and kept as low as possible.

The deer had no clue.

It stepped silently back from the water's edge and snuffled around in the grasses, taking a small mouthful and chewing it between its teeth.

Kiara levelled the pistol and aimed it at the deer's head and tried to steady her breathing, as her father had taught her.

She knew how to shoot, but it was a one-time shot. She had to hit the animal first time or the chance would be gone and the sound of the gunshot would scatter any other beast there deep into the woodlands.

She was toeing the doorway of death itself.

There could not be more riding on the shot.

She took the slow breath in and held it and, as the muscle in her trigger finger twitched and began to tighten, there was an explosion of sound and colour and movement from the undergrowth behind the deer, and in the blink of eye or less, a huge jaguar leaped from the bush. The deer scrambled on the spot with its feet skidding beneath it, and for an instant began to run into the river but thought again and began to turn.

Its hesitancy was its downfall, and within a second the jaguar was on it.

The two fell to the ground with the jaguar's huge jaw wrapped around the back of the deer's head and its colossal paws fixed firmly either side of its neck, the claws deep into the flesh. The deer kicked its legs for a moment but made no sound and a moment later it was gone, its eyes big and white and still.

The jaguar held it to the ground after it had passed, and even at that distance Kiara heard the cracking of its skull in the jaguars jaw. Blood seeped from its shoulders where the jaguar's claws held it in place and from the back of its head and then from its mouth and nose and eventually the jaguar relaxed its grip and stood back.

It licked the blood and looked around, smelling the air.

The deep red blood trickled down the bank into the water and the jaguar sniffed the dead animal and again licked the open wound where its teeth had been.

The Colt Python rung out in the late afternoon silence, echoing across the woodlands.

The jaguar spun and squatted and stared upriver to where Kiara stood, the pistol still outstretched before her.

It didn't move.

Its eyes were wide.

Kiara held her nerve and fired again, up into the air above the kill.

The jaguar twitched and glanced quickly to the undergrowth and again to Kiara.

She fired a third time and the jaguar spun, and in a flash of gold it disappeared through the trees and away,

Kiara waited, should it return.

She walked slowly upriver to where the deer lay in the dirt, her eyes flickering to the bushes for any sign of the cat, but it was gone.

She stood over the bloody deer.

"Now what?" she asked herself out loud.

She had prepared chickens and fish for cooking many times, plucking and deboning, but a deer was quite another thing. There was no alternative but to try.

She felt guilt for the jaguar, it may have been as starving as her and she may have resigned the thing to its death but it was the cat or her and that was that.

She took it by the back legs and picked it up from the ground. It was not heavy but it was dirty and bleeding and she hoisted it to the river and plunged the thing into the cool water, dipping as though it were a sachet of herbs in a pot, until it was clean.

She looked around.

Whatever she were to do with that carcass, she would need to find somewhere better to do it. She was near the road, not a well-travelled road by any stretch but she could not guarantee her safety there, and in a place where men killed for bags of rice, to be in possession of an entire deer was a liability indeed.

She lifted the deer from the ground and swung it around the back of her neck so that its front legs hung over her shoulders and the warm blood dripped down her red coat, and she walked to the road.

It was not far into the next village, a stretch of largely abandoned shacks at the roadside and little more. She took the deer carcass into the front yard of an aggregates facility where the trucks had long been abandoned and where big leaves and vines had reclaimed what was once theirs.

She carefully swung the deer down and put it on the ground, trying not to make a sound or to dirty the thing again, and set off on foot into the village.

Two men sat back from the road in the shade of a corrugated steel barn, smoking.

Kiara stood at the road.

They stopped and looked at her, a sight otherworldly, tight black trousers and work boots and an expensive black buffalo leather hat and a long swinging red coat dripping with blood, the shiny Colt Python hanging in her hand at her side.

The men said nothing.

"Buenas tardes" she called.

One man nodded and neither said a thing.

She waited.

"Come down" she called.

The men looked at each other and did nothing for a moment, before one rose and then the other and the two slowly made their way down the old stone steps to the road.

They stopped a short distance back, both visibly nervous.

"I have a deal to make with you"

The men still said nothing.

The front man looked left and right along the road, checking for any other people who may be with Kiara, or checking for any who could indeed help them were something about to happen to him and his friend.

He nodded his chin at her and watched through narrow eyes.

"I have a deal" she said again, "are you interested?"

He smiled nervously.

"What deal?"

"I need your help. It is in your interest, I promise you"

"What do you want?"

"I have killed a white-tailed deer, a female, she is quite large. I need to hang and skin her so that I can take the meat. But I am travelling alone and without any cart or pony, there is no way that I can carry the meat of an entire deer with me. What is not salted or cooked now will spoil within a few days"

The man looked at his friend.

"You want to give me deer meat?"

"I want to make a deal. If you let me hang the animal and help me to skin and butcher it without word to anybody else, you can take half the meat. More than half, everything I can't carry"

The man nodded slowly.

He looked up and down the road again. There was nobody in sight.

"Where is it? This deer?"

"Do you have somewhere we can do that?" she asked, ignoring his question.

His friend pointed at the barn behind them.

"What's in there?" she asked.

The man shrugged.

"Nothing"

"Does anybody else come here?"

The man pointed again.

"Here?"

Kiara nodded.

"No. Nobody comes here. There is nobody here"

He pointed along the empty road.
Kiara nodded.
"Ok. Wait there"
She left the men standing and went back along the road and returned a moment later with the deer around her shoulders. Her knees felt weak and she staggered as she walked.
She dropped it to the ground in front of the men.
"Can you carry up the steps please?" she asked, slowly removing the pistol again from her belt without trying to appear threatening.
The men carried the deer up the steps and kicked open the door to the old barn and the three went inside.
Kiara pulled the knife from the leather strap on her leg.
"Have either of you skinned an animal?"
The men nodded.
"A deer?" she asked.
One man said that he had.
Kiara pointed to the rusted chains on the ground
"Hang it"
Together, the two men and Kiara tied the chains around the deer's back legs and threw them over the wooden support beam across the ceiling, and hoisted the animal up from the ground, tying it off to a workbench to stop it falling.
She handed the knife to the man.
He made incision at the back of the knees and pulled the blade carefully and quickly down the back of each leg to the tail, and in a simple motion peeled the animal's skin downwards, making gentle cuts at the parts that needed it. When the skin was at the hips he cut the length of its belly to its neck and proceeded to take the rest of the skin down.
"Hold it here" he instructed his friend, who supported the animal to stop it swinging on the chain.
The man pulled the skin from the back haunches with relative ease and cut with force through the base of the tail so that most of the rear half of the animal's skin was hanging down, inside out over its head.
"Find a, er, thing for the guts" he said, peeling the white skin from the red meat and exposing the deer's ribcage, "everything is in here and it will fall"

Kiara left them and looked around the barn for something that could serve as a bucket and after a few minutes returned to them with an old plastic sink which had been removed from a kitchen and was browned and cracked.

"This?" she asked.

The man shrugged and continued his work.

"Is fine" he replied.

He cut the rest of the skin down to the neck so that the poor beast's head was all that remained, hidden inside the skin from the rest of its body which had folded inside-out over its skull to the ground.

"You want the head?" he asked.

Kiara screwed her face. She was not squeamish at such things but she could only carry what she could carry and had no interest in taking the head of the thing.

She shook her head.

"Sí" his friend said, "we take the head. Cut here"

The man rotated the blade back and forth at the knuckle at the top of the deer's spine, and cut around the flesh and finally through the oesophagus so that the head came free.

The carcass dripped.

The man stood back and surveyed his work.

It was not a tidy job, there were pieces of meat missing where the blade had gone too deep and there were patches of the body where the white of the skin was still attached, but ultimately the job was done.

"Hold this thing" he said, kicking the corner of the sink under the deer.

The second man looked at Kiara.

She shook her head.

"I'm not doing that. You can hold it" she said.

He paused and crouched and held the sink under the carcass as his friend cut along the sternum and pulled open the ribs.

The contents of the deer sat inside, grey and lifeless.

The man thought and looked about as though seeking some way to better handle his task.

He thought,

"Take it down from there"

Kiara unchained the animal and the chain whistled up to the beam and thumped against it and then took itself over the top, and the chain and carcass fell to the ground together in a crash.

They jumped back.

The man reached inside and carefully pulled the contents of the deer out into the old sink and unchained the animals legs and cut them at the knee and snapped its lower legs off.

The group stood and looked at the scene before them.

The beautiful wide-eyed deer which had taken an afternoon drink from the river was crushed in the jaws of a wildcat and had been reduced to a pile of meat on the ground in that old barn.

"Can you butcher?" Kiara asked.

The man shrugged.

"I can butcher as well as I can skin" he said.

"So not great" Kiara joked and the men smiled for the very first time.

As the sun was setting again on their jungleland hideout, the deer had been cut into pieces which were neatly lined up on the workbench, and the discarded bones and offal put to one side, already crawling with flies.

For the years since electricity, when the last of the batteries had faded and the lights had slowly gone out, one by one by one, the ability to refrigerate and freeze food had gone with them. The people returned to primitive methods of curing and salting and smoking and wrapping meat in leaves and burying it in sand.

"Do you have salt?" Kiara asked.

The men shook their heads.

She nodded.

"We can't smoke it"

The men said nothing.

"Ok" she said, jumping down from the rusted bonnet of the old Chevrolet farmtruck on which she sat, "so we have to cook it. I'll take a back leg and some of the smaller pieces down there. The rest is yours"

The men nodded and thanked her and set about making a fire.

They built a small round pit from rocks and filled it with dried grass and sticks and stoked it until it burned and added the cut pieces of dried wood and lay a metal grille over the flames. They wrapped the legs and the haunches in palm-leaf and hung them above the fire until the leaves turned black, and each sat back on the ground as the night drew in.

One of the men left and returned with a half bottle of mescal and they drank and talked about nothing and waited for the meat to cook, and by the middle of the night when there was no light but the flickering of the embers at the end of the fire, each portion of the deer had been cooked through and the three of them slept in the open beneath the stars.

Chapter Nineteen

For thirteen days she walked the trail of nothingness.

The villages each as insignificant and dead as the one which preceded it and yet the only thing to which she could pin her sanity. They lined up, miles apart through the endless green of the forested countryside, each a checkpoint on her journey that brought her another notch closer to her son. Between them, the road barely existed at all, and she lost herself many times, wandering in panic until again she found sign of the once-concreted surface, or caught the shine of a steel roof or the sound of a simple flute playing through the trees.

There was nothing there to take or to give. Many villages were long abandoned, used since as outposts for the travellers who crossed that land. Campfires had been made and made again and raincatchers set up and left and there were shell casings and smashed bottles and bones and little else.

She found shelter under the splintered roofs of old homes and barns and outbuildings where others had stayed, and she passed no other traveller for the first week.

But some towns were not abandoned at all.

Folk who had fled one village had regrouped in another, and in La Chinantla she found life.

The homes were intact, if little else, and there was organised society and men bringing timber on mules and hunting parties bringing back birds and monkeys and wild pigs for their meat, and the trees themselves cut back from their encroach.

A place cut off almost entirely from the country which hid it. A place forgotten by the nation and the government, as most were.

The people had built themselves a community there and they had water and food but it was not a safe place. On the edge of the town, a group of dirty weathered men in torn shirts dug graves in lines, and beside them a pile of bodies lay in the dirt, overdue their burial and swarming with flies, and the men watched her through their thin, crinkled eyes and when she greeted them they did not reply.

Yet despite the filth and disease and the unforgiving clutch of poverty, the town filled her with the hope that there could exist the place from her dreams. The people there were growing crops, catching meat and filtering water and there were indeed children running and music playing, such as in her fantasies. In that place, the lone guitar played with sorrow and the children were gaunt, but they were there and the potential was there too.

She left La Chinantla to the north and walked four days blindly across field and woodland with no knowledge whatsoever of where she was or where she was heading. She understood enough about the positioning of the sun and the moon to know her approximate direction but there was nothing more to give her indication of her whereabouts.

She passed by a group of men on horseback carrying ploughing equipment and stopped them and asked them where she was and they laughed and told her she was nowhere.

"Do you know Villahermosa?" she asked.

They nodded.

"Which way?"

The farmer pointed out across the land, away from the direction her current path led.

Kiara nodded.

"How far?"

"Too far" the man replied, laughing, "you can come with me"

Kiara's eyes lit up.

"Really? You're going that way?"

"Of course. Why don't you take off that pretty coat and get up on this horse"

The other men laughed.

Kiara turned to walk away.

"You don't want to come with us. We are very friendly, I'm sure you will enjoy yourself"

They laughed again.

She ignored them and set off up the road, her hand holding the pistol in her belt.

"Be that way, lady" the man said, kicking his horse to trot, "it's a damn long way to walk"

On the afternoon of the tenth day, her knees were beginning to give way underneath her and she was again suffering from hunger. The boots were wearing down at the heel and one had split at the side and she began to limp from time to time with joint pain.

She walked onwards like a lost animal, forgetting at times entirely where she was and even where she was heading and she sat and slept in the open and often woke with little or no recollection of her quest.

She followed a white dust track north until, from nowhere, she saw before her the sea.

It was vast and black and shining and she felt herself drawn to it like a magnet to iron, pulling her to its calm.

By the coast she saw across the pasture a small picturesque farmhouse, built in perfect white stone and shining with the luminescence of the sun itself. Around the garden were manicured bushes of white flowers and a polished black gate and smoke billowed gently from the chimney atop the red tiled roof.

She stood and stared at its beauty and questioned its reality.

She was transfixed, walking slowly towards it across the scrubby shore, until she saw in the garden an elderly woman with a broom of twigs, sweeping the stone path. She wore a dull floral skirt and her hair was tied in a scarf and Kiara walked yet closer.

The woman looked up and saw her and stood for a moment as Kiara neared the gate and at almost the last moment pulled a long-muzzled American revolver from nowhere and aimed it along the garden path at Kiara.

"Deténgase" she said softly.

Kiara had already stopped and she slowly raised her hands either side of her head.

The old woman said nothing.

Kiara very slowly removed her hat and held it to her chest and smiled at the woman.

"Can you help?"

The elderly woman watched her suspiciously.

"What do you want?"

"I am trying to get to Villahermosa but I'm very lost. I didn't mean to come as far as the sea"

The elderly woman smiled and lowered the pistol slightly.

"Oh my dear, you are lost. Are you alone?"

Kiara nodded. é

"Yes I am"

The woman lowered the pistol to her side.

"Come in here" she said, beckoning Kiara through the gate.

Kiara smiled

"Leave your weapons there"

Kiara stopped.

She hadn't left the pistol anywhere since she had left the farmhouse.

"Put it down, just there" the woman said, "you'll be fine, there's no trouble here. Come on dear"

Kiara fumbled the pistol around in her hand and then slowly stooped and laid it down on the grass, unlatched the gate and stepped through.

"Come my dear, sit. Look at you. You look like you've walked miles"

Kiara smiled.

"You have no idea"

The woman smiled and walked Kiara slowly up the stone path to the red wooden door.

"Where are we? How far north have I come to reach the ocean there?"

The woman laughed.

"That isn't the ocean, dear"

"It's not?"

The woman pushed the door open and allowed Kiara inside before her. She bolted it from the inside with three long iron bolts.

"This is La Laguna del Roasario. Beautiful isn't it? Where have you come from?"

"Everywhere. Monterrey, Cuidad de Mexico, Oaxaca" Kiara said walking into the hallway of the house, the polished wooden floor glinting the light through the window. On the walls hung photographs taken years before, faded in their frames. A young woman in the arms of a soldier, smiling with her leg kicking behind up behind her as she leaned in to him, and a school photograph taken of a younger boy, his hair messed and a forced smile.

"Oh my" the woman said, leading Kiara to the neat little lounge, "quite some way then. Maybe a better question to ask is where are you going?"

"Villahermosa"

"Ah" the woman smiled, "then you are doing quite well"

"Really?" Kiara asked, surprised. She had no idea where she was.

"You're a couple of days west. Three at most"

Kiara smiled a smile of relief. She felt foolish for having mistaken the vast lagoon for the ocean but she was tired and starving and her head had been spinning for days.

"Here my dear, sit down. I'll get you some bread"

Kiara thanked her again and took a seat on the yellow sofa. It was old and the arms were worn to the stitching but it was clean and well-kept. The room was charming, decorated in floral wallpaper that didn't match the carpet, bright ornaments and fresh flowers in a vase in the window and a stack of leather-bound novels and a tea-set that would have looked at home on the lawns of Europe.

"Do you live here alone?" Kiara called through the door to the woman as she stood in the kitchen.

"Oh yes" she replied, "I've been alone for, well, many years now. I lose count"

She came through with a glass board with bread and a sideplate and a cup of warm coffee and set them down on the table in the centre of the room.

"You do like coffee?" she asked.

Kiara smiled.

"I do, very much. I haven't had coffee for a long time"

The woman smiled.

"Here , drink my dear. Yes, my Alberto died thirty one years ago this winter, and since the boys left I've been on my own here"

"This place is amazing" Kiara said, her wide eyes scanning slowly around the room, "you've got bread and coffee, and fresh flowers. How have you kept this like this?"

The woman looked embarrassed,

"Oh it's just housework my dear. I like to clean, it keeps me young"

"It's beautiful"

She drank the coffee. It was perfect.

"Are they your boys, in the photos in the hallway?"

"Ah yes, Robert and Gabriel. That's them. Robert is married now. He has a boy of his own. I don't see them any more. And Gabriel, he has gone off too. He says he'll come and visit but I don't know"

Kiara smiled and ate the bread and the woman sat and the two of them enjoyed being there for a few moments and nothing more was said.

Eventually it was Kiara who spoke.

"So I can reach Villahermosa in two days from here?"

The woman nodded.

"Oh I would say so. Do you walk quickly?"

Kiara shrugged.

"I guess. If I walk east, where will I reach by the time the sun goes down tonight?"

"Tonight?"

"Yes. If I leave now"

"Oh, you shouldn't set out now, it's getting late. You don't want to be out on the road when it's dark"

"Thanks, but I'm fine. I'm a fighter. I haven't got all this way by sticking to daylight"

"Oh no, I won't have it. It's getting late"

"Really", Kiara insisted, "I'll be fine. You've been lovely to me, the coffee, the bread, but I need to keep moving. I'm going to find my son you see. I promised him"

"Oh, I have a son, Robert. He's married now. And he has a boy of his own"

Kiara just looked at her.

"You said. So you understand then"

The woman smiled.

"Dear you must rest. You can leave at dawn when the road is safe. Come, let me show you to a room"

She stood and placed a hand on the back of Kiara's shoulder and, with the very least amount of force possible, gently pushed Kiara forward from the sofa.

She stood.

"Thank you. You have been most kind, and your offer to stay here is very kind also"

She walked out into the hallway and towards the front door.

"But I am going to make the most of the last couple of hours of light while I can. Thank you again"

She reached for the top bolt on the front door.

"Please don't touch that" the voice came from behind her.

Kiara held the metal and began to slide it sideways.

"I'm just going to..." she started.

The woman spoke louder, the calmness in her sweet voice gone entirely and there was a growl to her and Kiara's hair stood on end.

"I said don't touch that" she barked.

Kiara turned slowly.

The woman, in her floral skirt with her hair tied in a scarf, was standing in the hallway with the long-muzzled pistol levelled at Kiara's face.

"Woah, ok, I'm sorry. I'm just trying to open the door so that..."

"Get away from the damn door and get down on your knees"

"I'm sorry, I'm sorry. Listen, if you can just open the door then I'll be gone"

"Get on your knees now"

Kiara paused.

Her hands had involuntarily raised again to either side of her head and she didn't move.

The woman barked and her voice cracked.

"I won't ask you again"

Kiara slowly lowered herself to her knees by the door as the woman watched.

From behind the elderly woman, a noise came from behind the door, a low wooden hatch with a ribbon tied across it that led to a space under the stairs, a cupboard or a staircase to the basement or a crawlspace. It was chained and locked with a combination lock.

The voice called something out in Spanish that she didn't hear properly, anguished and scared and warped as it reached her ears.

The woman slammed the butt of the pistol against the wooden door.

"Shut your damned mouth, you. What have I told you?"

The voice called out again, unrecognisable.

She smacked the wood again, harder.

"If I have to come down there" she bellowed at the door and the voice said nothing more.

Kiara watched the chained door.

"Stay there" she said to Kiara, "move and I'll shoot you in the face"

The woman leaned sideways to the door and began to flick the numbers over on the combination lock, her bony fingers fumbling with the dials as the other hand held the pistol out at Kiara.

It wavered in her outstretched arm, swinging loosely as she concentrated on the lock.

Kiara saw the opportunity.

She thrust herself forward from her knees and launched straight at the woman's outstretched arm.

She pulled the trigger and thumped a round into the wall.

The mumbled voice behind the door called out again as Kiara twisted the pistol in the old woman's hand. The woman grabbed the back of Kiara's hair and heaved it downwards and Kiara screamed out and the voice behind the door screamed again and the woman shot and shot again as the pistol flailed wildly around her pretty hallway, lodging bullets in the polished woodwork.

The two women wrestled across the hallway and crashed into the wall, knocking the photos to the ground. The glass smashed and the photographs floated out, the image of the soldier and the girl fluttering across the hallway. On the back of it was printed text and half of another picture, not a photograph at all but cut from a magazine.

The woman's pretend life unravelling before her.

Kiara reached down and pulled the rosewood hunting knife from her leg, hidden the entire time from the woman, and sunk it into her arm and the old woman screamed an ear-piercing scream that shook the windows of the place, and her bony white hand seized open and she dropped the pistol to the floor.

She let go of Kiara's hair and staggered backwards as Kiara ripped the knife back out of her, the woman's blood dripping from it through the dried deer blood that had not yet been cleaned.

She fell backwards to the floor as blood pulsed from her arm, the whites of her eyes piercing and bright.

Kiara picked up the pistol from the floor and turned and pointed it at the woman.

She was crumpled helplessly in the corner, blood pooling around her bent legs.

The muzzle of the pistol shook in Kiara's hands.

She was about to squeeze the trigger and stopped.

Only the woman knew the combination to the lock.

Kiara steadied her breathing and her muscles relaxed very slightly and the gun stopped shaking.

"What's in there?" she asked, flashing her eyes to the small locked door.

The woman glanced over, shaking and whimpering and said nothing.

"Open it"

The woman frantically shook her head.

"Open the door"

The woman began to cry.

"Open the damn door or there'll be hell to pay. You have no idea what I'm capable of"

The woman shook and slumped sideways to the floor and crawled across the hallway, slipping in the blood, until she reached the lock. She took hold of it, her hands shaking and her face white. Some of the numbers had already been flicked at her previous attempt, and again her thin fingers fumbled and she dropped it against the door and Kiara kept the pistol on her.

She watched.

The woman flicked the last of the numbers into its correct position on the lock and it clicked. She paused before opening the lock and looked back at Kiara.

"Please" she managed, breathing heavily through her tears.

"You were going to put me down there" Kiara snapped, "with whatever it is that you keep in there. You deserve what you get. Open the door"

The woman clicked the latch of the lock open and the chain swung to the ground with a clang and the women fell backwards to the floor.

Kiara stepped forward and slowly took hold of the top of the small door and opened it. A smell poured out of the darkness. Inside, the wooden steps led from the hallway down into a blackened basement beneath the house.

Kiara peered down but the darkness was absolute and her eyes could barely see the stone floor beneath.

She waited, the pistol still on the woman.

"Please close the door" the woman begged.

Kiara ignored her

Below, the sound of shuffled footsteps came from the dark to the foot of the stairs, and against the black she saw the silhouette of a young man, thin and dark and filthy. He looked up at her and the light hit his eyes, desperate and sad, peering up from his bearded face.

He said nothing.

"Hola?" Kiara said into the dark.

The man watched.

A young girl appeared next to him, her short summer dress thick with grease and dust and her leg cut and bandaged and her wispy hair clinging to her face.

She looked terrified and confused.

"You can come out of there" Kiara said.

The girl clung to the man, who held her with his big dirty hand.

He arched his neck to see better through the doorway into the hall.

Kiara turned to the woman.

"Who the hell are these people? What in god's name have you done here?"

The woman didn't reply.

"You can come out. It's safe" Kiara said again.

She stepped back into the hallway as the sound of the man's footsteps slowly and tentatively climbed the steps, the gentle sound of the young girl following a few steps behind him.

Kiara pulled open the heavy iron bolts from the door and let it fall open, the late afternoon sun flooding in from the beautifully manicured garden outside where birds could be heard and the shimmering of the lagoon hung beyond.

The man appeared at the top of the stairs and looked at Kiara and then at the elderly woman laying on the floor, twisted and red.

Kiara picked up the bloodied knife from the ground and spun it in her hand and offered it out to the man. He looked at it as though he did not know its purpose.

"Here" she said, "do what you need to do"

He looked up into her eyes.

The desperation fell from them and they narrowed and he cocked his chin to her.

"I will not need it"

She nodded.

"Thank you" he said.

She turned to walk out of the door as the girl stepped out into the hallway and the man picked up the elderly woman by the leg and began to drag her down the wooden steps into the black underbelly of the beautiful house to what fate she was destined.

Chapter Twenty

Kiara walked into Villahermosa on the thirteen day and felt as though what weight had burdened her thus far had been lifted, and each step was light as though she walked on a cushion of air.

She was wrecked.

Her boots were split and her jacket was torn and frayed and thick with dirt and the dried blood of the deer and the elderly woman. Her husband's hat, which she still wore proudly, was missing stitches and was scuffed beyond repair and her pockets were bare.

She wore the rusted knife at her thigh and the two pistols in her belt, hers and the old lady's, not six rounds between them, and she limped and coughed and could not think straight. The only thing she still held of value with which to trade was the wedding ring on her finger and she knew it would go into the ground with her no matter what.

Villahermosa was not a large city, but it was a city nonetheless and it felt vastly larger than any place that she had passed through since Oaxaca, and was in substantially better condition. No fires had burned there and the extensive network of freshwater tributaries and waterways that snaked down from the Mexican Gulf had kept the land fresh and the people alive, and had allowed small boats to bring in fish and seafood.

The place was as unsafe as any city in that land, crawling still with the stricken and desperate who fought and stole, but Kiara had walked through the very cauldron of the underworld, and in comparison the place seemed almost utopian. The roads were cracked but there were roads, the trees and bushes had overcome the homes there but they were lush and flowering, and she felt peace.

She walked up the riverbank of the Rio Carrizal as it took her up into the very heart of the city.

There was only one place on her mind.

The name which had been written in that letter to Dylan by her husband's own hand. Etched into their history. A place she had never been to, but which she had learned about from her father who always told her that he would one day come south into Tabasco to visit. Not a grand place, not renowned in that country or elsewhere, but a place that she knew existed and a place she knew would surely survive fire and plague.

El Parque Museo la Venta.

The only open-air museum in Latin America, her father had once told her.

He had loved to study his history books. He read all manner of dusty old texts and recited facts to her about the great history of that nation which, as a young girl, she had readily shrugged away with disinterest. But she had listened nonetheless. She may not have let on at the time that she cared, even one bit, but she had heard him when he spoke and his passion was infectious to her.

He told her of the Olmecs, the first people to build civilisations in that land, the fathers of the fathers of their country.

"You should see what these people built, Kiara" he would say, "great pyramids to rival the Egyptians, carved stone animals that a man could not carve by hand today if he tried"

She would be playing, combing the hair of a doll or weaving or waiting for him to finish so that she could play again on the land.

"The number zero, my girl. Do you know how to count anything without also knowing the value of zero? These people created that. You have everything to thank them for, Kiara. One day I will show you"

It took her years to appreciate what he was saying.

He would explain, at times in depth, and she could remember to that day facts that he spoke of, but the weight of his words and the true impact of the forbearers of their nation did not truly resonate with her until years had passed.

"We'll go down to the Gulf, dad" she would say, "we'll all go. We'll take a couple of weeks and we'll see it all"

But they never did.

The farm was there to be run, the crops and animals could not be left, and that financial windfall that was so often dreamed of never did come, and before they knew it the years had passed and Kiara had moved on and her father had grown old and the time had gone.

She was going there for him.

To complete the circle.

The only place on the entire Gulf coast that she knew by name.

And so it was written in the letter to her son, and so that would be the place that she would go.

She would pray that Dylan too could make it there.

The city was as busy as anywhere she had been in a long time. There were men leading horses and people going about their businesses and a musician played in the street and people threw him coins of no value.

The roads were open and the buildings still stood and it reminded Kiara of the towns and cities of the north through which they had passed many months ago. She followed the main highway into the city and stayed with it as it drove further into the very heart of the place.

She approached a group of travellers with mules and carts and asked them if they knew of the park there and they nodded and told her to continue onwards.

She had not seen so many abandoned vehicles in a long time, more indeed than in the capital city itself. They were abandoned there along every lane of the road, which at times was three lanes wide in each direction. A huge exodus from the place that had been seemingly paused in its progress. Cars and minivans and trucks of all sizes, bumper to bumper, their windows smashed out and their wheels taken many years ago.

As she reached the underpass at Paseo Tabasco, she saw where the great fire had been. The concrete of the tunnel and the ramps at either side of it were blackened with oil smoke and each vehicle in the queue, some forty vehicles back from the tunnel to the north and the south, had been torched completely and beyond recognition.

She stood and surveyed the absolute obliteration.

An old man passed, smoking something in a wrapped leaf.

"What happened here?" she asked, pointing to the explosion of blackness that emanated out of the underpass. The concrete of the road above was cracked through.

The man looked slowly over and shrugged and walked on.

Little more than half a mile further north, her tired eyes which had seen more in their time than they should and which flickered forever with terrible tiredness, lit up in her head with pure tingling excitement and true relief.

On a tall steel pole at the edge of the road hung the rusted and faded roadsign of that previous world, once a deep green with reflective white lettering, it was dull and rifle-shot and browned at the corners as though it were wet cardboard.

The wording was clear enough.

It read *Centro* in large letters and there was the symbol for the airport, and underneath it clearly read *Parque Museo la Venta*.

Kiara stood and stared at it and smiled.

She remembered all the conversations with her father, all the things he had dreamed of, longed to see and the places he longed to visit. That place had always been at the top of his list, ahead of any Mayan or Aztec historical site.

She felt a sorrow at his loss, and at her own losses for they were many, but she still smiled for she had walked the coals of hell to be in that place and lost everything for doing so. Yet she was there.

She followed the road to the entrance where the first of the colossal stone carved heads stood proudly on a plinth next to the sign. It was beaten and worn and looked as though it may have been grafittied and then cleaned again, and as she neared it she was intercepted by three men in blue shirts with pistols.

"Hola" the man said, his tone alone questioning what she wanted there.

She nodded.

"Hola señor"

They didn't stop her moving to the great stone head, but they made their presence and their protection of the gate very evident to her, and thumbed at their pistols as they watched her,

She looked at the great Olmec head and saw, looking back from its eyes, the soul of her father.

She reached out to touch it.

"Ah" snapped one of the men.

She turned and he shook his head at her.

"Can I go inside?"

"What do you want there?"

"Inside? To look. I am meeting someone here"

The man nodded.

"Please, be respectful"

She said that she would, and thanked them and they nodded to her without smiling and watcher her as she entered the park.

The sounds of the city drained away almost immediately.

She recounted the words of the letter to her son.

In that place, there is the grandest of ceiba trees, much like the one your grandfather cherished so dearly. I will sit under it until you are there.

As she took the path, overgrown with all plantlife, dead leaves carpeting the small white stones of the walkway, mosquitoes swarmed around her and bugs in every tree chirped and small birds hopped secretly between branches.

She had taken no more than ten steps into the park when she stopped.

It was directly in front of her, greeting her as it had greeted all others, the towering whitened trunk of the majestic ceiba.

Its bows stretched endlessly out of sight, over all the bushes and trees which grew there, twisted and old and ribbed with thorns.

"The tree sees", she heard her father say.

The tree her father grew had been huge, imposing, and always kept from her touch as though laying a hand on it took some of its magic. Its stature had been undeniable, but only as she stood there before that ceiba did she feel, flowing through her, the true energy of the ancient thing.

She felt her father, and she felt all who had come before him and she felt again the warmth of her family and of Mia and Ryan.

She stood mesmerised for some time as the sun danced down through the canopy of huge leaves.

She was broken from the trance by a coati who walked brazenly towards her along the old rugged pathway. Its nose to the ground and long tail swinging behind it like the rudder of a boat, it approached. It saw her and looked up and she did not move and it watched her for a second and no more before returning its attention to the ground, and on it walked.

She looked back to the tree.

She had made it.

It was there and it was standing and it was where her father had always described it to be. The tree of life.

The sacred tree of the Olmecs.

The grandfather of every tree, as he called it, including his very own.

She sat down and waited and she sat there as the sun slowly dropped away. She knew that there was very little chance of her son arriving that day or the next or the one that followed, and she was entirely prepared to have to wait there in that spot for a week or more. Though, at the same time, she had walked so far, through so much, at such pains, to sit in that spot that she felt scared to leave again in search of food and water, should something occur to prevent her from returning.

But she knew she had to eat, though she had come to care little as to what. Leaves, grasses, fruits or berries at best, the deer meat a rare exception.

She walked the park, overgrown as it had become and drank from the waters of Laguna de las Ilusiones. The water there was not clean but it was water nonetheless and it was better than not drinking at all. The cages and pens and pits in the rear section of the park where animals had once been on show, were long vacated and the place was filthy and old and rotten.

That evening she ate from the trees there and drank from the lagoon and found a place near the entrance, within sight of the great ceiba, where she made her camp for the night, wrapped in the coat with the two loaded pistols in her hands.

On the second day, the security guards with the blue shirts came to her and asked her why she was still there and she told them again that she was waiting for somebody and they asked her to move on.

She told them that she would not, and that she was waiting for her son and they had agreed that very place to meet, and that she was doing no harm and valued and cherished the place with the love it deserved. She said that, if anything, she would protect the history of it and not the opposite.

They shrugged and called her crazy and let her be.

She waited for seven days, walking slow laps around the park and standing at each of the stone monoliths and observing them in detail, clearing from them the fallen leaves and the green residue of the encroaching trees. She repeated her route throughout the day until she knew well the locations of each of the trees bearing fruit or berries and which of the leaves not to eat.

Another week passed. As she walked the pathways, once lined with little white stones, she pulled away the overgrowing vines and kicking away the leaves. The security guards would come and go and they would ask her why she was walking circles around the park, clearing it as though she were the caretaker and she would reply that, for the short time being, she was.

She knew well each of the statues and the altars and assigned each of the great carved heads a character and spoke to them playfully, for she had little else.

The guards would ask her, mockingly, when she was meeting her son there and they would laugh to each other, regardless of her response.

Occasionally there would be other travellers, men and women who would visit that place and would walk slowly and contemplatively around the ancient artefacts and they would nod and smile to her and move on.

She sat each night under the canopy of the ceiba and thought about her life and about her parents and about her children. She remembered every good time they had spent together and she remembered things that she had not remembered in many years which she believed forgotten to time and she smiled at each of them.

Another week passed by as the nights became lighter and the air warmed and the berries on the trees dwindled in number.

One afternoon, a security guard who she had come to know better than the others, came to her alone in the park.

"Hola" he called.

She smiled.

"Listen señora, I think is time for you to move on from here. Your son, he is, maybe not coming here"

She shook her head.

"He is"

The man sighed and shook his head very gently in reflection.

He sat on the stone wall and looked down at his feet and turned a stone around in his hand.

"You have been here, you know, a long time now. You should find some place to go. I know people here in the city who could help you, they have food. Good people"

She smiled.

"You're kind. But I don't need help, I will wait here until my son arrives. Then we will go. Thank you"

He nodded and sighed again and stood, and took a moment as though he may say something more or protest to her further, but eventually he just said *ok* and waved and left.

She went on, slowly clearing and cleaning the park for there was nothing more for her to do, eating the leaves and the fruits and drinking from the lagoon and spending each night camped by the tree of life, dreaming all there was to dream and waiting with the patience of a mother.

On the beginning of the fifth week, the security guard brought her bread and a cup of tequila and sat with her.

"Thank you" she said to him, "very much"

He smiled.

"Yesterday it is my birthday. My wife left the city to a farm she knows, and they have made bread. I want you also to eat"

"That's incredibly thoughtful. Happy birthday, really. Bless you"

She raised the cup to him and he nodded and she sipped the tequila and passed it to him and he drank.

"To your son"

He passed it back.

She smiled and drank.

"Who employs you?" she asked.

The guard cocked his head and his brow furrowed.

"Employ me?" he asked, his translation not exact.

"Here. Who employs you to work here, as a security guard?"

"Ah" he said, "here. Nobody does. I, we, all, we work here as security guard before. So we still do it"

"Just for the love of it?"

He nodded and looked at her as though her question were foolish.

"For this", he said, passing his hand across the park, "the Olmec history, the heads, the altars, the statues. Is our history. It needs protection, always. Why do you think is here now, standing the way it always has"

She smiled again, deeply, at the nobility of it.

Her father would have been proud and tremendously grateful.

"You're a good man", she said.

He smiled.

"You're a good mother"

As she sat that night, she felt thankful for everything she had, even though she had nothing at all. She smiled to herself and felt for the first time in many, many months, the warmth of her faith returning to her soul and she sat in contemplation of it all, lost in her head and her heart.

She didn't hear the footsteps behind her.

He walked from the front gate of the park and stood a few feet back in the dusk, shadowed from face to boots, a long rifle hanging from his hand.

As he shuffled on the stones, she snapped back to her reality and her heart jumped and she leaped up and spun around to face him, instinctively pointing the Colt at the darkened figure.

She burst into tears on the spot.

He stepped forward and grabbed her and held her as hard as he could. "I was starting to think you wouldn't come" she sobbed, holding him tightly.

"Of course I would come mom" he said, tears in his own eyes.

She held him for what felt like a lifetime, crying and stopping and crying again until eventually she stepped back and looked at him.

"You found it"

He nodded.

"Belo's tree" he said, looking up at the great white ceiba before him

"The tree of life"

She nodded and smiled the proudest of smiles.

"We made it Dyl. I'm sorry about your father, I am, so much. I'm so sorry this was how it was, we tried so hard. He loved you so much son, so much"

He shook his head.

"Don't be sorry mom. I've seen so much, so much death, so many people dead that you can't even imagine. I know how difficult it is to get by, to survive. I know. I know now, I understand how life is and how it has to be. I understand. But we'll go to dad, yeah? You know where he is?"

She nodded.

"I do"
"We'll go there"
She nodded and wiped the tears away.
He walked slowly away from her to the tree.
"So what now, mom?"
She stood next to him.
"I don't even know any more"
"The border?"
She shrugged.
"Do you want to go north to see where your father is?"
He shook his head.
"One day. Sure. Not now. We are not finished yet, mom"
She looked at him.
"Are your platoon here, the others? Will they find you?"
He shook his head.
The moonlight flickered down through the leaves.
"No. I left them a few days ago. There's no way they can move together as quickly as I can move alone. Even if they sent out a smaller group to get me, they have no idea where I am. We'll stay here tonight and go for the border at dawn"
She thought for a while and looked at him and looked at the tree.
"So that's the plan?", she said.
"Amatique Bay?"
She smiled.
"Yes. Let's do it then"
"That was always the plan, mom"
She nodded.
"It was son. It was always the plan. It will be good down there, I know it will. We'll come back one day"
"Maybe"
"Yeah, maybe"
They stood together beneath the immense arms of the tree of life, its bark shimmering white beneath the stars and the moonlight bouncing red from her long coat.
She took the hat from her head and placed it on Dylan and adjusted it slightly and smiled, and he smiled too and each felt the hope and the

energy from the ceiba flow out over that place, and they each knew that, in that land of uncertainty and brutality and ruthlessness and sorrow, their days were not done and there was yet more for each of them to give.

If you've enjoyed this book, you can delve deeper into Kiara's world and explore the route and the places visited, along with more of Mark's work at

www.marklwatson.co.uk

Printed in Great Britain
by Amazon